T0028747

Wildcat

Wildcat

Amelia Morris

FLATIRON
BOOKS
NEW YORK

This is a work of fiction. All of the characters, organizations, and events portrayed in this novel are either products of the author's imagination or are used fictitiously.

WILDCAT. Copyright © 2022 by Amelia Morris. All rights reserved. Printed in the United States of America. For information, address Flatiron Books, 120 Broadway, New York, NY 10271.

Grateful acknowledgment is made for permission to reproduce from the following:

Excerpt of "Working Together" from David Whyte's *River Flow: New & Selected Poems*, printed with permission from Many Rivers Press, www .davidwhyte.com. © Many Rivers Press, Langley, WA, USA.

www.flatironbooks.com

Designed by Devan Norman

Library of Congress Cataloging-in-Publication Data

Names: Morris, Amelia, author.
Title: Wildcat / Amelia Morris.
Description: First edition. | New York : Flatiron Books, 2022.
Identifiers: LCCN 2021037754 | ISBN 9781250809216 (hardcover) |
    ISBN 9781250809230 (ebook)
Subjects: LCSH: Motherhood—Fiction. | Female friendship—
    Fiction. | LCGFT: Humorous fiction. | Novels.
Classification: LCC PS3613.O75548 W55 2022 | DDC 813/.6—dc23
LC record available at https://lccn.loc.gov/2021037754

Our books may be purchased in bulk for promotional, educational, or business use. Please contact your local bookseller or the Macmillan Corporate and Premium Sales Department at 1-800-221-7945, extension 5442, or by email at MacmillanSpecialMarkets@macmillan.com.

First Edition: 2022

10 9 8 7 6 5 4 3 2 1

FOR TEDDY AND ISAAC

THE WORLD IS LONELY FOR COMFORT, AND
FOR THE HIPS AND BREASTS OF WOMEN.

—CLARISSA PINKOLA ESTÉS,
WOMEN WHO RUN WITH THE WOLVES

WE COULD BEGIN BY UNDERSTANDING
OURSELVES AS DANGEROUS.

—EULA BISS

Wildcat

She can't remember where she read it, but the point was that the number one factor that determines the successful care of an infant isn't cleverness or intellect but devotion. She thinks of this now with her almost ten-month-old son on her hip. She's standing just outside the front door of her house, watching Maxine and a woman named Taffy, whom she just met moments earlier, bring cat after cat after cat into her house.

Is this an act of devotion? The question almost makes her laugh. It must make her smile because when Maxine looks up at her she smiles as if in reply.

Pregnant Leanne would not have considered this anything close to devotion. Pregnant Leanne would have been panicking, would have been very concerned about the cat hair on the upholstery. Back then, to be devoted to a child had meant something singular, something à la the Virgin Mary: statuesque, haloed, with the slightest tilt of the head. To be devoted to a child had summoned something pure, like a white beam of light.

"What are we going to do with all the cat carriers?" she asks as Maxine approaches.

"Oh, Taffy will just put them back in the van, I think."

Leanne nods. When Maxine had come up with the idea, Leanne

hadn't imagined the carriers. She also hadn't considered the sound of them—of a room full of cats. She's actually never owned a cat before, at least as an adult. Growing up in rural Pennsylvania, they had farm cats (though they didn't have a farm). Their purpose was to keep the mice at bay. They all lived outside. Well, all except Lazarus, who had gotten hit by a car one afternoon and broken her hind legs. After that, she got her name (Lazzy for short) and an invitation to come inside to mend. But then her dad and stepmother grew to love Lazzy apparently—Leanne had moved out by then—and there, indoors, she spent the rest of her days.

But thinking of her dad makes her reconsider her past, pregnant self. He'd died one week before she'd gone into labor. He'd had a massive heart attack late at night, and by the time that Beth—his second wife—had realized something was up, that he had never come to bed, he was already gone.

What she's saying is that for the vast majority of her pregnancy or her life, she wouldn't have allowed thirty cats into her house. But that maybe in that last week, in that hazy period, when she was still pregnant and he was dead, when things had felt both real and unreal, when she was actively rewriting the story of her life, she might've acquiesced, might've welcomed them in.

Now she understands that devotion can take many forms. It can look like the opposite of purity. Like mud, like filth, like that layer of grime on your bathroom sink. It can look like pain, like suffering. And sure—why not?—like a living room full of mewing cats.

PART
1

1

SIX MONTHS EARLIER

I t was six a.m., possibly earlier. Leanne was breast-feeding Hank on her side of the bed, which wasn't just her side of the bed anymore. It was cozy nook and strenuous office. It was where she kept the important pillows. The life-giving pillows. It was where she secreted fluids: milk, blood, and sweat. It was the place she'd spent so much time in the past four months that she joked to friends that she'd created a divot in the mattress.

And so it was the same this morning. She was fastened, *rooted* to the spot even though a bizarre sound pulled her eyes up from her phone. "Fuck," she whispered. Their dog was heaving at the foot of the bed. She nudged James with her elbow. "She's gonna throw up! June—she's gonna throw up!"

James sat up abruptly, still half-asleep and just a second too late to relocate their little dog to the hardwood floor in the hallway just outside their room. She'd already vomited all over the duvet cover.

But fifteen minutes later, Hank was done nursing; James had sopped up the vomit, removed the duvet cover, cleaned up June's furry beard, and crawled back into bed. Leanne placed the baby into the crook of his arm and watched as James singsonged, "Good morning!" and Hank slowly turned his head, found his dad's face, and smiled—a huge, shoulder-shrugging smile.

"Who wakes up like that?" Leanne said. She nuzzled her face into her son's neck and gave him a quick succession of kisses.

"Not *June*," James said.

"She probably knows we're leaving this morning."

They were going to Palm Springs, a two-hour drive away, for the night for her friend Regina and her husband Val's anniversary party. "She's *so* sensitive," Leanne said with faux sympathy. And then: "Are you dropping her off at WagVille or am I?" She pulled on a pair of shorts and a t-shirt.

"I thought we'd do it on our way out."

Leanne nodded. "After Hank's nap."

"Of course." The way he said it implied a firm awareness of Leanne's ritualistic way of handling the baby's nap, which took place about an hour and a half after he first woke up: she tucked him in on the couch, sat down right beside him, pulled up *The Best of Debussy* via YouTube, and started in on the day's work session as he dozed. It was something she'd done in the weeks after he was born, when she didn't know she could put him down in the crib and walk away from him, and something that she apparently couldn't keep up for much longer. He wasn't a newborn anymore. She knew she was supposed to celebrate this milestone, but now everyone—mostly her mother and Ofelia, their nanny who came twice a week—talked about getting the baby on a schedule and napping in his crib, and what was celebratory about that? She liked being near him when he slept, liked listening to his breathing change. A slumbering baby at her side was like being pregnant again: she could do what she pleased for the most part *and* be a mother.

"I gotta rest up myself," James said. "So I can *maintain* consciousness while talking to Val about amateur stair running or that one guy with the Woody Allen glasses who—"

"Woody Allen glasses?"

"Yeah, and the curly hair."

"Chip?"

"I think so."

"I don't think those are Woody Allen *glasses*."

"Well, whatever. I don't like talking to him."

"He likes you, though," Leanne said, smiling, scooping Hank into her arms.

But why your *fourth* anniversary? Leanne had wanted to ask when Regina first told her about the planned party months ago over speakerphone, but she'd held back. Their friendship hadn't typically included questions like that—questions that emphasized the discrepancies between their lifestyles. Like the fact that Regina owned a high-end homeware shop located in West Hollywood, whereas Leanne, at least up until her eighth month of pregnancy, had worked part-time at a similar but different high-end homeware shop (also located in West Hollywood).

Both stores catered to an elite set of clientele, many of whom were celebrities. Each time a famous person came in, it surprised Leanne how exciting it was. Why was it exciting? They were strangers. But that was—she guessed—the whole trick of it. They didn't feel like strangers. *She* was the stranger. One time Jimmy Kimmel came in with his fiancée. They were going to register at the store. Normally, Leanne hated registries. It was a lot of work that amounted to zero sales, at least on that initial visit. But with Jimmy and his fiancée, Leanne had been happy to do it. And as she walked them through the various dinnerware lines, she could feel herself performing.

"Is it all dishwasher safe?" the fiancée asked.

"Absolutely. Dishwasher, microwave, and even oven safe up to four hundred degrees."

"*Up* to four hundred degrees?" Jimmy said.

"Yes," Leanne said.

"So it's not really oven *safe*."

"It *wants* to be. It's aspirational."

Jimmy had smiled and laughed the smallest laugh that made Leanne feel like a champion for approximately one hour. She also felt dumb for falling so easily and uninterestingly into the role of admiring fan.

This, in a way, also came to describe her friendship with Regina.

The other reason she hadn't asked *why the fourth anniversary?* was more logistical. Regina had called her via Bluetooth on her drive to spin class, and there was something so depersonalizing about talking to someone via speakerphone, the way they always sounded like they were being flushed down a toilet.

Even so, Leanne liked hearing Regina's voice, liked hearing her talk *at* her about her life, a life that had also recently gone through a major transformation; Regina too had had a baby, a little girl named, embarrassingly (for Leanne at least) Ursa Major. Ursa on its own was fine, and it was what she and Val seemed to call her the most often, but the two together? To be named after the night sky? It wasn't something Leanne would want to have to live up to.

That's why she'd chosen Hank. Plain as day. Plus, you could add the letter *T* and get *Thank*.

They'd first met years and years ago at James's work Christmas party, back when Leanne and James weren't even engaged. They were twenty-three, *maybe* twenty-four. They'd hit it off at the party, but nothing really came of it until much later when they discovered a shared enthusiasm for group exercise classes—an enthusiasm born of another shared pastime: a lifetime of attempting and/or maintaining thinness. (Ideally, with some level of tone.)

But slowly, geologically, the workouts led to getting drinks led to going to the movies led to becoming women who called each other up whenever something they felt like sharing popped into their heads, who had even spent Christmas Eve together at Regina's parents' house in Beverly Hills. It was lovely, yet Leanne could admit she was after something better—that rarer kind of friendship, the kind that came so much more easily when she was younger, back when that self-protective outer layer of human ego fell away more readily, leaving two exposed animals seeking warmth in each other. Like what she had with Mary Anne, her college roommate. They'd danced naked in her room to the Talking Heads together; they'd slept in each other's beds; they'd told each other harrowing details about tampons they'd inserted toward the end of their periods and then forgotten about. But you can't rush these things, she'd told herself. They would get there. Eventually.

So instead, when Regina told her about the party in Palm Springs, Leanne responded with a decisive "Great!"

It *was* great for her. She'd come to love attending Regina's parties, standing shoulder to shoulder with the rich.

But James would sooner have stayed at home. Leanne had convinced him that it was going to be fun, that it would be their first road trip as a family of three. They could get date shakes! "Fine," James had said. "But we're not getting them an anniversary gift. It's gonna cost enough for a hotel and babysitter."

"It's not all fun and games," Leanne had said. "It'll be good for the book." Leanne's first book, *Diary of a Home Cook: A Year in Recipes*, was coming out in August, five months from now, and she knew for a fact that one of the women who would be at the party wrote for *T* magazine.

At this, James had sighed. "Sometimes I worry about you." He was kidding. He was not kidding.

2

Leanne wouldn't say it outright to anyone, but her son was special.

It wasn't quite fair because technically and physically speaking, he *was*: he had a streak of pure white hair sprouting out at the very crown of his otherwise brown-haired head. Like a superhero.

In her last post on the food blog that had gotten her the book deal, she'd made Butter Chicken and then, at the end, included a few photos of Hank and his nursery. Since then, she kept getting questions on her blog or Instagram about Hank's stuff: what kind of crib, who makes the sheets, where did she get the toy accordion, and so forth. But Leanne knew it wasn't the products that were special. She and James couldn't afford the expensive, particularly twee baby stuff. It was the *baby*.

This morning, she had two emails waiting for her from inquiring women. The first wanted to know about the bronze brackets holding up a shelf in his room. The second asked about his baby quilt, which James's mom had made for him.

Another email confirmed the time and dates of the writing class she'd be teaching that summer. The reminder set off a faint tremor of panic. She hadn't thought of her time away from teaching as a maternity leave, especially since she'd never stopped working toward the release of her book; she'd had essays to write and publicity to plan. But teaching felt definitive. To instruct other humans she would need to be showered, dressed, and not open to interruption. She forwarded the email to James—her way of reminding him that he'd agreed to watch Hank those mornings when she'd be working.

But there was another email that interested her the most. It was from a famous writer, Maxine Hunter. A few months ago, Leanne had read her most recent novel and become mildly obsessed with it. The book was like nothing she'd previously encountered. It felt deeply personal—the main character's name was Maxine—but also somehow detached, like reading her diary, though a version that had been edited by a Buddhist monk.

On Maxine's website Leanne had found that Maxine apparently sent out a newsletter, or rather, what she called "An intermittent note about what I am doing, or sometimes a story or a piece of writing."

Leanne signed up right away and was now getting her first missive, not exactly a personal email, but a thrill all the same.

Dear Readers:
I'm writing to ask you a favor. I'm going to ask you a question, and I want you to be honest with me. I want you to give me your very first response. Your instinctual answer. In fact, if you only have time to simply read the question but not to answer it, please stop reading and come back later when you have time.

Leanne paused to take a look at Hank sleeping next to her. He looked very sleepy. She kept reading.

Here's the question: What do you think of a married couple (they've been married for about six to ten years) in their late thirties or early forties who don't have children?
I look forward to reading each and every answer.

Maxine

Leanne began typing right away:

Hello Maxine,

The first thing that comes to mind is a woman who lives in my neighborhood. She's forty-one, and her husband is at least a couple of years older. She's not just my neighbor. We're friendly (?). She makes these caftan-like dresses, and I've purchased a couple of them. Anyway, they don't have kids. Before I got pregnant, I kind of assumed that they couldn't—or that they were still trying but so far it hadn't worked out.

When I was pregnant enough to start telling people, I told her the news and then asked if she wanted kids. She said, "Maybe, someday. Although it's getting a bit late."

In short, my assumption remains the same. That they tried, that it didn't work, and so now they're going to have a really aesthetically beautiful life. Maybe an internally beautiful life too? #bestofluck

But seriously, in the past year, they've embarked on a bunch of home improvement projects, and their house looks spectacular. She also has an amazing wardrobe, drives a black BMW, and always smells like a botanical garden. I imagine that if I didn't have a child or wasn't going to, I would try and go this route too. Specifically, I would hire a landscaper to plant jasmine all along our backyard fence. I would also buy my hand creams and face lotions at small boutiques instead of CVS. I would get really good at yoga and be sure to go to the Korean spa at least once a month.

On another note, I recently read your book Koala Life *and LOVED it. I actually read it while my son went from being a few days old to a month old. He's four months now. I look very forward to reading whatever it is you send us or publish next.*

All the best,
Leanne Hazelton

Leanne struggled as to whether or not to mention that she had her own book coming out, but ultimately she decided not to. She didn't want Maxine to think that she wanted anything other than some sort of conversation. Even if she did.

She hit *Send*.

She moved on to Facebook, which was typically next in line after Gmail, followed by Twitter, before opening whichever Word document she was supposed to be working on. (How often she checked Instagram depended on the handiness of her phone, though occasionally she found herself on the desktop version of the site.) But Facebook was where she first saw the video. It caught her attention because a few people, none of whom held any kind of relation to one another except that they were all friends with Leanne, had posted it. A woman she used to work with had posted it with the caption: "Weirdest outfit ever." Regina's husband, Val, wrote, "The art of getting dressed y'all!" and then someone James had gone to college with simply wrote, "#thanksInternet."

She looked at Hank next to her as she turned the volume almost all the way down on Debussy and then clicked on the video for it to play. Hank stayed asleep as the video opened with a shot of a man with his back to the camera. The man wore nothing but a pair of gray boxer briefs; he looked to be in decent, normal shape if not a little thin. He was standing in the middle of a sparsely furnished mid-century modern living room with floor-to-ceiling windows. It was a room Leanne immediately recognized as Val and Regina's living room. The camera then swooped around him panoramically, dramatically—revealing his face. *Oh.* It was Val, she realized. His face was bearded as per usual. But he looked quite serious. He held a saucer in one hand and a teacup in the other. He took a sip and then looked out the window with purpose, like Batman patrolling Gotham from atop one of its skyscrapers.

A voice-over kicked in: "My name is Val Pincher. I am a media consultant, and I live in Los Angeles, California."

Some jazz-like music trickled in as the screen went black. Then the title "Why I Dress the Way I Dress" appeared in white block print.

The next shot opened in a different room—their bedroom, it looked like. Val stood in front of a mirror, tight jawed. The voice-over returned: "I'm not afraid of evolving," it said while Val pulled on a pair of shorts, and then the camera cut to a close-up of his face. His brow was furrowed. "I think style should be fluid. I think we *should* look back at photos of ourselves from ten years ago and laugh. Sure, that was me then, but this is me *now*."

Leanne's front teeth pressed against her bottom ones, the onset of a cringe—whether it was for herself or Val, she wasn't sure.

He put on a white cotton shirt. This was followed by another close-up of his face. He was concentrating on the task at hand. "I think it was Oscar Wilde who said that beauty isn't always beautiful. Don't quote me on that [laughter]. Maybe it was Camus."

"Oh, Lord."

He put on a dark-blue long-sleeved cotton shirt—on top of the white one. Then the focus shifted to an open window, blue sky and sun. "I hear people say that men's clothing is limited, that we don't have much in the way of choice, but I disagree. Men's clothing is all about *choice*."

He buttoned up a classic blue-and-white-striped Oxford shirt. He tugged at the collar and looked into the mirror. At this third shirt, she shook her head. It couldn't be comfortable. She thought particularly of the area at the inside elbow, all tight with cloth.

And then, suddenly, he was pulling a gray V-neck sweater over his head and smoothing it atop his chest. What was he trying to do—set a world record for layering?

"My rules for don'ts? Don't try and be something you're not. And don't forget to get your wife's opinion. In my experience, the wife *knows* about these things [laughter]."

The camera followed as he left the bedroom and picked up some keys from the table by the front door. He slipped on a pair of loafers without socks and reached for a jacket. As he drove away in his vintage pickup truck, he was actually wearing the jacket. He also tipped his hat to the camera—though he was not wearing a hat. The credits ran.

Leanne scrolled down to the comments section below to see what it was she seemed to *need* to see.

Either his legs are going to be cold or his torso is gonna be hot.

Aaaaaaaannndd my jacket, just in case.

This BRAH's so top-heavy he might tip over.

Everyone needs to chill. Did he need the jacket? No. But this is fashion. It's not always a needs-based approach.

The video had been up for only three hours, but there were already eighty-six comments. She read every single one. Most of the world seemed to agree on the horribleness of Internet trolls, but what about all of the online commenters who made you feel seen, made you laugh out loud? They were the opposite of trolls. They should get a name too.

3

Before they left for the desert, she made James watch Val's video.

"Don't try and be something you're not. I'll remember that one," James said once it was over.

Leanne smiled. "But what about all the shirts?"

"Yeah, I mean, *I* can't wear that many shirts."

As they drove, Leanne pulled up *This American Life* on her phone. They'd almost finished the second act, a story about complaints the show had gotten regarding the voices of some of the young women on their staff, when Hank started to cry and they had to turn it off. Leanne crawled from the front seat to the back to wave various things in his face.

James flipped on the radio. NPR was playing a clip from one of the recent primary debates. She leaned forward and semi-shouted over Hank's crying: "Can we not?"

James pressed the CD button. Van Morrison groaned sweetly.

Hank had stopped crying. "You just needed to know you weren't alone," she whispered at him, and then looked back up. She caught James's eye in the rearview mirror. He smiled, and she smiled back. He was really quite handsome, his face angled and unshaven. They'd been married six years, and sometimes she forgot this—that he was a good-looking person. Something about being out of the house together usually reminded her. At home they were faceless, nameless.

Their terms of endearment for each other the same: Sweetie. Sometimes Swee, which was better, though not by much.

"Vocal fry," Leanne said over the music. "My mom's complained about that, though not in those words."

James nodded. "Oh yeah. Winnie definitely prefers a man's voice."

During her mom's last visit, a month ago now, they'd gotten in an extended argument stemming from an offhand comment she'd made while in the car. Referring to some other public radio story, she'd said: "Well, they should at least be able to speak our language."

Her mother's identity as a Republican couldn't be overstated. It showed up in the way she held her body, in the way she asked a server for a Splenda packet, in her name: Winnie Wenderson. (She'd once been Winnie Hazelton but changed it again upon marrying Leanne's stepdad.) And of course, it showed up in her stance on immigration.

And because she was always visiting from the East Coast—specifically from North Carolina, where she and Leanne's stepdad had recently moved—she would come for a week and stay at the house. This made the visit stretch out endlessly, each day involving countless moments of Leanne holding her tongue to keep the peace, until just like that, she couldn't anymore.

This time, she had guffawed theatrically. "It's a good thing you were born in the U.S.!"

"What's that supposed to mean?"

"That it's a good thing you don't have to emigrate anywhere. My god, can you imagine yourself in Mexico, starting from scratch?"

"I could work at a clinic!" she'd said, and the sheer predictability of this response made Leanne roll her eyes. Yes. Her mother *was* a pediatrician. Yes, she had a skill set.

"But you won't even *drive* in suburban Los Angeles! You won't eat lentils!"

"I don't like the texture," she'd said, her teeth clenched. And then, a few hours later, Winnie announced that she would not be visiting again until she was "invited."

This was very Winnie. Winnie's love was conditional. She wielded it: offering it up when Leanne was obedient and taking it away when she wasn't. The problem—for Winnie—was that this tactic was losing its edge.

Some eight years ago, however, it had worked to great effect. That was when Leanne had announced her engagement to James, a *Jew*, and her mother's main response had been to hang up on her mid-call. This was followed by silence and an adult version of pouting. Eventually, her stepdad became the mediator between the two. "Your mother's main concern," he explained in a robotic tone that made Leanne crazy, was for her *soul* as well as the souls of their unborn children, who would inevitably grow up confused—"with no faith at all."

The women's relationship ultimately resumed, but it had taken a combination of time, James's oversized heart, and therapy—a favorite moment of which was when Leanne's therapist asked, seemingly flummoxed: "What *did* happen to your mother?"

As for her father, he was dead.

It was strange. Ever since he died four months ago, she almost enjoyed announcing it. "My dad's dead," she would say to James, seemingly out of the blue. She didn't know if she said it as confirmation or public rebuke. Probably both. He had been only sixty-five, but he'd never treated his own life as a precious commodity. After a visit with his mother, he'd once told Leanne to "shoot him" if he got that old. He was one of those rare doctor smokers (though he never smoked openly in front of Leanne and her brother Charlie). When she thought of him eating, it was Italian hoagies, regular soda, mashed potatoes, and roast beef.

In this way, the heart attack—his first and last—while shocking, had also made sense.

There'd been no chance to visit him in the hospital or anything like that, though Leanne thought that might've been sadder. At the very least, harder.

And of course she *was* sad. She might have even been devastated.

She'd been nine months pregnant. She remembered her belly shaking as she cried. But in the hours after her brother had called her to tell her the news, she'd had a series of recurring, selfish thoughts:

1. Her dad wouldn't be able to read her book.

2. Her dad wouldn't be alive to serve as fact-checker to the bygone but still disputed family history as laid out in the book.

3. Her dad wouldn't get to meet her baby—who would have been his first grandchild.

4. This wasn't going to change her life. At least not her day-to-day life.

She'd definitely been wrong about the fourth thought. Her day-to-day life *had* changed. Or at the minimum, her week-to-week life.

Her phone rang. "Can you see who it is?" she asked James.

He grabbed it from the passenger seat and glanced at it. "Ah, the queen herself."

"Oh, c'mon," Leanne said. "Let me take it."

"Bow down!" he said in a high-pitched English accent, handing her the phone.

"Hellooo," Leanne said into the receiver.

"Are you guys here?" Regina said, sounding a little panicked.

"Not quite. We're a little over halfway. What's going on?"

She exhaled breathily and then said in a hushed tone: "Do you know about this video of Val? He's getting dressed."

Leanne didn't know whether to admit to it or not. "I saw something on Facebook this morning."

"Fucking Facebook. Did you watch it?"

"Just a little."

"Mole!" Mole was a nickname that had arisen at a baby shower they'd both gone to during which a toddler kept pointing at a large mole on Leanne's chest and announcing quite loudly: "Mole!"

Regina kept talking: "It's so stupid. It's this men's fashion site, and they reached out to Val, and he really wanted to do it. I helped him pick out his outfit, but I didn't stick around for the fucking shoot. And then I see the video, and he added two extra shirts to the outfit we'd already picked out. It's going viral right now, as we speak. It's up to four hundred thousand views. The comments are so mean."

As she was talking, Hank writhed in his seat. Leanne looked at her watch. He was getting hungry.

"And that's a lot of views for that site? I mean, isn't it a really popular site?"

"All of the other videos have like fifty thousand or seventy thousand views *at most*."

"What does Val think?"

"He doesn't care! He's totally shrugging it off."

"Well, that's good."

"I just wish I didn't even know about it."

Leanne caught James's eye in the rearview mirror. He was motioning for her to wrap it up. She nodded knowingly. *I'm trying.*

"Look, we're going to be there in less than an hour. Let us check into the hotel and then I'll come by. Okay? It's gonna blow over, and people will move on to the next thing."

"Okay, fine."

Leanne hung up and looked at James in the mirror. He was smiling.

"What?" she said.

"Nothing," he said, still smiling.

4

At first, Leanne hadn't thought too much of Regina except that she'd laughed at Leanne's jokes. At the end of that first party, as they were saying their good-byes, Regina said, "You guys have to come over for dinner! I'll email you."

She did. And they did.

It was the first couples-based dinner party Leanne and James had ever attended. They were twenty-four. No one they knew cooked. No one they knew even had a dining room table. The people they knew had house parties in houses with wall-to-wall Berber carpet and mouse infestations.

But Regina and Val's place didn't have Berber carpet. The walls were freshly painted in a crisp white, the floors a light hardwood. They had properly tailored curtains. The kitchen was stocked with colorful enamel-coated cast-iron pots, the brand name of which Leanne would soon discover and, two years later, put on her wedding registry.

Los Angeles was like this: matryoshka dolls of wealth. Or at least, that's how Leanne had come to think about money in the world. In Middleton, the small Pennsylvania town where she'd largely grown up, Leanne's family *were* the rich people. Although her dad hadn't played the part. He hated money, and it mostly showed. While he and Winnie were separated (a long, drawn-out process), he moved even deeper into rural Pennsylvania to live with his then-girlfriend,

Beth—as well as Beth's son from a previous relationship—in an old farmhouse. He drove a rusted-out Previa minivan, wore his Oxford shirts with holes in the elbows, and made a point of making fun of Winnie's consumerist habits.

But he also ended up having two more kids with Beth. And so suddenly, when Charlie and Leanne weren't at their mother's, they were a family of seven. He and Beth put a giant addition on the farmhouse. Soon after that, Winnie remarried and moved to Pittsburgh. Leanne and Charlie were in fourth and sixth grade, old enough to decide where to live full-time. Leanne didn't remember choosing to stay with her dad as much as choosing to go wherever Charlie went. Either way, they ended up staying in Middleton with their father. And so it was at Middleton Elementary School where Leanne began to understand that their house was different from the houses of her peers, where she once heard it referred to as a mansion.

But then, as a teenager, when Leanne's relationship with her stepmom had deteriorated beyond repair and she realized that her older brother would be graduating—leaving her in Middleton without a familial ally—she moved to live with her mom and stepdad in the suburbs of Pittsburgh. It was only then that Leanne came to understand that her family's financial standing was actually quite average. That the farmhouse in Middleton was only an outlier because everyone else in that town was so plainly poor.

College opened up another doll. There she met people who hailed from "the City." She met fellow eighteen-year-olds who played sports like water polo and drove Range Rovers. College also introduced her to James, who came from the suburbs of Chicago and a similar middle-class background (minus the stint in rural America).

After graduation, and a bit of respective traveling, she and James decided to drive out to Los Angeles. James wanted to be a filmmaker, and Leanne wanted to see him do it. And so now here they were, peering into yet another level of affluence: at a dinner party in West Hollywood being hosted by people their age who had clearly skipped the postcollege phase of buying secondhand couches on

Craigslist and thinking that adding chopped bell pepper to the contents of a Zatarain's box was a legitimate home-cooked meal. It felt a little bit like magic. Like proof that Leanne was somehow on the right track. Did these people see something in her? (And if they did, could they please relay it to her boss at the stationery store where she was paid $11 an hour?)

Either way, Leanne liked the feeling. And soon, she began fielding other email invitations from Regina.

"I hope you're all having a fabulous day," one such email began, and went on to explain that Regina had recently learned to crochet and wanted to host a craft night. The signature included a link to her blog.

This was the mid-2000s. Leanne didn't know people with blogs. Crocheting didn't interest her, but she liked being invited to things. Leanne wrote back declining the crochet invite but also asking if Regina wanted to try a yoga class. "I go to this amazing teacher with a bit of a cult following."

"I'm interested!" Regina wrote back.

In her workout clothes and clutching a yoga mat, Regina was not the same self-assured person she'd been the previous times Leanne had met her. It reminded Leanne of that thing fashion people said about clothes—how they could act like armor. In just leggings and a tank top, Regina seemed timid, porous.

"So a lot of people are afraid of her," Leanne said just above a whisper. She unrolled her mat. "But I think most of her cold edge is a cultural thing—she's Romanian. I think she and her family had to flee. Plus, she was a gymnast. And Romanian gymnasts are *for real*."

Regina nodded as she sat down on her flattened mat. Leanne studied her. She was curious to see how she'd do. She held her body like someone who knew how to look but not how to *be*.

But once class started, it was so hard that Leanne almost

forgot about Regina's presence completely. Although about halfway through, she watched as Regina stood up and excused herself from the room. She didn't take anything with her, so Leanne assumed she was coming back. And indeed she did, returning with a hand towel and dabbing at her very flushed face.

Toward the end of class, as they prepped for Savasana, Catalina began to sermonize: "You have to ask yourself: What do you want? And be specific. Be specific with what you're asking of your body, your mind."

What Leanne wanted was always a variation of the same: to be a successful writer. She'd recently given up on getting her humor book published and was focusing on getting into a really good MFA program. The book was a compilation of letters Leanne had actually written to a famous female comedian, but the comedian had never written Leanne back.

"That really was insane," Regina said when it was over, looking sweaty and spent.

"I warned you," Leanne said, smiling.

The women rolled up their mats, and when Leanne turned around Regina was already across the room talking to Catalina. In the year Leanne had been going to Catalina's class, she'd only ever thanked her; she'd never wanted to bother her. But there Regina was—nodding and chatting with her. This was Regina, as she would slowly learn. Everyone was a potential friend.

Each Tuesday and Thursday for roughly the next year (until Leanne *did* get into grad school, which upended their schedule), they went to Catalina's class. In that year, they enjoyed this strange island of a friendship, one where Leanne avoided all mentions of her stationery store job and daily humiliations as a gift-wrapper for rich women. Instead, she focused on her school applications and writing aspirations. And Regina walked Leanne through the process of quitting her office job and opening up her very own homewares store.

Perhaps because she believed that graduate school would pull her more firmly into a separate friend realm, or maybe she already knew they were simply ill matched (there were no fairy tales to pull from where the poor girl and the rich girl team up to slay a dragon), but for whatever reason, Leanne had never treated the relationship like it had legs, like it had a chance beyond workout accountability. So: so what if she didn't assert herself fully?

But then, Leanne hadn't foreseen Regina's stickiness—the way Regina always had an event that she presumed Leanne would attend. Neither had she foreseen her own desire to *adhere*. She didn't yet understand the ways she was willing to make herself small so that a female figure *might* love her. And so the friendship had survived through the years. Then, eventually, it grew.

Which is all to say that Leanne hadn't realized she was setting a precedent when they were twenty-four—the median age of *Bachelor* contestants, when her youth felt unquestioned and everlasting—and Regina mentioned "her" Realtor. They'd just finished a yoga class. Leanne was walking toward her used Toyota Corolla and Regina to her newly leased Prius. Leanne considered her friend in that moment. She saw so clearly a young woman playing grown-up. A little girl talking about meeting with her Realtor. She wanted to ask her, laughing: *How can you afford a house? I can hardly afford these yoga classes!*

But instead, she said, "Exciting!" and got into her car.

5

Her dad died on Sunday, November 1.

The memorial service for him was held on Saturday, November 7.

Leanne gave birth to Hank the very next day: Sunday, November 8.

On that Wednesday in between, she received a package in the mail. It was a gift from her dad for the baby. It was spooky.

Her dad had been a horrible gift giver her entire life. His typical pattern was to call on Christmas or her birthday and ask if she wanted anything. Her response was almost always the same. "Oh, I don't know. Maybe some books or something?" Sometimes, a week or so later, she would get a package from Barnes & Noble with an assortment of strange books on semantics or chess theory or something written by Neil Gaiman.

But he'd also been a gynecologist, and the closer to the due date she got, the more often he seemed to call. Truthfully, he'd been starting to bug her. Her entire life he'd been unavailable, and now, all of a sudden, he had advice to give. A younger Leanne might have lapped it up. But the thirty-three-year-old version was much less interested. Plus, he talked *at* her mostly. He was cynical about the current state of obstetrics. Doctors made decisions to evade lawsuits, he said. He didn't believe in the endless ultrasounds and casual C-sections. He'd delivered plenty of breech babies, which he described as "no big deal."

She didn't understand how he and her mom had ever been together at all. They shared nothing in common. Her dad had seemed to believe in health, in the body's ability to take care of Itself, whereas her mother—the pediatrician—believed in sickness. All throughout her pregnancy, her mom reminded her of the ways things could go wrong. She hounded her about folic acid supplements, made sure she got the flu shot and the Tdap vaccine. She begged her not to have a homebirth.

But the combined effect, Leanne supposed, was a positive one. Leanne trusted her body *and* medicine.

The other thing he kept on about was Brittany, his other daughter and Leanne's half sister. She was six years younger than Leanne and also pregnant, just a few months behind Leanne. "You should call her!" he kept saying. It wasn't like him. Brittany had been born when he was still technically married to Winnie, which was one thing. The other was that he'd hidden the entire pregnancy from his estranged wife. The family story Leanne had grown up with was that *she* had told her mother one day during a tantrum: *Daddy and Beth have a baby!* Though he eventually married Beth, and Leanne would end up living with them for a long stretch of her childhood, the sisters had never been close. And until then—until the two of them were pregnant at the same time—he'd never seemed to care. At the time, she'd explained it away as an atypical (for him) fatherly urge for the cousins to know each other. But now she wondered if some part of him had known that he was about to die. He seemed to be working from a long-standing to-do list.

This theory would also explain the baby gift.

Just a few weeks before the heart attack, he'd asked her if there was anything he could get for the baby. She'd sent him the link to the registry with zero expectations. It was a list of practical things she believed she would need—blankets, bibs, a diaper bin—but she'd also put a few impractical things on there. The homewares store where she'd worked had introduced her to a Japanese children's toy line that made the most beautiful toys she'd ever seen. They were expensive and unnecessary, but the high-end store had also introduced her to the type of consumer who *wanted* to spend a certain amount of money, especially on registries—these people would announce it plainly: "Hi. I want to spend $300."

Surprisingly, her dad had chosen one of these toys. It was a wooden telephone with an old-school rotary dial. And when it arrived, the note attached read:

Happy baby day! You know I can be "on call" if you want!

As soon as she'd opened the box, without thinking, she'd picked up the receiver and spoken into it. "Thank you."

Somewhere, somehow, she heard him respond. *It would've been funnier if I hadn't died.*

6

By the time Leanne arrived at Regina's family's Palm Springs house, it was one-thirty in the afternoon. She brought Hank along because he was due to nurse.

Regina opened the door, smiling. Regina had an outfit for every occasion, no matter how fleeting or particular. Right now, it was a floral-patterned lightweight silk robe. She held a glass of champagne. "There you are!" she said. And then matter-of-factly, motioning toward Hank who lay at Leanne's feet, fastened snugly into his removable car seat: "And there's your child."

"Are you drunk?" The question came out before Leanne had a chance to censor herself. She had seen Regina with a drink in her hand on hundreds of occasions, but she had never seen her noticeably, plainly drunk. It was something she'd wondered about from time to time: how Regina never seemed to let herself go, how no matter what had happened the night before, she would be ready to get up and go to spin class. Regina, the automaton.

She only shrugged as she turned around and waved for Leanne to follow her. Leanne grabbed the handle of Hank's car seat and hoisted it. They walked through the foyer, which opened into the dining room, which spilled into the vast kitchen. The giant marble island was covered with makeup products, tools, and camera equipment. Three women sat nearby on the chairs talking.

"This is Justine and Megan, and you know Margarita, obviously."

"Of course. Hi, Margarita." Margarita was Ursa's nanny.

"They're doing my makeup. Justine and Megan." Regina pointed at them in a way that made Leanne feel deeply self-conscious. "This is my friend Leanne and her baby, Hank."

Leanne felt awkward. "Nice to meet you guys."

"She and I are going to talk about something, and then we'll get started, okay?" Regina smiled weirdly, her eyes squinting.

The women nodded. "Sounds great. We're ready whenever."

Regina turned again and headed to the bedroom, but before following her, Leanne looked at the women and shrugged apologetically.

Inside the bedroom, Leanne felt a bit more at ease. "This house is pretty insane," she said as she propped Hank and his car seat atop the nearby dresser. The ceiling must have been at least twenty-five feet high, and one wall consisted of floor-to-ceiling windows that slid open to the pool outside.

"It's pretty," Regina said, nodding. "Can I get you something to drink?" She gestured to a bottle of champagne in an ice bucket.

"Sure," Leanne shrugged. "So where's Val?"

"He's 'training' with his brother. So stupid." She used air quotes and rolled her eyes.

Leanne unfastened Hank from the thick black safety straps and placed him down on the white wool rug on the floor at the foot of the bed.

Regina handed her a glass of champagne. "Thank you," Leanne said, sitting down on the floor next to her baby. "Cross-training?"

Regina nodded, rolling her eyes once more.

"Relatively harmless activity."

But Regina didn't seem to hear her. She was reaching for her phone. "Can you just watch this video and tell me what you honestly think?"

"Sure, but . . ." She wanted to ask her how much champagne she'd had, but instead she said, "Where's Lila?"

"They're not coming." She frowned. "Martine has a fever."

Lila was one of Regina's oldest and best friends and someone who at this point Leanne knew fairly well by proxy. Regina handed Leanne the phone with the video cued up. "Great, it's up to five hundred thousand views."

Leanne took it with one hand as she reached past the edge of the rug to place the champagne glass down on the polished-cement floor. "But has Lila seen it?"

"Yeah."

"And what did she say?"

"She told me to relax and have a glass of champagne." Regina held up the glass.

"Well, okay then."

Regina smiled with her eyes closed. "Just watch it please."

Leanne pressed play.

As she watched, Regina sat down on the floor and made faces at Hank. Occasionally, she mocked her husband: "He's not afraid of evolving, Hank." And: "I've got an idea, Hank. Let's put on another shirt!"

"So the outfit itself doesn't make a ton of sense," Leanne said once it finished. Regina stood up, exhaling loudly.

Leanne watched her as she crossed the room to pour herself some more champagne. "Reej, you're gonna be trashed before the party even starts!"

"I don't *care*! And I don't want to renew my vows." She was now looking at herself in a full-length mirror and raising her eyebrows up and down. "Not with *that guy*." She turned suddenly and motioned toward her phone.

"It's going to be hard to renew them with anyone else," Leanne said, watching Hank, who was trying his best to roll over—his one arm reaching hard across his body.

Regina fell forward onto the bed and groaned into the mattress. "And I'm going to have to have another kid with him because she needs a sister. You know he bought a pizza oven, right? One you have to put together yourself." She'd picked up her head and was looking at Leanne with her jaw hanging.

"I did know. But hold up. You obviously don't have to have another kid with him."

"Yes I do," she said, popping up onto her elbows. "I have to have at least two. And it *has* to be with him because I'm already thirty-five."

"Thirty-five is nothing."

"Easy to say when you're only thirty-three and already have one." She pointed accusingly at Hank, who had begun to whimper. He'd rolled over onto his stomach but now was sick of it—his arms and legs swimming in the air in frustration.

"He gets stuck."

"Yeah, Urse used to do that." Regina was now hanging her head over the edge of the bed to see.

No one spoke. It wasn't that Leanne herself hadn't thought about these things. She herself wanted a sibling for Hank and by a certain age and with one father. But it felt so gross to say it aloud. Or to hear it said to her from someone with so many options at her fingertips.

"I think I'm going to nurse him," Leanne said, and began unbuttoning her shirt.

"Nurse away. I already pumped twice today," Regina said, sitting up and reaching for an opened bag of chips perched on the bedside table.

Leanne stood up. She first moved her champagne glass to the top of the nearby dresser and then picked Hank up and sat down with him in a giant white leather armchair. She could feel Regina's eyes on her and felt mildly uncomfortable.

"You're lucky," she said.

"Why?"

"Because James is tall. If our next one is a boy, which I don't want, he'll be short because Val is short and I'm just average-sized."

Leanne didn't even know where to start.

"So why would you say I'm lucky? I have a *boy*. Plus, I can hardly afford a nanny even just two days a week. I have no family nearby to help. By the time James comes home from work at seven, I feel insane."

"But James *goes* to work!" She dropped back into her mocking tone: "*I'm a media consultant.* Please. He does *some* social media work for people I introduced him to." She pulled back the covers and crawled into the bed. "When we first got together, it was fine. But now . . ." Her sentence drifted off into a yawn as she rolled onto her side.

"But now what?"

"But now he's almost forty."

"Yeah, but it's not like you guys have money problems."

"No . . ."

Leanne could tell that she wanted to say more. "What?"

"I don't want to take care of him for the rest of my life." She yawned again.

"You mean, like, pay for him?"

Regina flipped to her other side, so that she now faced away from Leanne. "Yeah," she said.

"But wait." Leanne was suddenly so curious. "Don't you guys have joint accounts?"

"He wouldn't let me." The answer came out softly, barely audible.

"He wouldn't let you?" Leanne said, but then thought about it. "Who wouldn't?"

"Mmm" was all she said.

Leanne stood up, cradling Hank, and walked to the other side of the bed. She was beginning to get an idea of their specific situation. She sat down on the edge. Regina's eyes were closed. She shifted into a more supine position. "He would be fine if we got divorced. It's fair."

"Are you really considering that?" Leanne said, though her mind was elsewhere. The blinders were suddenly, frighteningly off. She stared at her friend. She looked peaceful, pretty. Just asleep instead of drunk and irresponsible. Instead of ridiculous.

The questions kept coming, one after the other: How much did her store even *make*? Or did it lose money? Leanne had always assumed Regina's parents helped her out, something she knew other people's parents did, too, but she didn't know anyone who admitted to it less or talked about *work* more than Regina. Regina was always having "crazy" workdays. She talked so much about it that Leanne didn't realize until this moment how much she had believed her.

Now she saw everything so plainly. She saw her role: the inferior friend, the friend who worked a retail job in her thirties, the friend who, until recently, lived in a small two-bedroom apartment and drove a used Toyota Corolla. There was no competition to be had, only safety. Up until recently, Leanne had served to make Regina feel better about herself.

She'd been living a Jane Austen novel: Regina was Emma. And Leanne, Harriet.

But then Leanne had sold her book proposal—she still remembered the way Regina's eyes had shot downward when she'd first told her that she'd gotten an agent. And also when she told her she was pregnant. It was almost as if she hadn't asked for permission from Regina to do these things, to *also* make progress. And then the promise of a grandchild led to her and James's parents helping them scrape together enough money to buy a house they could never have afforded on their own. She quit her retail job. She became a mother.

She sat there on the bed, trying to remember the end of *Emma*. She knew that Emma married Mr. Knightley, and that Harriet married that man she'd originally wanted to marry, a resolution that resolidified the women into the roles they had played from the novel's beginning.

Regina lay on her back and began to snore. *Jesus*, Leanne thought. *Should I prop her on her side in case she vomits?*

Hank pulled off her breast and looked up at her. He looked so happy, content. Leanne moved him upright and gave him a few gentle pats on the back. She stood up and walked back toward the car seat. She tucked him back in, knowing that she had one more question she needed to ask.

She sat back down on the king-size bed, grabbed Regina gently by the shoulder and pulled it toward her so that Regina lay more on her shoulder than on her back. Then: "Reej?" she said softly. She squeezed her arm and gave it a little shake. "Regis?"

"Mm," she said, taking in a breath. "Twenty minutes."

"I have a quick question."

"Mm," she said.

"Have you read my book?" Leanne had given her a copy of the manuscript months ago.

"Hmm."

"My book—have you even glanced through it?"

She shook her head.

"Why not?"

"I don't want to."

"Just like you don't want to vaccinate Ursa?" It was another unspoken agreement between them. But of course, Leanne had clocked the semi-horrified look on Regina's face when Leanne, pregnant, mentioned she'd gotten the flu shot. It had bothered her in the moment, but she'd frozen, done nothing. She hadn't known how to oppose Regina. How to be herself.

Now Regina showed a version of the same look. "Gross."

"Vaccinations?"

She shook her head, as if disgusted. "I won't."

The worst part was that she already knew. She'd known all of it, but in the way she "knew" about stillbirths and chemotherapy. Because she didn't want to know more about these things, because they were sad and upsetting and scary and common. Stillbirths and cancer weren't contagious, but to let them into your psyche did require work, a kind of calculus that Leanne didn't want to do.

But now here it was. Her friend was not a good person.

Regina had been attracted to Leanne in the way someone is attracted to a stray kitten. The kitten is cute. The kitten is vulnerable. But if that were true, then Leanne had to admit something else: that she'd been attracted to Regina for similar but of course opposite

reasons. Up until this moment, Regina had been confident—
perhaps not as confident as Leanne had wanted to believe—but
still, it was a kind of confidence that Leanne had never possessed. A
kind Leanne wanted.

She couldn't remember anything else about the conclusion of
Emma. Surely the denouement alluded to whether or not the women
remained friends. In the short term perhaps, but Leanne couldn't
imagine it lasting, couldn't imagine Harriet and her blue-collar husband having Emma and Mr. Knightley over for dinner.

But then again, Val was no Mr. Knightley. And Leanne wasn't a
classic Harriet. Leanne had a book coming out, a book she'd made
happen via the low art of blogging. She had a tall, assured husband
(a man much more closely resembling Mr. Knightley, thank you),
a beautiful son with a magical strip of white hair on the top of his
head, and a dead father who possibly spoke to her from the grave. If
anyone was leading a charmed life, it was *her*. Right?

She took a deep breath in.

She stood up. She grabbed the handle of the car seat, heaved it
upward, and then she spotted Regina's phone lying there on the
floor where Leanne had left it.

She got an idea—a strange, wonderful, horrible idea. She put the
car seat back down.

7

She picked up the phone. If it were locked already, the almost-certainly bad idea wouldn't even be an option. She pressed the circular button. She pressed it again. No lock screen appeared. She was in, just like that. Her chest tingled with adrenaline. She felt it move through her body to her fingers. She glanced up at Regina: sound asleep.

Ever since Hank had been born, Leanne had noticed a significant drop-off in likes from Regina on Instagram. Ditto on Facebook. She also knew for a fact that Regina unfriended people who bothered her. (Leanne's own personal policy with friends who annoyed her on social media was to simply endure.)

She clicked open Instagram. Regina had 18K followers to Leanne's 3K. The bottom of the screen lit up with new likes and comments. She typed her handle into the search box. She clicked on her own name and there was her answer: the blue button read, *Follow*. It was sadly *just* like her best friend to un-follow her. "So lame," Leanne whispered, looking up again at Regina. And then at Hank. His eyes were drooping.

What happened next Leanne could only explain as a version of her base instincts taking over—like when she'd been deep into labor, trying to make her way into the hospital, unself-consciously bellowing as she leaned on car after car in the parking lot.

First, she clicked on the *Follow* button to follow herself.

Next, she closed the app and opened up Regina's email. She didn't know exactly what she was looking for. She just scrolled down reading the subject lines. She stopped when she hit upon one from Thea McManus with the subject *Santa Barbara Girlz Weekend?* Leanne hadn't heard anything about this.

Hank whimpered. With her left hand, she began rocking his car seat while with her right she held the phone, swiping her thumb down and down as she quickly absorbed the information that Regina was going to Santa Barbara with a group of women that didn't include her—all seemingly organized by Thea.

Leanne knew Thea. She was a newish friend of Regina's who up until this moment hadn't threatened Leanne at all.

Now she closed out of Regina's email and instead opened up her text messages. She saw her own name at the top, quickly followed by Lila and then Thea. She clicked on Thea and scrolled. She scrolled and scrolled, looking for *something*.

At last, she found it: her own name. It took a minute to find it spelled out in chronological order, but once she did, there it all was.

> **Thea:** So then we'll shoot for that weekend at the end of March. Sound good? I'll send out an email to you, me, Lila, Agnes, and Leanne.

> **Regina:** Sounds perfecto. Though I doubt Leanne will be able to make it. She doesn't have a full-time nanny ☹

> **Thea:** I sort of figured, but also thought since you guys are so close, it was rude not to invite her at all.

Regina: I adore Leanne! But it's
your birthday. You should invite
whoever you want! 👋

Thea: I was just thinking of the usual
suspects.

Regina: Totally.

Thea: I don't have to invite her.

Regina: It's up to you!

Thea: I actually don't know her very
well. 👻

Regina: That's what I thought. But
I wasn't sure.

Thea: Yeah.

Thea: OK, so let's just make it you, me,
Lila, and Agnes. That's four women,
which should be plenty. ☺

Regina: Sounds divine. Can't wait!

"'She doesn't have a full-time nanny'?" Leanne whispered. "Jesus Christ."

She moved back into Regina's email. This time, she searched
for "password." She'd begun to sweat a little. She looked at Hank.
He seemed moments away from falling asleep, which felt akin to a
blessing from god—the god of spite? She took a breath through her
nose to try to calm herself. She didn't have any specific plan beyond

the desire to prove that Regina was not who she appeared to be. She scrolled quickly. Then she saw an email from Regina to herself. The subject was simply: *IG password*. She clicked on it.

Orange04!

Leanne grabbed her own phone. She opened Instagram. She clicked on *Add an Account*. She logged in as Regina. (She was familiar with this process because she had a separate account for her food blog.) She waited until the email about *a new log-in from a new device* showed up in Regina's account. She clicked on the link that would allow this other device access. She deleted the email and then went into the deleted emails and deleted it there. She told herself she wasn't necessarily going to *do* anything. It would be mostly harmless. She would make Regina "like" an occasional post or two.

An image from Roald Dahl's *The Twits* popped into her head. It was a book she'd loved as a kid. The Twits were a married couple who played progressively larger practical jokes on each other. She hadn't reread it in over ten years. Were they jokes or were they simply cruel stunts?

As soon as she'd done all this, she wanted out of there. *What were you thinking? Who are you?*

She placed Regina's phone on the rug where she'd found it. She heaved Hank and his car seat upward, and with one last glance at sleeping Regina, she slid out of the well-appointed bedroom suite.

8

As she drove the flat, wide streets of Palm Springs back to the hotel, she took a deep breath. She looked in the rearview mirror at Hank, asleep.

She looked at the clock on the dashboard.

In a few hours, she would have to attend Regina's party. She would have to act as if all were fine, as if Regina were her friend. Her *dear* friend. Which she still was?

This was slated to be her and James's first night out without Hank since he had been born. She'd been looking forward to it for months. She'd wanted to get dressed up and eat food served to her from a tray. She'd wanted to feel pretty.

She still wanted those things.

9

When Delia, the sitter she'd booked on a website, showed up at the hotel, Leanne could feel the relief hit her skin. She was young and soft-spoken and deferential. She would not hurt a baby.

Leanne had already made the bottle with the breast milk. "I'm hoping this will be enough," she told her. "I've never actually left him at night before, so I don't know how much he drinks."

Delia nodded. "It's good, ma'am," she said.

In the car, she wanted confirmation from James. "She seemed very nice," she said.

He nodded. "Very nice."

"We're good people?"

He smiled. "Yeah, for the most part."

She hadn't told him a thing about her afternoon with Regina. She'd briefly considered it, but there was no way of framing it so that her behavior was excusable. In fact, if she really let herself think about it, there was no way of framing the entire course of their friendship in which Leanne came off well.

She pulled down the sun visor and looked at her face in the mirror. She'd put on black mascara and pink lipstick. She had wanted to get a new dress for the party, but all the ones she liked were over $300. She'd given up, deciding to wear a roomy magenta shift she'd gotten for a wedding when she was about twelve weeks pregnant. It was the only appropriate thing in her closet that fit her postpartum breasts. It was fine. She looked pretty.

She flipped the sun visor back up and scrolled through her phone, stopping at a photo Brittany had just posted. "Oh," she said; the sound came out involuntarily.

"What?"

"MyKayla's up to eight pounds."

"Oh, that's great," James said.

She thought her dad would be pleased to know that his death *had* brought the sisters slightly closer. Finally, they could share the same narrative: their father was dead. On the day of the memorial service, Leanne had sent Brittany a long condolence via a direct Facebook message. Brittany had responded in kind and included her cell phone number. And then, when Hank was born the very next day, Leanne had texted her a photo of him. Ever since, the two communicated via their phones, Facebook, and Instagram—mostly with variations on the heart emoji.

And so, about three months ago, in early December, it was through social media that Leanne found out that Brittany had gone into labor five weeks early. The baby—a girl they named with curious capitalization MyKayla—was mostly fine. Her lungs were developed enough to breathe on her own, which was apparently huge. The main problem was with her suck/swallow/breathe coordination. Brittany had posted about all of this and then Leanne had Googled it. Basically it meant that the baby had trouble eating. Leanne had texted Brittany, offering support, but living across the country there wasn't much she could do. Mostly, she stared at Hank and felt guilty for having birthed a full-term baby who'd nursed for thirty minutes straight almost immediately after having come out of her. His birth weight had never even dropped. He'd only gained. Her pediatrician had been so impressed.

Now in the passenger seat, she typed her comment: *This news is giving me life!* ♥ ♥ ♥

10

I t was a little after six—the sun had just set moments ago—when Leanne and James arrived at the party. It was being held at a sprawling resort hotel that Leanne had been to a couple of times before, though never to spend the night, only to eat at one of the restaurants. Despite being firmly in the desert, the grounds were lush and green with pockets of manicured grass, rows of orange and grapefruit trees, and Leanne's personal favorite, palo verdes with their mossy-colored trunks and branches.

Servers with trays of champagne greeted them at the entrance along with a photographer, a man who must've been part of the team. A well-known lifestyle magazine had featured Regina's wedding, but Leanne knew that Regina wanted more for this party. She was older now. She wanted to show her growth, her development, that she was going up, up, up! An image of Regina as a kind of cartoony Thanksgiving Day parade balloon came to mind. And then herself as one of the people on the ground, sweating, holding on to a gigantic tether.

Moving deeper into the venue, she and James met servers with trays of hors d'oeuvres: ice-cold ceviche on a single blue-corn tortilla chip, baja-style fried shrimp with a spicy aioli, and spoons of limey cubes of avocado mixed with pomegranate seeds. Everything oozed effortless wealth.

Within a few more minutes, James and Leanne found themselves chatting with a couple they often ran into at these events: Sabine and Joshua. They were both artists and much older. Joshua must've been fifty, but he had this lithe skater-boy youthfulness about him. Leanne liked looking at them, the ease with which Joshua held his drink and the cut of his understated navy suit. And Sabine, with her smoky eyeliner and neither straight nor wavy hair. This was just another event on their calendar.

And then a pair of violinists began to play. A woman who must've been hired to do so encouraged the crowd to form a semi-circle around a simple, white cloth chuppah, which Leanne hadn't even noticed until now. People were still arriving, which somehow only added to the feeling of ease of the event—*Come or don't come. We'll be having a good time no matter what.*

Regina and Val emerged. Regina looked striking if not a tad overly made-up. She wore a peachy-coral floor-length dress with a gold trim that, paired with her tanned skin and dark-brown hair, gave off a vaguely Elizabeth-Taylor-as-Cleopatra vibe. The two of them stopped and faced each other underneath the chuppah. A friend of theirs, a poetry professor at UCLA Leanne had met a couple of times, entertainingly and quickly walked them through a renewing of the vows.

"To four more years!" the poet shouted as a way of wrapping up, and Val and Regina raised their hands in triumph.

Everyone laughed and raised their glasses. "To four more years!"

Leanne shouted it too. She was on her second glass of champagne and feeling warm and buzzy; she looked at James as if to say: *I know they're horrible, but goddammit I'm having fun!* James winked back.

The speakers kicked on loudly to that Taylor Swift song with the refrain about the couple never being off-trend. Val and Regina danced. It was sweet; it was funny; it was a show. How long would they be able to keep it up? Leanne wondered for them. For herself.

The answer was nine o'clock.

That's when James began pinching Leanne on the back of her arm. But he hadn't needed to. Leanne was ready too. Her breasts tugged at her bra, aching with too much milk. Though before they could leave, she felt compelled to talk to Regina, to actually say hello and good-bye.

Leanne found her deep in conversation with Laura, which was the only kind of conversation Laura had. She was a photographer who had just launched her own line of cotton underwear.

"Oh, are you leaving?" Regina said. Laura turned her head as well.

Leanne nodded. "Yeah. Sorry to interrupt. Just wanted to say good-bye and hello, too."

Leanne nodded as Regina said, "You've gotta go home and nurse?"

"Well, pump."

"I'm going to refresh my drink," Laura said to Regina, squeezing her on the shoulder. And then to Leanne: "Nice to see you!"

"You too!" Leanne said, and then to Regina: "Hey, you did it."

Regina nodded but not in a way of acceptance. "Well, I'm glad you guys made it." Would anyone else standing there watching have been able to see it, the coldness emanating from Regina's body? To Leanne, it was plain, as if she were busy erecting an invisible steel wall between them. "Are you heading straight home in the morning or are you going to stick around for the afternoon?"

Propelled by an almost unconscious desire to fit in, Leanne attempted to match her tone: "We'll probably get breakfast and then head out."

"Cheeky's?"

"Maybe. It might be too crowded on a Sunday."

"King's Highway?"

"Probably safer."

"Yum," she said, pulling Leanne in for a hug. "Thanks again for coming! It means a lot." It felt like embracing a robot, the way their bodies angled mechanically toward each other from the hips.

"Of course," Leanne said. And then one more time just because she couldn't think of anything else. "Of course."

"I'll see you soon." She was already turning to walk away.

Run, Leanne, run! she heard her dad say.

Yes, she said back. *I am.*

11

B ack at the hotel, Leanne and James paid Delia and then stood
over Hank's Pack 'n Play, which they'd tucked into the corner of the room. They watched his chest rise and fall. Everything was okay.

They got into their pajamas. Leanne set up the breast pump in
the bathroom. She grabbed her phone, and as she sat on the lidded
toilet, she scrolled through Instagram while the machine churned
and spat air.

Not surprisingly, half of her feed consisted of photos from Regina's party. Leanne herself was probably going to post one. Maybe
the one James had taken of her from dinner—she was biting into
a taco. It gave Leanne an uncomfortable pleasure to know that
whatever she chose would show up in Regina's feed. She *wanted* to
show up there, to be unavoidable. Mindlessly, she toggled over to
her email. Her heartbeat jumped. Maxine Hunter's name was in her
in-box. She clicked on it right away.

Leanne,
Thanks for your response. Clearly, it's all very interesting to me: a
life with a child versus life without. You have to choose one way or
another without a trial run. Even if you become a parent at a late
age, like sixty, you will spend the rest of your life as a parent. There
is no going back!

I wonder if your friend would've answered the question about wanting kids differently if it had come from someone more like herself, someone who didn't have children either. Right now, I'm probably—almost certainly—writing to you differently than I might to someone without children.

Right?

Max

Here's what Leanne learned about Maxine in the inspired Googling that ensued:

She was thirty-eight. She lived in New York City. She'd gotten her start in performance art. Then she'd written a play. And then her first book. She'd divorced four years ago, after only two years of marriage, and then started a relationship with a woman. All of this mirrored the plot of *Koala Life*. So maybe Leanne already knew much of her life story?

She could feel that the pump had done the work it was capable of. (It never did as good a job as Hank.) She pulled the tubes out, removed the plastic funnels from the inside of her sports bra. She placed the two meagerly filled bottles on the counter. She caught a glimpse of herself in the mirror. She was just drunk enough to find herself pretty and to laugh at the way her nipples poked through the sports bra. She then rinsed all of the various parts under hot water and laid them atop a white hand towel she'd arranged there for that very purpose. She looked down at her phone and toggled back to the email from Maxine. She liked the question mark after the word *right*. Maxine Hunter was asking her something. And Leanne would answer. She looked back at her own reflection. *Fuck Regina*, she thought. She didn't need her.

PART

II

12

It wasn't as simple as that.

During the next week, Leanne came to the frustrating conclusion that she needed Regina for a bit longer—just until her book came out.

Plus, there were the logistical problems. For example: Carmen's baby shower, which was *tonight* and to which both women were invited. There was book club to consider—Leanne was hosting the next meeting at her house. She couldn't just cut her out of her life with one swing of the ax. It was going to be a process.

There was also the strange emotional element—the various urges Leanne got to text Regina about something inconsequential. It confused her to no end that she could still *want* the friendship, although it did occur to her that maybe she just didn't want the lack of it.

It reminded her of when she'd lived in Costa Rica for a few months right after college, and she'd briefly dated a boy named Gabi. He wasn't her typical choice. He was muscled and manly. He drove a motorcycle. He didn't seem overly interested in her. But she'd been teaching English in a small town and actively trying on a personality that could cut loose. He was the third guy she'd ever slept with, and she'd done so after only two dates, if you could call them that.

Afterward, when he didn't call when he said he would and then not even after that, she was so disgusted. With him but also with herself. She'd become a woman with low self-esteem, a woman contingent on a phone call. She avoided everyone, wrote tirades in her journal for days. Weeks later, still hurt, she ran into him at a party.

Most people were hanging out and drinking in a group in the living room. A few were in the kitchen making dinner. Eventually, he pulled her aside into an empty room. He had the look of an eighties pop star: tight-fitting jeans, white sneakers, and a subtle mullet. But in Costa Rica, it worked. She backed herself against the wall. He grabbed her waist and pulled her in for a kiss. Leanne let him. It was part of her plan.

"I think we should just be friends," she said, inches away from his face.

"Yeah?" he said, and kissed her again, pressing himself against her. His jeans were so thick. They had to be uncomfortable. They kissed for a while, and the whole time, Leanne kept telling herself that she had to be the one to stop first.

Finally, she grabbed his cheeks and held them. "We should get back to the party."

"Segura?" he said, pulling her to him.

"Yes," she said definitively, and turned to leave.

The rest of the night, she could feel his eyes on her but refused to look back. She left the party alone. She'd been proud of herself. She'd been strong. She had self-respect! But now, thinking about it for the first time in almost a decade, she felt something like regret. The guy had looked like Daniel Day-Lewis's sexier brother. But her thinking had been so firm, so tit for tat: He had hurt her, so she had to hurt him back. Now she wanted to go back in time to that party. She wanted to talk to her past self, to tell her that she didn't need to extract everything from this one person. She wanted to befriend herself, to guide her younger self into a softer existence. Not for Gabi's sake—his heart had hardly been broken—but for her own.

As soon as Hank finally went down for his morning nap, she opened up her email in order to reference the shower invitation. It wasn't a normal baby shower. She remembered instructions being involved.

But she was immediately greeted and distracted by a message from her brother. The subject read: *Guess she called dibs on this too.* She clicked it open to find a screenshot of what looked like one of Brittany's Facebook posts. Leanne must have missed it, and it took her a second to put everything together. It was one of those mirror photos where the person held up their phone to their own reflection. It wasn't anything special. Brittany was smiling as she wore baby MyKayla in a sling. But Charlie had doctored the photo, circling something in the background with a red digital line. Leanne squinted and then understood: it was an oil painting that had hung in Dad's study—a landscape of a busy harbor.

This had become the joke between them. That they hadn't received anything of their father's in the wake of his death because they'd forgotten to call dibs. The truth, that their dad had simply left everything to Beth, who in turn hadn't considered them at all, was, she guessed, not as funny.

But that wasn't entirely accurate. Leanne *had* called dibs on something.

Right after the memorial service, fully pregnant, she'd called Charlie. She'd wanted him to tell her every single thing she'd missed, but her big brother hated talking on the phone, hated talking in general it always felt. He tried, though.

He told her how there was no body or casket. He'd gathered from Jordan—their other half sibling—that Dad had been cremated. So instead, there was an easel holding a poster with an image of him in a suit and tie. Charlie had taken a photo of it for her and texted it. She spent a long time staring at it, wondering who decided to put the weird tapestry effect on the image. Who had wanted the poster to look like fabric when it was clearly a poster?

Below his name—Charles Scott Hazelton—and the years he'd lived, 1950–2015, was a quote by Stephen Hawking: "It is not clear that intelligence has any long-term survival value."

She wondered who'd chosen the line. It was so good.

But an hour or so after this conversation, she'd called her brother back. Something had dawned on her. "Did you get any of his ashes?"

"No," he said.

"Why not?"

"I didn't even think of it," he said.

"Oh." Her first thought was that he could reach out to Beth and ask her for a portion. But she knew that he'd just checked into his sad hotel for the night, that the request was a bridge too far, both for her to ask it and for him to do it.

"One thing I forgot to tell you is that Brittany did give me a box of some of the things from his office. It's nothing much, but there's a framed poem you made for him. I'll send it to you."

But days later, with newborn Hank at her side, she'd emailed Beth asking about the ashes. And then a month later, when she hadn't heard back, she'd followed up. Then Brittany went into early labor and Leanne knew she couldn't pursue it. But now the baby was fine. And Leanne was curious. She searched her in-box to see exactly what she'd sent to Beth. She wanted to read her own words and listen for the tone. She found the two emails bundled together; she'd sent the second one as a reply to the first.

On Wed, Dec 2 at 11:51am
Leanne Hazelton leannehazelton@gmail.com wrote:

Hi Beth,

Not sure if you saw the below email that I sent last month. I'm sure that you are busy and still grieving Dad's death. I know that I am, but as I wasn't able to attend the memorial service, I was hoping that you could please send me a portion of his ashes. At the very least, if you could respond and let me know you got this email?

Thank you,
Leanne

On Wed, Nov 11 at 1:07pm
Leanne Hazelton leannehazelton@gmail.com wrote:

Hi Beth,

I know we haven't spoken in a long time, but I was hoping that we might find a moment's solidarity given Dad's recent sudden death. As you know, I was too pregnant to attend the memorial service. (In fact, I went into labor that very night and have a newborn baby right here as I type this.) But I would still like to hold some kind of private service for him. It's my understanding that he was cremated, and I was hoping you might be able to send me via mail a portion of his ashes. It would mean so much to me.

Thanks for your time and many condolences for your loss.

Leanne

Rereading them sent fresh indignation through her. She *knew* that that was Beth's email too, since her dad had once forwarded something to the both of them. (Leanne had quickly responded, only to him with: *Don't forward things to both of us at the same time!*)

She had to assume that by this point, Beth, Brittany, and Jordan had already released the ashes somewhere. But she wanted Beth to have to at least *say* that to her.

Leanne and Charlie had never expected money from their father, not even when he was alive. His boundaries had been so clear, and they knew not to overstep them—but did he put *nothing* in writing for them? A chess set? A stack of books? In her mind, she and her brother had been the originals—the *true* offspring. Brittany and Jordan had come second. They were the weirdo ancillary family that her dad had fallen into as opposed to having chosen. She still wasn't ready to admit that maybe she'd been wrong.

So, angry and with her sense of entitlement revived, she typed up a third email.

Hi, Beth! she wrote, deciding on "freakishly cheerful" for the tone. *Glad to see that MyKayla is doing so well. Gah! What a scare and what a relief! Was wondering where we're at in terms of Dad's remains?*

She hit *Send* just as Hank began to stir.

13

Dear Ones,

It is with great excitement and pleasure that Damian and I invite you to celebrate the 120th day of my pregnancy.

In Yogic tradition, this is the day in the pregnancy when the woman becomes a mother. It is the day the woman becomes the vehicle for the soul of the baby to fully incarnate.

In the words of Yogi Bhajan:

"The purest thing in the world is the heart of the mother, the heart-chakra, the center of the mother. It is the purest thing in the world. It can move God. It can move the universe. It can cause an effect beyond limitation."

To celebrate this special time and to show your support, we ask that you bring a momento [sic] that has some kind of sentimental meaning to you. It can be anything you find yourself drawn to: a rock, a shell, a photograph, a wooden carving, a textile, a hand-made object, whatever. All of the offerings will be kept as reminders of your love and support as we bring this child into the world.

Please join us Monday, March 14 at our home at 7 p.m. for reflection, meditation, and, of course, celebration.

Also, come hungry! We will be serving a great Argentine feast.

With so much love,
Carmen and Damian

P.S. A photographer from Kindred *magazine will be here shooting the event.*

Leanne had handed Hank off to James the moment he stepped inside the front door. She was already going to be late.

As she dressed, her phone pinged. It was a text from Regina, the first since the party: *Is your wood carving finished for Carmen's 120-day-old fetus?*

Leanne smiled and texted back instinctively—without reminding herself that she hated her: *Lol. Yes. I carved it myself. It's quite pure.*

Regina texted back: 😄

A few minutes later, Leanne emerged from the bedroom to sort through James's personal rock collection, most of which James had arranged on an upper shelf in Hank's room. There, she found James as well. He was putting Hank's pajamas on. "Do you think he'll be warm enough in that?" she said. "It's kind of cold tonight."

"He'll be fine," James said. "What are you doing with my rocks?"

"I need one for this baby shower."

"You need a rock?"

"It's like a Buddhist thing."

"It's funny, isn't it? You always hate when I bring rocks home, and now you're taking one of them."

"I don't *hate* when you bring them home. What about this one?" Leanne held a smooth gray rock in between her thumb and forefinger.

"Yeah, I mean, that's a really nice rock that I handpicked from the Russian River."

Leanne smiled. "Can I have it?"

"It's not for Regina?"

"No!"

"Fine then."

Within five minutes, Leanne had kissed the boys good-bye and was driving to Carmen's.

14

Julianna greeted Leanne at the door. Julianna was the woman Leanne had referenced in the email to Maxine—the one who lived close by who didn't have children.

"We're just getting situated," she said, and motioned toward the living room off to the left.

Leanne turned the corner to find Regina sitting in the middle of the couch with four women forming a sort of horseshoe shape around her—Lila and Carmen on either side.

"Guys, I'm fine, really," Regina was saying. "I guess I just didn't realize how hard I'd hit it."

"What happened?" Leanne asked, looking first toward Regina and the women, but when they continued to talk among themselves, she turned to Julianna: "What happened?"

"Regina hit her head against an open cabinet at home right before she came here and then felt dizzy once she got here and had to sit down."

Leanne nodded. "Oh."

Carmen stood up. "Hi, love!" She walked over to Leanne and planted a crushing kiss to her cheek. Of all the women Leanne had met through Regina, Carmen was by far her favorite. If she were to judge her femininity on a scale of ten, Leanne would give her the ten. Her hair was wavy and storybook long, falling to the middle of her back. She'd grown up in Brazil but had an Argentinean father who had eventually moved them to the States. She spoke Portuguese, Spanish, and a subtly accented English that Leanne found so compelling. It made her beauty somehow approachable.

She talked in aphorisms of her own making. "A woman's power is in her pleasure," she'd once said, which at the time had called to Leanne's mind an image of her mother eating a chocolate éclair. The groaning, the nodding, the chocolate drip drip dripping down her chin, which she eventually, *finally*, pseudo-addressed via a swipe of her thumb and the announcement: "I like creamy things."

But now Carmen was asking about the baby.

"Oh, he's at home. Seven o'clock bedtime."

"Oh." She looked truly deflated.

"How are you doing?"

"I'm great." She clutched her lower belly, though there was still no visible mark of her pregnancy. "It's Regina we're worried about."

"No, I'm fine. I just—"

"She might have a concussion," Lila said, almost appearing to be excited by the notion.

"Honestly, it *does* sound like a concussion. My son's friend got one playing soccer," a woman named Jenni said.

Another woman chimed in, apparently reading from her phone: "It says that the best thing we can do is just monitor her and make sure she doesn't pass out."

Everyone agreed.

"Okay, well then, I guess we should eat!" Carmen announced. "There are empanadas in the kitchen. Champagne too. Damian's at the grill. We hung all these pretty lights out there on the porch, so hopefully we'll get some good shots. Oh, and this is Malena, the photographer." She gestured to a woman standing in the corner of the room with a camera.

Leanne had been to Carmen's once before—with Regina. They'd wanted to check out and possibly buy one of her handbags. Leanne had really wanted one, even since before she met Carmen, but wasn't willing or able to pay the $450. She'd been hoping for some kind of in-person, wholesale discount, but Carmen didn't offer any. Even so, Regina had left with one, plus a matching wallet.

With a few women still surrounding Regina, Leanne followed Carmen presumably to the grill, passing through the kitchen. The floor consisted of squares of green, yellow, and blue Moroccan tiles; the walls of open wooden shelving were heavy with copper pots, earthenware bowls, and glass jars filled with colorful spices and dried beans. The kitchen opened up to the deck, and with the door propped open, the air smelled thickly of smoke and meat.

Through the window, she could see Malena taking photos of Damian heaping grilled meat onto a plate that Carmen held. Leanne could already see the feature coming together: "West Meets South (America)." There would be photos of all of these pretty women in their off-white linen shirts and balloonish pants eating ribs, gnawing on bones. Leanne hated that she still wanted to be one of them. It reminded her of being thirteen and flipping through *Teen* magazine's Great Model Search, of wanting so badly to be one of the teens in the running to be the next Great Model. When would she stop wanting things that were so clearly not meant for her?

Once everyone had a plate of food in front of them, Romina— Carmen's younger sister—took charge of the ceremony part. But as she explained the yogic basis for what they were about to do, Leanne couldn't follow. Instead, she focused on Romina's thin, muscled legs. Despite the chilly weather, the younger version of Carmen was wearing a black cotton miniskirt so short it barely covered her ass. Leanne was mesmerized, not just by her legs, but by the confident way in which the woman held herself. If Leanne were to wear a skirt that short and tight, she would have one hand permanently tugging at the black material to make sure it wasn't riding up. But Romina didn't seem to care. Also notable was the fact that the skirt *wasn't* riding up.

Soon enough, she was done speaking, and the woman to her right was explaining the item that she'd brought and why it was important to her. The woman had a one-year-old at home and began choking up. "You want to protect them as much as you can, but you can't protect them from everything. Or so I hear," she said with a little smile.

The next person up was Damian's mother; she'd brought Damian's original baby blanket.

Jenni held up a massive piece of pink quartz she'd found in Quartzsite, Arizona. Carmen's eyes lit up when she held it. "This is incredible."

Romina brought a bundle of lavender she'd picked in Ojai and dried.

When it was Leanne's turn, she held the rock in her right hand. It was shaped in a kind of cylinder and so smooth that it had the look of a piece of driftwood.

"James collects these rocks," she said. And then, without a second's warning, her throat closed; her eyes welled. What was happening? She had barely said anything. She didn't even care about this rock! "I've honestly never cared about them until I guess *now*." She shrugged as a way of conclusion—wanting rid of the spotlight—and set the rock on the coffee table among all the other items that had been offered up. It looked lonely there, dull and dwarfed next to the shiny piece of quartz.

When she looked back up, Carmen was nodding at her. "Thank you. It's lovely." Leanne scanned the rest of the faces. Regina was looking at her phone. The other women appeared to have moved on already. *I brought a rock?*

Lila brought a scented candle—one of those sixty-dollar ones. She leaned forward to add it to the table, but Carmen intercepted it and brought it to her nose, inhaling deeply. "Ah, it's divine. Thank you, Lila."

The last person to go, as she was sitting directly to the right of Carmen, was Regina. "I didn't technically make this either," she said, reaching deep into her giant bag, "but I did *have* it made." She pulled out a thickly folded quilt. Carmen gasped, taking it in her hands and unfolding it.

Everyone cooed.

"Ah."

"Wow."

"It's beautiful."

The quilt looked mostly white with thick azure stitching around the border.

"Is this going to be part of your line?" Carmen asked.

"Well, not this exact one. This one is *exclusive*," she said, winking. "But yeah, baby quilts very similar to this one."

Exclusive. Please! Leanne thought, and wished she could shout. *The only thing exclusive about it is the price point.* She was bothered for endless reasons. Sure, because she couldn't afford a quilt. But even if she could afford one, would she want it because she liked it or because she just wanted to belong? But mostly, she was bothered because she'd already been excluded. She was already out of the loop. She'd known that Regina had wanted to expand her line to include baby blankets, but she hadn't known they were *now* in production. And of course, she was bothered that this bothered her.

With the ceremony ostensibly over, the women began to mingle and chat once more.

A queue formed in front of Regina and her new product, and Leanne considered waiting in it, paying her own respects. But no. Those days were over.

15

At home, halfway through breast-feeding Hank in the dark of his room, while the white noise machine mimicked ocean waves crashing, she pulled out her phone and began scrolling. Looking at the pictures of the party, she saw well-dressed women in muted tones next to vibrant plates of food. She momentarily considered un-following Jenni—the biggest Regina sycophant?—though didn't. She kept scrolling. She hit a post by Brittany. It was a picture of MyKayla, all swaddled up atop a mess of blankets. The caption read: "Baby MyK is getting the hang of this thing! #blessed #fighter #MyKaylastrong #babygirl #miraclebaby."

Leanne commented: *YAY!!*

She put her phone down, switched Hank to the other breast, and then picked it back up.

She tapped on the search box and typed in "Maxine Hunter" to see if she had an account. She did.

Leanne went through her photos, randomly clicking on the ones that interested her. There was a bizarre series from her trip to the eye doctor, which concluded with a selfie of her *and* the eye doctor. There were photos of strangers in airports. Of her and her Uber driver. There were a few photos of her and the musician/actress Giulia Stein. Apparently, in one of those strange twists of fate, as if god forgot to shuffle their talent-and-luck deck, Giulia and Maxine had known each other since childhood. And they'd both separately grown up to be famous artists. Or maybe it wasn't a strange twist of fate? Maybe they'd pushed each other in their respective arts. Perhaps alone, without the other, neither of them would have made it. Perhaps alone, both would have given up at that first impasse, would have bowed out as soon as push came to shove.

Push coming to shove. The saying rolled around her mind. She imagined pushing Regina—her own hands flattened against her shoulders. She imagined the indignation spreading across Regina's face. Surely, she would shove back. It reminded her of a tweet she'd clicked on, which had led to an article highlighting a study of preschoolers. The results showed that three- and four-year-old girls were just as physically aggressive as the boys, but the boys were corrected for their behavior three times as often. Correction was a form of attention, the article stated, and so it perpetuated the behavior. It didn't say what happened to the girls, what behaviors of theirs were unwittingly perpetuated. But Leanne could imagine.

She looked back down at her phone. She tapped on the web browser. The first tab that came up was this dense *New Yorker* book review covering a book about the history of vaccination. She'd found it yesterday while looking for more information on the topic. She knew she should just read the book itself, but she really didn't want to. She wanted the CliffsNotes. According to the reviewer, one of the points the author seemed to be making was that people who resisted vaccines displayed less faith in the "system." It made no sense to Leanne in terms of Regina. The system had served Regina well. So well that Regina couldn't see it? Or maybe so well that she had to deny its existence? The more Leanne read, the more she learned, like the phenomenon of herd immunity—that as more and more people within a population were vaccinated, the better protected everyone was: that the vaccinated protected the unvaccinated. The more she learned, the more annoyed she became: that Hank's immunity would protect Ursa. That some people could evade the rules and suffer no consequences.

She quietly seethed.

And then she had an idea.

She switched to Regina's account and went straight to the search bar. She typed in a username she'd heard about: *KNOWvax&OK*. Leanne tapped on the latest post, a spare image of some dried bundled flowers lying next to a straw hat on a white surface—maybe a kitchen countertop. The accompanying caption began in all caps: "IT IS OK TO: 1. Ask questions about what goes into your baby's body!" The list continued, but before Leanne read on, she saw that what she had come here to do had already been done. Regina had already *liked* this post. Leanne tapped on the username again. She could see that Regina wasn't following the account. This post must've come up for her according to an algorithm. She followed the account for her and then went to the next most recent post—an impassioned soliloquy for feeding your baby "whole foods" and liked it on behalf of Regina.

Then she logged out as Regina and back in as herself. She re-followed Regina so that when she clicked on the tab that showed you what your followers were up to, Regina's recent anti-vax *follow* and *like* would pop up. As soon as she saw it, she screenshotted it. What would she do with this? She didn't know, but it felt necessary. Other parents should at least *know* that Ursa wasn't vaccinated. Right?

She logged back into Regina's account and deleted the notification that Leanne had re-followed her. As she did so, Regina received a direct message. *Ah, yes. Direct messages!* Leanne tapped the in-box. The unread message was from Carmen. She knew enough not to click on it. Instead, she clicked on the one below it, which had already been read.

It was a message from a woman named Helen. Leanne read it and quickly gathered that the women had recently met for lunch. When Leanne clicked on her profile, she saw that Helen worked for *À la Table* magazine.

The next exchange under that was with Regina's mother, Mimi.

Regina had shared an image of a couch from Design Within Reach. The caption with it read: *What about this one?*

Mimi, whom Leanne had met on a number of occasions, had written back: *Yes, I think that will work nicely in the new office. Go ahead. Daddy and I were going to add more to your account this month anyway.*

She took another screenshot. She wanted to look up exactly how much the couch cost so that she could choose an appropriate level of resentment, but she'd have to do it later. She could feel that Hank had fallen asleep at the helm. She placed her phone down on the armrest and then stared at her son in the darkness. She felt the accrued tension in between her shoulder blades while she stared at her baby's slightly agape mouth; his body looked the opposite of hers in every way. So open, so trusting. She touched his cheek with the back of her finger and promised to do better for him. She promised not to let him turn out like her. "No," she whispered. "When you grow up, you won't even *like* overpriced mid-century modern furniture."

The next morning, Leanne texted the screenshot that read:

Regina Mark followed KNOWvax&OK

Regina Mark liked a post by KNOWvax&OK

to Mary Anne, her best friend from college. Though Mary Anne lived in Brooklyn, she knew all about Regina (and her textiles) and now—after a stream of texts from Leanne—she knew the basics of the women's falling-out.

She moved on. Hank was napping, and she had other things to do, like write back to Maxine Hunter and work on this essay her editor thought they could place with the *New York Times* as part of her book's publicity strategy.

She began with Maxine.

Hi Maxine,

It's true. My neighbor might have felt uncomfortable saying she didn't want children—plainly and flat-out—to someone newly expecting.

Right now, if I'm being honest, I'm writing you under the assumption that you are leaning towards not *having them. Right?*

I've recently realized how much my decision to have a baby wasn't a decision at all. I can't ever remember giving the alternate option (not having one) any consideration, which is kind of crazy.

I might just be writing you at a low point, but it's been making me think. I mean, in certain socioeconomic brackets, babies can almost be like a well-designed house or a carefully put together outfit—they can be just another way of expressing ourselves, another way of asserting our point of view. I don't know.

Yours,
Leanne

16

Leanne's dad wasn't the only family member who had died while she was pregnant. At the beginning of the pregnancy, she'd also lost her maternal grandmother.

Soon after, Leanne learned that she'd left her thirty thousand dollars. By the time she got the check, she was seven months pregnant. The homewares store didn't offer any kind of maternity leave as she was technically a part-time employee (no matter the hours she actually worked). She'd also recently received the first half of her book advance, which amounted to about ten thousand dollars, after agent fees.

Between this money, her teaching gig, and freelance writing work that she assumed would happen more and more often, especially once she was a published author, she'd felt nearly invincible. She gave notice at the store and worked her last day a month later.

Now it was six months later. She was shocked by how quickly she had spent the money, how much time it took to pitch story ideas to editors, and how often no one wrote back. She was equally shocked by her own lack of foresight—the way she simply hadn't imagined that without that biweekly paycheck, that of course her bank account would only get smaller and smaller. She and James had never joined their accounts. She knew that he would help her if she ran out of money entirely—that he would *have* to.

One day, she sat down with a calculator and worked out how

long she had before she was broke. Probably another six months, maybe seven.

She could see a lot of things now.

Like how she never should have hired a nanny, even one who came just twice a week. But when she was pregnant, she'd been surrounded by women with nannies or women hiring nannies. It had seemed standard.

Now it mostly seemed expensive. And complicated.

Ofelia's heart was open. During the interview, she'd taken Hank into her arms and pressed her cheek against his. She talked to him in a singsong Spanish, bouncing him around the room, and then, almost suddenly, she turned to Leanne and touched her on the cheek with an open palm. Looking right into her eyes, she said, "Usted tiene la cara de una muñeca."

Leanne used to speak Spanish almost fluently, and she could feel her face redden as she translated. *You have the face of a doll.*

"Sabe muñeca?" she asked.

"Sí," Leanne said, nodding.

"Como una Barbie!" she said, smiling.

Leanne had hired her happily, but she soon learned that when Ofelia was in the house, she couldn't remove herself enough to get any work done. Their place was small, and making her body available to Hank, she learned, also made her body available to Ofelia. When Hank was otherwise preoccupied, Ofelia roamed from room to room and talked on and on. Mostly about her two adult children, especially Cindi, with whom she wasn't getting along.

"Cindy?" Leanne had asked during one of the early days. It didn't sound like a Guatemalan name.

"Yes, Cindi. Like Cinderella."

"Oh."

After a few weeks of this, Leanne tried a different approach. She asked her if she could start her day at nine-thirty a.m. instead of eight-thirty a.m. That way, Hank could take his morning nap,

Leanne could drink her coffee, then nurse him, and then leave the house for at least two and a half hours.

Typically, she went to a coffee shop and couldn't wait to get there. But today after leaving Hank, Leanne sat in the car, not wanting to do anything but sit there. The morning had been so rushed and hectic. She breathed in the feeling of being alone. It felt so good. Out of habit, she reached for her phone and toggled it awake. She heard the chime of a new email. Lo and behold there was one from Maxine:

I read this interview the other day in which the interviewee said that we are living in an "ascension culture." By this, he meant that our culture is by and large consumed with the idea of our lives getting better, of us improving over time. He seemed to conclude that we do this because we think that the better we become—and this is usually most easily expressed in material ways—the more people will like us. And we all want to be liked.

But really, if you think about it, we are always descending. At least, on one level.

Plus, what's so wrong with descending? There is a YouTube video titled "Women bloopers" that has hundreds of millions of views. (I am at least ten of them.) Everyone loves watching other people's bloopers (bloopers = people falling aka descending), but for the most part, we don't like being the blooper.

Yours,
Max

She tossed her phone on the passenger seat, turned the key in the ignition, and began formulating a response.

17

Dear Maxine,

Thank you so much for that email.

Do you want to start a descension culture with me? (Gmail is acting like descension isn't even a word. That's how much our ascension culture rejects this idea!) Point being, I feel myself going down, down, down.

Speaking of, are you going to get pregnant or what?

From the bottom *of my heart (get it?),*

Leanne

From her usual table at the coffee shop, she closed her laptop and opened up her journal. She wanted to scrap the essay she'd been working on and start something brand-new.

The essay was supposed to center on love. She'd been writing about herself and James—a version of what she'd already written about in the book—about their circuitous road to coupledom.

But now she wanted to take a different approach. She wanted to write about *the end* of love, the end of a relationship. She wanted to write about the thing she hadn't been able to tell anyone. Kept in her mind, the memory still thrilled her some four months later.

* * *

She had just given birth. Hank was on top of her chest, breast-feeding for the first time. She had no idea what she was doing. She had every idea. She was still in the delivery room itself and not the actual hospital room where she would spend the next day and a half.

James must have stepped out to call his parents. She'd gotten a walking epidural, and though her doctor was actively giving her two stitches, she couldn't feel anything but joy. It was not happiness. It was so much larger than that. A distinct image of her heart came to her. It was broken. It had hatched actually. Inside was another heart—a shiny new one. It was fresh and beautiful and open, open, open.

And that's when she felt it. She didn't know what to call it. Her dad's spirit? He stood behind her. He bent down and pressed his cheek against hers in a way he'd never done while alive. He smelled like smoke, like he always had. He was admiring her baby. He was proud of her.

Now she wrote in her journal at the top of the page: *Visiting Hours.*

18

Leanne had hoped that Mary Anne would have spread the news that Regina didn't believe in vaccinating to all the Brooklynites who inevitably came to Los Angeles. But she knew that was a long shot, and nothing seemed to be happening.

She felt restless. She wanted to *work out*. She was sick of the long walks around her neighborhood, dragged down by the weight of Hank in the carrier.

She was ready to feel strong and lithe again, to sweat profusely, to press her fingertips into her lower abs and not lose them in a layer of softness. Someone online had mentioned Tracy Anderson videos as the only way to "get their pre-baby body back."

Today, she would try. She put Hank on his back on his activity mat in the living room. She then jogged to her bedroom. She threw on two sports bras and a pair of shorts and hurried back, singsonging, "Are you ready to sweat, Hank?" Hank had already rolled over. He looked up at her, his head bobbling. "Yeah!" she said. He smiled.

She pulled up a janky, bootlegged version of a Tracy Anderson workout on YouTube called *Maximum Burn* and pressed play.

"Here we go!" she said as the video began. She'd wanted to match Tracy's enthusiasm, but the sound of her own voice only emphasized the room's emptiness. She shrugged the feeling away—once she started sweating, she would feel different.

But after ten minutes she didn't. Her body felt so heavy. Stiff. She looked over at Hank. He had army-crawled off the mat and was reaching for June, who lay underneath the couch. She made it another five minutes before pausing for some water. As she drank, she grabbed her phone and mindlessly tapped open Instagram.

In the next minute, she slunk down to the kitchen floor. A few minutes after that, she scooted herself out toward the living room where she could check on Hank. He had wormed his way over to the book they'd been reading that morning—*Knuffle Bunny*. "You see Knuffle Bunny?" Leanne called. He slapped at the book, smiling.

She swung her legs out wide and leaned forward, stretching her hamstrings and inner thighs.

She continued to scroll until she came upon a photo that thrust her upward, as if hit by an electric shock. It was of Lila, Agnes, and Regina. They held wineglasses to their lips. The caption read: "Lovely ladies. #santabarbara #pinotnoir #girlstrip." Thea had posted it. Her chest swirled, like a child in the deep end who didn't quite know how to swim.

Leanne tapped on Regina's username—she didn't actually log in as her. Her most recent photo was of a cocktail in a martini glass set directly in front of her bikini cleavage. Regina's head was cropped out so that it was literally just her cleavage and a martini.

Leanne scrolled through the comments. Thea—who was there, who possibly even *took* the photo—commented with a string of five of those salsa dancer emojis. Regina's sister: *Red hot*. Agnes, who was also there: two salsa dancer emojis and two fire emojis. Lila, present as well: *Want that bathing suit*. To which Regina commented back: *Not sure they make it in children's sizes* 😊😊. (Lila was so petite she sometimes bought clothes in the children's section.) A few people Leanne didn't know had also chimed in, affirming Regina's cleavage and cocktail to be hot.

19

From: Leanne
To: Regina, Carmen, Lila, Miriam, Laura, Sara, Agnes, and Jenni
Subject: Book Club 7:30 p.m. next Tuesday at my place

Fri Mar 25 at 1:07pm

Hi guys,
Just a reminder that book club is next Tuesday at my place.

If there's a spot in the driveway feel free to take it. Otherwise, there's ample-ish street parking.

I'm going to make a giant pot of soup for our entrée. Just reply with what you're bringing so we don't overlap.

Looking forward to it!

Leanne
www.diaryofahomecook.com

From: Regina
To: Leanne, Carmen, Lila, Miriam, Laura, Sara, Agnes, and Jenni
Subject: Re: Book Club 7:30 p.m. next Tuesday at my place

Fri Mar 25 at 1:20pm

I'm so sorry, but I'm going to have to miss this one! One of my best clients is in town that night and we have dinner plans. Perhaps I can swing by after? I hate to miss!

x

Kind regards,
Regina Mark
R.M. GOODS
8400 Beverly Blvd.
Los Angeles, CA 90036
www.RMgoods.com
www.RMarksthespot.com
see our latest story in *C Magazine*!

From: Regina
To: Leanne
Subject: Re: Book Club 7:30 p.m. next Tuesday at my place

Fri Mar 25 at 1:22pm

I'm so sorry to miss. Last time this client was in town, she bought two 25K light fixtures so I don't want to blow her off. ☹☺ Though I'd like to!

Kind regards,
Regina Mark
R.M. GOODS
8400 Beverly Blvd.
Los Angeles, CA 90036
www.RMgoods.com
www.RMarksthespot.com
see our latest story in *C Magazine*!

From: Miriam
To: Regina, Carmen, Lila, Leanne, Laura, Sara, Agnes, and Jenni
Subject: Re: Book Club 7:30 p.m. next Tuesday at my place

Fri Mar 25 at 1:50pm

Oh no! I'm going to have to miss this one too! I just got pulled into a work dinner myself.

Miriam

From: Carmen
To: Miriam, Regina, Lila, Leanne, Laura, Sara, Agnes, and Jenni
Subject: Re: Book Club 7:30 p.m. next Tuesday at my place

Fri Mar 25 at 3:41pm

I should be able to make it. If I do, I'll bring something sweet.

From: Sara
To: Carmen, Miriam, Regina, Lila, Leanne, Laura, Agnes, and Jenni
Subject: Re: Book Club 7:30 p.m. next Tuesday at my place

Fri Mar 25 at 4:03pm

Oof. I'm out too. Sorry!

sarakgreen.com

From: Agnes
To: Sara, Carmen, Regina, Miriam, Lila, Leanne, Laura, and Jenni
Subject: Re: Book Club 7:30 p.m. next Tuesday at my place

Sat Mar 26 at 9:23am

You'll have to count me out again. One of these days I do hope to make it. Or at least buy the book. xA

From: Leanne
Toι Agnεs, Saιa, Carmen, Regina, Miriam, Lila, Laura, and Jenni
Subject: Re: Book Club 7:30 p.m. next Tuesday at my place

Mon Mar 28 at 12:44pm

Hi again:
Just wanted to see if the rest of you were planning on coming tomorrow. . . . If it's going to be a small group, I'll make less soup. Thanks and hope to see you soon!

Leanne
www.diaryofahomecook.com

From: Jenni
To: Leanne, Agnes, Sara, Carmen, Regina, Miriam, Lila, and Laura
Subject: Re: Book Club 7:30 p.m. next Tuesday at my place

Tues Mar 29 at 4:05pm

Ladies,
My sincerest apologies for canceling so last-minute but I cannot make it tonight. Without sharing too much, a very close friend of mine is going thru something very difficult right now and I need to be available to her and her family.

From: Laura
To: Jenni, Leanne, Agnes, Sara, Carmen, Regina, Miriam, and Lila
Subject: Re: Book Club 7:30 p.m. next Tuesday at my place

Fri Apr 1 at 7:24am

Hi Everyone,

I wanted to apologize for missing our last meeting and not even RSVPing. That's not like me at all and frankly a bit ridiculous. Between finals and a nightmarish dental situation, book club got lost in the shuffle. I really am sorry.

Let me know if we are on for another book and feast. I promise to do better next time.

There was no book club that night.

Regina had started this book club, and Regina would end it. Of course she would.

Leanne had always seen herself as offering something Regina couldn't get from her other friends. Val had even put it into words once. Right in front of Regina, he'd said to Leanne: "You bring out the best version of Regina."

Regina had seemed almost embarrassed by the comment, but Leanne had smiled and nodded, agreeing, though she didn't realize exactly what version of Regina she had brought out until now. A human one.

It made her remember the time they'd gone to the movies together to see a stupid romantic comedy, only they'd gotten the times wrong and ended up seeing a documentary about this famous fashion photographer. It was upbeat and not too serious until the very end, when it became clear that the photographer was gay but had spent his life repressing it—that he'd not had one single romantic relationship. Leanne had cried.

Afterward, the women went to a nearby restaurant and sat at the bar. They ordered glasses of wine. The heaviness of the movie's ending had followed them.

"I hate my job so much," Leanne had said.

"You do?" Regina had seemed so surprised.

"Of course," Leanne had said, almost laughing. "I fantasize about quitting, about walking out *all of the time*."

"It's funny. I just see it as your day job. But everyone knows you're really a writer."

"That's funny. I don't see myself as a writer at all."

No one said anything for a solid minute. And then Regina leaned in close and—almost whispering—said, "I want to close the store."

"Really?"

She shrugged. "I want to make something myself."

"Yeah? Like what?"

"Clothes, mostly."

"You should do it."

"Yeah," she said, exhaling. "Please don't tell anyone."

Leanne shook her head. "I wouldn't."

"My mom had a failed hat business in the eighties. It was clearly this thing she loved, but I guess she couldn't maintain it once she had kids. I don't know what happened really."

Leanne had never seen Regina look so sad. She didn't know how to react. She said: "Oh."

"All I know is that she never went back to work." She looked up from her wineglass and shrugged.

"Do you think she wanted to?"

"I don't know. It might have taken some pressure off. Like, if you're only a mom, you have to be a good one."

They didn't have kids of their own yet at this point. They weren't even pregnant. They didn't know anything about mothering first-hand. All they knew was what they'd grown up to think or not think about moms.

An urge to text Regina, to somehow make up with her and get things back to normal, hit Leanne hard. The two of them were good for each other. Without Leanne, Regina would become as impervious as marble, and without Regina, Leanne would become soft and shapeless, like melted wax.

Leanne grabbed her phone and searched for Regina's name. She clicked, pressed the phone to her ear, and waited.

It rang twice before Hank woke up from his nap with a shriek and shook Leanne out of her panic. She hung up and went to him.

If Regina called her back, Leanne would give the friendship one last shot. If she didn't, Leanne would move on. For real.

* * *

Regina never called.

Leanne cut out a portion of a poem she found in the Sunday *Times* magazine that compared an enemy to a Buddha:

Meaning, you ought to learn to attain tranquility
From having someone against you. . . .

She tucked it into the flap of her journal and then wrote down the two things she believed would help her attain the most tranquility:

1. Sell tons of books / get tons of publicity

2. Get back to my pre-baby body except more muscle-y

She pictured herself like a hibernating bear. But instead of hibernating, she was doing the work. She'd *been* doing the work. She'd already written a book. She was emailing her publicist with ideas. She'd gotten the necessary blurbs from writers who were much more successful than she was. And when her book came out, she would emerge from her lair: thin and hungry, ready to receive spring's bounty.

20

What did it mean that one of Leanne's favorite activities to do with a baby was grocery shop? But really, what activities could one do with a baby, and not *to* a baby or *for* a baby? She'd tried a "parent and me" yoga class once but was so bored. She didn't enjoy pretending other people's babies were cute and/or hearing the general tone new mothers took with other new mothers. Everyone was too polite or too clichéd in their exhaustion. At least with grocery shopping, she was accomplishing something she needed to do anyway. At least at the grocery store, she could interface with nonparents or her favorite sector of humanity: old people. Plus, she liked buying things. She noticed that when she tried to curb her spending on things like clothes and restaurants, she ended up "shopping" at the grocery store, lingering within the beauty section at Whole Foods, suddenly curious about the sorry-looking vegan sandals they sold there. She once bought a cookbook at Target titled *One-Pot Yum*. Later at home, seeing the cover in the light of day with its dumb font, she thought: *This is what happens to depraved people.*

But today, she and Hank had already gone to the grocery store. Now it was the afternoon, and she turned to her next favorite hassle-free parent-friendly activity: walking the neighborhood. She clicked the baby carrier around her waist and then strapped Hank into it. For some reason, she turned down the street instead of up, which was her usual route. It was sunny but not oppressively so. She could feel the slightest of breezes in the air. At the bottom of the hill, she made a right and almost immediately ran into Julianna—her neighbor of sorts, the one with the caftan line—walking her dog.

Oh, Christ, she heard her dad say.

She's not that bad, Leanne thought back, not sure why she was defending her.

The women made eye contact. "Hey," Julianna said. Leanne smiled and gave a wave. They were going the same way and began walking side by side. "I didn't see you at the reception for Mona's new jewelry line," she said.

Leanne was still on Regina's mailing list and had seen the invitation in her in-box, but of course she would never go to another event at R.M. Goods. She needed to decide whether to lie or tell the truth. *Actually, Regina and I broke up.* She ran the sentence through her head. Wouldn't that be nice? To say it plainly. Why *was* there no good language around the end of female friendships? Everyone loses a close friend at some point.

She settled somewhere in between. "I haven't seen much of Regina lately."

"No?"

"No," Leanne confirmed.

"Did something happen?"

"Well," Leanne started.

But Julianna stepped in, launching into a story about a flower-arranging workshop Regina had hosted at her store and an RSVP gone awry. Leanne remembered the workshop in question because she remembered thinking she wouldn't pay money to learn how to arrange flowers. But she hadn't known anything of the specifics Julianna was talking about.

"So what happened between you guys?" she said at the end of it. And then: "Do you want some coffee?" She motioned to her house. "I'm right over there."

Leanne grabbed her phone from her pocket to check the time.

But as she did, she realized she had no excuse. She had nowhere to be, as per usual, and Hank seemed content to be carried. She shrugged. "Sure."

They passed through Julianna's living room with its gigantic shaggy off-white rug and perfectly broken-in brown leather couch on the way to the white lacquered and marbled kitchen. Leanne took it in. Her first instinct was jealousy, but then she did an about-face. She felt sorry for her. Suddenly convinced that this was the basis of all of these women's problems. That their houses were designed more for magazine profiles than as places of refuge, that they were set up to be photographed instead of actually lived in. Could a soul flourish in such sunny, pristine conditions? She doubted it.

Julianna heated a kettle for coffee. Leanne sensed that she was waiting for the answer to her question, but that she wasn't going to ask again.

"So back to the topic at hand," Leanne said. "I mean, we weren't a match made in heaven, but at her anniversary party—the one in Palm Springs—she got drunk and told me some things that I think she regretted."

"What things?"

Leanne inhaled. She peeked down at Hank whose eyes were now closed.

Be direct. Like headline news.

"Well, that she hasn't vaccinated Ursa."

"Oh!" Julianna crinkled her nose, but in a way that made Leanne think she didn't quite get it.

She clarified: "Like, she's an anti-vaxxer."

Julianna flattened her lips and shook her head. "Well, my friend Mona—the one whose event it was this weekend—she probably won't work with her again. She wasn't at all happy with how she was treated."

"Yeah?"

At this, Julianna was off. She began describing the night, as told to her through Mona's eyes. The details were so particular and the slights so insignificant to Leanne that her mind began to wander. She wondered about Julianna's posture; she sat so upright. Where did she learn that? She considered her complexion; she wanted to know her skincare routine. Did her husband desire her? She looked too collected, too poised to muss up.

In this way, she felt less like a part of the conversation and more like a witness to it.

And yet it did feel good to know she wasn't alone, that Julianna was tramping around in the same squishy terrain: trying to prove Regina's guilt in a case without evidence. No. Apart from a possible screenshot or two, the evidence remained sadly—*only*—a feeling.

21

By mid-June, Leanne hadn't achieved what she might call *tranquility*, though she *had* set a time limit on her social media use via some app. They'd also sleep trained Hank. She'd questioned the practice every single second he'd cried, but then, after four days, when he'd apparently learned he could skip the crying and go straight to sleep, she believed it to be the best decision they'd ever made. In all, her life felt much less insane than it had just months ago. James had caught on to the fact that she wasn't hanging out with Regina as much, and when he asked about it, Leanne took the same tack that she had with Julianna. She said she found out that Regina wasn't vaccinating Ursa, and that it had driven a wedge between them. Everything else she left out.

Her gossip sessions with Julianna had helped—had loosed some of the built-up resentment—and apart from lunch with her and her own book's release date, now just six weeks away, she had very little else going on. Well, that and it was her birthday.

She was thirty-four today. It didn't sound old to her except when she thought about having another baby, and the fact that if she didn't get pregnant in the next two months, the pregnancy would be deemed "geriatric." And she knew she didn't want to get pregnant in the next couple of months. So geriatric it would be!

The good news was that it was an Ofelia day, and Leanne had decided to forsake a morning of writing in favor of the Korean spa.

She hadn't been since before she was pregnant, and a visit felt well overdue.

For a measly fifteen dollars, you got access to *the spa*. This included a steam room, sauna, cold-plunge tub, hot tub, and these other two bonus rooms: the jade and clay rooms. Leanne liked spending time in the latter ones even though she had no idea what the benefits were. The floor of the jade room was covered in these small translucent pale pink rocks while the walls and floors of the clay room consisted of yellow, almost-glowing bricks made of what Leanne assumed was clay. She'd Googled "clay room Korean spa" as well as "jade room Korean spa" a couple of times but could never find what their exact purpose was or even how to best enjoy them.

For another thirty dollars, you could get a scrub—an amazing if not painful and humbling experience, during which you lay naked on something akin to a waterproof massage table in close proximity to about eight or nine other tables while a woman wearing only a black bra, black underwear, and Brillo-pad-like gloves scrubbed 99.8 percent of your body. The first time Leanne got scrubbed, she could believe neither how much dead skin flew off her body in tiny lint-like pieces nor the places on her body the scrubber had scrubbed. For the most part, she kept her eyes closed during the process, but sometimes if she were lying on her side, she'd open them to momentarily peek at one of the other women getting scrubbed on a nearby table. It was almost violent the way the scrubber worked on her patient, as if she were cleaning a dirty fry pan in a sink. Only instead of using a faucet, she'd intermittently chuck a bucket of hot water on top of the body to clear off her work surface.

Leanne couldn't speak for others, but she definitely did it more for how she felt by the end than for how she felt during it.

On the drive there, she tried to listen to NPR, but they were reporting on a measles outbreak in San Diego: seventy-three cases less than two hours away from her. She didn't want this information, to be made to feel angry and helpless; Hank couldn't get this vaccine until he was one. She switched over to the country station, something she did with more and more frequency now. In Middleton, everyone had listened to country music. Well, everyone except for her, her dad, and her brother. "Redneck music" her dad had called it. Leanne winced at the memory, though it wasn't the only one like that. Her dad had been, well, an asshole. A few days after the memorial service, Leanne had even asked her brother: Of the people who had spoken, who had actually gotten him right? That is, had anyone actually addressed the bad bits?

"I think the word most used was 'difficult.' That one doctor who worked with him the most—Barnes. He called him a 'real piece of work.'"

"Hmm," Leanne had said to her brother. "How did you say it?"

"I didn't say anything."

"But I thought you spoke?"

"I did. But I didn't *say* anything. Those things aren't for the dead person. They're for everyone else."

In the days that followed, Leanne kept wondering how she might have put it had she been there. Would she have told the truth?

Because truthfully: he *was* an asshole. After all, it had been his decision, after he and Winnie married, to move away from Pittsburgh where they'd both grown up. He'd wanted to be in a small town. He enjoyed railing against snobs, elitists, which almost made her laugh now. As if Pittsburgh—Steel City—were this beacon of intellects. But then he also wanted to make fun of rural America, of hunting, of Christianity, and the annual demolition derby at the county fair. It was like he needed to draw a line in the sand between himself and everyone else. But then, in doing that, he'd drawn one between Leanne and Charlie and the rest of their peers in Middleton; he'd drawn one between Leanne and Charlie and Beth, who *was* Middleton—born and raised. Even if their dad had done everything the right way. Even if he'd divorced Winnie before getting

Beth pregnant, even if it hadn't gotten so ugly between him and Winnie, Leanne doubted that things between his first family and second would have turned out any better.

No man was an island, but you could aspire to be.

But recently, despite her upbringing, she'd found comfort in the world as presented in country songs. Country songs were stories, usually set in a place where Daddy done his best and women (presumably wearing cut-offs) rode in the passenger seat.

She pulled into the lot and found a parking space. She turned the car off and out of habit checked her phone for messages. She watched as her email updated and then scrolled through the new ones, spotting Regina's name right away.

From: Regina
To: Undisclosed Recipients
Subject: Anniversary Party to be featured in À la Table Magazine

Fri June 17 at 9:15am

Hi friends,

I'm very excited to say that Val and my anniversary party is going to be featured in the October issue of *À la Table* magazine. Can you please sign the attached release form in case they choose any recognizable (lol) pictures of you to include within the feature?

Thanks so much for your cooperation.

Regina Mark
R.M. GOODS
8400 Beverly Blvd.
Los Angeles, CA 90036
www.RMgoods.com
www.RMarksthespot.com

"Oh, how exciting! Do they know you don't believe in science?" Leanne said aloud to no one, and then typed her response.

That's awesome! Will sign and send back later today. If they do choose any "recognizable" pictures of me, could they please use my name and include that I'm author of the recently published DIARY OF A HOME COOK? By the October issue, the book will be out.

She reread it, briefly considering how she might throw in a mention of her birthday, of the strange passing of time. Last year, Regina had thrown her a birthday dinner. She'd made paella. They couldn't drink. They'd both been pregnant. And now look! One year later and they were mothers. Also silent, mortal enemies. But after one more moment's thought, she gave up on the idea. She pressed *Send*.

As Leanne undressed at the spa in front of her locker, she reminded herself that this was a spa and spas were filled with naked bodies and that hers was just another one of them.

But just as she was pulling off her t-shirt, a woman in a white robe walked by. *Was that?* She walked to the edge of the lockers. Leanne couldn't be sure, but the woman looked a lot like Maxine Hunter.

In another minute, Leanne was naked with only a towel wrapped around her, walking into the spa as well. She spotted the woman in question right away at the showers. (A shower was the mandatory first step.) As the woman looked to the left, Leanne could see her whole face. *Oh my god.* It was definitely her.

Three of the six shower stalls were taken. Leanne walked to the one furthest from Maxine, feeling it unfair to shower next to someone she knew but who didn't know her. But then again, she reminded herself, neither of them really *knew* each other.

Leanne soaped up and wondered: If the situation were reversed, would she want a fan she had corresponded with a couple of times over email to introduce herself while she was naked? Probably not.

Although, Leanne counterargued, she was also naked, which did level the playing field.

In the sauna, they'd rigged a flatscreen TV up against one of the walls. It was always set to some Korean television station. Leanne liked to lie on her back on the first step of the stadium seating and put her legs up against the wall (facing away from the entrance in case anyone walked in) and listen to the calming sound of a language she couldn't understand.

Sure enough, as she was lying there, someone did walk in. Leanne looked over her left shoulder to see that it was Maxine, fully naked with a towel slung over her shoulder. They made brief eye contact. Leanne smiled. She was worried that Maxine hadn't cold-plunged after the steam room. It was a beginner's mistake, and one that Leanne had experienced. But again, Leanne stayed quiet, not knowing what to do.

Maxine took a seat on the same first stadium step Leanne was lying on. Or at least that's what it felt like. Either way, she was directly behind her now; Leanne couldn't see her.

Leanne remained supine for a few more minutes before the tops of her ears felt like they were burning. She slid her legs down the wall, rolled to her side, and sat up. She was now sitting just a few feet away from Maxine. She felt keenly aware of her own body, as if it were outlined by a thin hum of electricity.

She turned her head and Maxine looked over. "Maxine?" It came out involuntarily.

"Yeah?" She looked confused but calm, sitting up straight, her short dark-brown hair slicked back.

"I'm sorry," Leanne said, pulling her towel up with one arm to haphazardly cover herself. "I thought it was you, and it felt strange *not* to say anything, but of course it's also strange to say something."

Maxine stared at her.

"My name is Leanne. We've never met but we've emailed a few times. You told me how we're living in an ascension culture—I'm sorry if this is too weird."

"Oh, right. Yeah, of course I remember that." She made no effort to cover herself up. Instead, she spoke normally, her small breasts and pubic hair completely exposed.

"Do you live here in Los Angeles?" Leanne asked, touching the tips of her ears, trying to momentarily protect them from the heat.

"I do, actually."

"Oh. I thought you lived in New York."

"No, no. I used to. I've been here for about six months now."

"Oh, well, I'll have to update your Wikipedia." Leanne said, and then immediately felt her heart race and her stomach buzz.

Maxine smiled. "Would you?"

Leanne dropped her arms back down. Her desire to flee and to stay felt equal. "The sauna always burns my ears. I've gotta go cold-plunge." Leanne stood up and as unself-consciously as possible, wrapped her towel around herself. "You know about cold-plunging, right?"

Maxine moved her eyebrows downward.

"In between the sauna or hot tub or whatever other hot thing, you're supposed to cool down. Otherwise, it's too much heat. At least, it was for me the first time."

Maxine nodded. "Oh, okay. Yeah, this is my first time here."

"Ah, okay, well. There's your tip." She made her way to the door. "The cold-plunge tub is this one right here." Leanne motioned to the tub immediately outside the sauna. "Or I see some women kind of just dump the cold water on themselves in between."

"Yeah?" Maxine said, standing up to get a peek and revealing her entire nakedness. She was much more muscular than Leanne assumed a writer would be. "Well, I'll go there next."

Leanne nodded. "It's pretty intense. FYI." She held up an open palm as if to stop herself from going further. "Okay, I'll leave you alone now."

"Hey, no. I appreciate the advice."

Leanne smiled and gave a little wave before pulling the door open and sliding out.

Leanne cold-plunged as quickly as possible—it stunned her; the water felt like a steel knife cutting right through her—and then studied the clock on the wall. She still had twenty minutes left before her scrub. She decided to spend it primarily in the jade room. She hated the feeling that she'd created—an energized self-consciousness. The entire conversation ran through her head.

In the jade room, Leanne lay on her back on top of her outstretched towel and took a deep breath. Her mind continued to spin. Because of their emails, Maxine had her full name. What if she Googled her later? Leanne sometimes Googled fans who emailed her. If she did, Leanne wondered if Maxine would see that she had a book coming out. She wondered if she might want to read it.

Just then the door opened. Leanne was facing away from the door, so she couldn't see who it was. She could feel the person entering the room.

"So what's this room all about?"

Leanne turned her head. It was Maxine!

"Oh hey," Leanne said, attempting normalcy. "I actually don't know. I just like it."

Maxine unfurled her towel so that it lay right next to Leanne's even though there was enough room for them to be further apart if she'd wanted.

"So I guess you didn't bring your baby with you," she said, lying down on her back.

Leanne smiled. "Nah. Not this time." Even though no one else was in the room, they spoke softly, barely above a whisper.

"I remembered your recent email. It took me a minute. You asked if I was going to get pregnant, right?"

Leanne turned her head. Maxine faced the ceiling. The awkwardness she was feeling moments earlier seemed to melt away. She had come *to her.* "I guess I just assumed that's what you were wrestling with." A moment passed between them. "Sorry, it's a very heteronormative assumption, I realize."

Maxine smiled and then turned her head to face Leanne. "I don't know. You have this window of time to consider doing something, so you almost *have* to consider it when the window is closing."

"Right," Leanne said. "You're thirty-eight?"

"Mmm-hmm." She'd turned back toward the ceiling.

"Well, you don't really look thirty-eight. Not that it's that much older than me."

"How old are you?"

"Thirty-four. Today actually." Her voice cracked.

"It's your birthday?"

Leanne felt Maxine turn toward her again. She looked at her briefly and nodded. "Yep."

"Well, happy birthday. I had you at thirty-one."

Leanne smiled. "Well, with clothes on, I look older."

"Right. Of course."

"Though, ever since giving birth, I've noticed that I look best naked. Because my old clothes don't quite fit me right. And since my breasts are bigger, it makes everything else look smaller." Leanne didn't know why she couldn't shut up.

Maxine turned her head to face Leanne again. "I'm not trying to get pregnant. The question was for a book I'm working on."

"Ah," Leanne said, looking away.

"I'm very curious about being pregnant and giving birth. But not the part that comes after."

Leanne laughed and then said nothing. She felt too much, split between wanting to stay there forever and wanting to run away. "I hope you believe me when I say I really hate to cut this short, but I have a scrub appointment." She turned back toward Maxine, who was propped up on her elbows.

"Ah, of course."

Leanne waited a beat, and then as smoothly as possible, she rocked herself up, grabbing the edge of her towel as she went so that by the time she was standing it was almost wrapped around her.

Maxine remained in the same position. Leanne looked down, making sure to keep her focus on her eyes. "It was really so nice to meet you," she said with a smile. "I can't tell you how much I loved *Koala Life*."

"Thanks."

"And you can keep me in mind as a case study for your book," she said as she side-stepped Maxine's head and made her way to the door.

"I just might," she said.

Leanne smiled at her. Maxine smiled back.

An hour later, when she got back to her car, her face almost hurt from smiling. What a great birthday she was having.

In the driver's seat, she toggled open her email, quickly seeing that Regina had replied: *I will definitely forward this info to the editors. And remind them of the book!*

22

That night, Leanne couldn't fall asleep. She kept running over her conversation with Maxine. James began to snore, and so she grabbed her pillow and copy of *Koala Life* and made a makeshift bed on the couch in the living room.

The thing about *Koala Life* was that it was categorized as a novel, but the narrator's name was Maxine Hunter, and the other character names were the names of people in Maxine's real life; for example, the character of Maxine gets divorced, falls in love with a woman named Gilda, and then the book itself is dedicated to Gilda, who, as far as Leanne could gather, was a real-life woman whom real-life Maxine had a relationship with.

All of it fascinated her. To be that open with your art, to be that open in love, to allow yourself to change your mind and then cement it into a book. It seemed to go against everything the world and her family had, both silently and loudly, taught her, which was to choose something and then stick with it. To pick a side—that everything *had* a side. To never cause a scene, whether in happiness or pain. To *look* pretty but say nothing.

She found Gilda's Instagram account. She swam her thumb across the screen over and over until she was a year and a half deep into her feed and found the last photo posted of her and Maxine together. Prior to that, ninety percent of the photos must've been of the two of them.

Gilda looked young. And the way she used social media made her feel young too: so many serious-faced selfies, like she'd grown up taking them and wasn't self-conscious at all. She had these warm light-green eyes. Leanne could also see Maxine's comments on the photos. One of them was *Why you so beautiful?* She was beautiful. Leanne thought that if someone were to change sides, Gilda would be an easy person to do it with. One photo showed their matching tattoos. They were small, located on the inside of their forearms: a childlike, very simple 2-D drawing of a house and a sun overhead.

What had happened between them? Who broke up with whom?

She got the urge to email Maxine, to ask her, to keep their conversation going somehow. But no, not at one in the morning. Wait until tomorrow, she told herself. See if you still want to then.

23

Hi Maxine,

Do you ever watch The Bachelor? *If not, surely you know the premise, right? How twenty or so different women vie for the heart of one man—typically a man they essentially view as a celebrity because they watched him as a previous contestant on the sister series,* The Bachelorette? *Each season, there are a bunch of recurring themes that emerge, but two main ones are that TIME with The Bachelor is everything, and that OPENING UP during that TIME is highly lauded behavior. This ends up creating a pretty stressful environment, because each woman has only so much TIME with The Bachelor; many of the women worry that they didn't get to OPEN UP enough during that limited TIME, or that they managed to OPEN UP only partway. These women then feel weird about it. They feel unfinished. Semi-heard. So then, the next time they see him, they are worked up. They've spent their free TIME (of which they have loads) in their heads, admonishing themselves for not having OPENED UP more efficiently. They're vulnerable and trying to clarify what they said, and as a viewer, it's both compelling and difficult stuff to watch. You want to take the woman aside and tell her:* Don't worry about OPENING UP right now. Just ask him normal, first-date stuff like, Are you a cat person or a dog person?

I bring this up because I find myself feeling strange about our whole Korean spa experience. (Also: Are you a cat person or a dog person?)

The good news is that I now feel more empathy toward those Bach-elor contestants. They're just trying to communicate with someone they like in what little TIME they have.

Okay, off to the park with Hank.

All in good TIME?
Leanne

Leanne hit *Send*, which brought her back to her in-box, where she saw she had a new email *from* Maxine. She looked at the time stamp. It had just arrived, basically the same moment she'd sent her email to *her*. She opened it immediately.

Hi Leanne,

I wanted to let you know that I'd marked your last email you sent me as "unread," which is what I do when I mean to write back to some-one. The system is not foolproof.

I clicked on your link—diary of a home cook. You didn't tell me you're a writer too. And you have a book coming out. Congratula-tions!

Yours,
Max

Leanne wrote back quickly.

Looks like we were writing each other at the exact same TIME. Geez! Get off my wavelength, Maxine! Just kidding. We can share.

I really wanted to tell you that I'm a writer too, but my book is a lot different from yours.

A few hours later, she got the following response:

Do you want some more TIME with me? I'm going out of town for ten days over the fourth, but what are you doing the following Mon-day, the eleventh?

Also, I'm a cat person. In fact, the times that I've watched The Bachelor, *I've wondered what the show would be like if they substituted the contestants for cats—the bachelor or bachelorette would be human, but they'd be choosing the cat they were going to live with for the rest of the cat's life. Just an idea . . .*

24

Leanne was early, but within a moment of sitting down outside at Marigold, Lila arrived; she had texted Leanne last week asking if she was free for lunch sometime. It had been strange to see her name appear on her phone after all this time, and at first, Leanne had wanted to make up some excuse and say no. But then she asked herself: What had Lila done wrong? She'd been silent. She'd done nothing. Which was of course the problem.

In the end, Leanne realized she wanted the opportunity, wanted to be seen. She'd texted back: *Sure! How about Wednesday? I'll have Hank with me.* (She didn't want to spend half an Ofelia day having lunch.)

It had been more than four months since they'd last seen each other. No one she had encountered recently—not even Julianna—looked as thin and as cleanly put together as Lila. (*Did* Lila grocery shop, stand in the pharmacy line at CVS, feel her own mortality?) She had this pale skin with the faintest of freckles and thick dark-brown hair, which she wore in a low ponytail.

They hugged, and Leanne caught the scent of her perfume or face cream. It was sweet and citrusy. Lila leaned over the stroller to greet Hank, who smiled, his chin glistening with drool. Leanne could feel the absence of Regina looming over them, but plowed forward as if she couldn't, immediately asking about Lila's eighteen-month-old daughter. "What's Martine up to?"

"Oh, everything. She's so busy." Lila went on about her nanny, Lupita, and how she'd been sick, so she had had to take Martine with her to her latest shoot. In turn, Leanne talked about prepping for the book's release and how she was getting back to teaching soon.

A few times the conversation came to a slow, energy-less halt. *An object at rest will stay at rest*, she heard her dad's voice say.

I'm not at rest, Leanne thought.

But then, after the server dropped off their plates, Lila did set *something* into motion. She asked: "So what happened between you two, between you and Regina?"

The energy between their bodies shifted instantly. They leaned in toward each other. The rapid change made Leanne question why gossip between women had such a bad rap. She would have to look up the etymology of the word—if it had started out as a pejorative or become that way over time. And why was it always associated with women anyway? James loved gossip. He just didn't have any male friends he was close enough to to do it with. Gossip was con-nection. At the same time, she knew she had to tread lightly. She knew that probably no matter what she said, Lila's allegiance would be and would remain with Regina, that Regina was still her queen, that she gave order and clarity to Lila's life, and wasn't that what people wanted most? To believe that their version of life was the correct one?

But then wasn't that true for Leanne as well? Prior to this very moment, she had considered herself loosed, an electron gone wild. She'd pictured herself sparking her way out of the atomic wall, but that's where the image had ended. What happened to the electron next? Was it free, or did it simply attach itself to another atom? She didn't know. She suddenly saw her own shortsightedness. She saw all the ways Regina was still giving order to her life. Still defining her life? Maybe there was no such thing as freedom. At least not in politics. Or stories. Didn't every hero have to choose a side and then defend that side to the death? If not, what was the point? She tried to think of a famous, serious story that included a wavering, vacillating hero protagonist. The Buddha? She didn't know enough about his story to say, just that he was a proponent of the Middle Way, or so she'd read on Wikipedia at one point. Even still, that was *a way*, a choice.

Vaccines are a kind of middle way. It was her dad again. He was referring to something Leanne had read online from a long interview with the author of that vaccine book. She'd been talking about how vaccines are not one thing. They're not static. Because they rely on our bodies to respond. Our bodies must break the virus, like a horse.

"Well," Leanne finally said, confused by her own mental rambling. "You know she hasn't vaccinated Ursa, right?" It was the only thing she apparently could say.

But Lila was no longer looking at her. Her face had broken into an awkward, self-conscious smile. And then she stood up and called out, "Regina!"

Leanne looked over her shoulder and saw the woman herself. (Val was also present.) The host had seated them just two tables away. Lila was already standing up, walking over. How was this possible? Was she being *surveilled*? Had Regina implanted one of those GPS trackers into Lila's skin? How? Why? And should she go over as well?

But she was sandwiched in by Hank's stroller and the chair behind her. She made the quick decision to give Regina a wave and a smile from her twisted position. Regina waved and half smiled back, looking a bit confused.

Leanne turned back around, grateful for Hank and the chicken parmesan sandwich she'd ordered. She took a giant bite, staring at her baby as she chewed. She dabbed at the corners of her mouth and then turned around again.

In another moment, Lila was back at the table. "Oh my god. That was funny," she said in a low tone.

"She's everywhere!" Leanne said, her hands on her cheeks.

Lila shook her head. "I was here with her on Monday."

Neither of them seemed to know how to pick up the conversation again, not that it had ever truly begun.

"Anyway," Leanne finally said after swallowing another bite. "I think we're just too different."

Lila nodded. "I'm guessing you didn't see her blog post yesterday?"

"No, why?"

"Uhm, she wrote a whole thing about vaccines."

"What?"

"Yeah, I guess because of the San Diego stuff everyone's been talking about it."

"Oh, wow. Does she say she doesn't vaccinate? Do her sponsors know? I mean, I don't think most of them will be into that. And what about you? Doesn't it worry you—in terms of Martine?"

Lila shrugged. "You should just read it. It's good."

"What's good?"

"She's got some good ideas." Lila shrugged again.

Leanne nodded. Her face felt hot.

The call is coming from inside the house!

"So, so you don't vaccinate Martine?"

She finished chewing. She had the face of a ballerina. "I've done some of them, but she's still breast-feeding and has only ever eaten organic food."

"Right, but breast milk and healthy food—it's, it's—" She was having trouble formulating a sentence. Didn't Lila know that half of the food labeled organic actually wasn't? Hadn't Lila heard that NPR story? Was Leanne the only one suffering through public radio? "Those don't a vaccination make, Lila."

Lila only continued to shrug as she forked at her food.

Leanne's tongue had gone dry. When she saw the server, she asked for more water and the check as casually as possible. The women noted how good the food was, fawned over Hank, and then paid the bill. They stood up. Leanne, with stroller and child, and

Lila, without, made their way to where Regina and Val sat, both on their phones.

Leanne had no recourse but to smile. "Hey, guys."

Val looked up. "Hey!" He stood up, innocently, stupidly. He gave Leanne a hug. "Haven't seen you in a while."

Leanne received it. "Yeah," she said.

Regina remained seated, still looking at her phone. "Leanne's book is about to come out," she said.

"Oh, right! Right. And how is this guy?" Val leaned over the stroller.

"Oh, he's good." The air around them was dead. "Anyway," Leanne said. "I better get him home."

At this, Regina looked up. "It was nice seeing you guys."

"Yeah," Leanne said, zombie-like, already pushing the stroller away.

25

She put Hank in the car seat and tried to gather her thoughts. The baby grabbed at her face as she clipped the buckles into place. Without thinking, she breathed in, smelling to see if he'd pooped. She didn't think so. She got in the driver's seat, turned the key in the ignition, and dialed James's number. When he picked up, she shouted into the car's Bluetooth. She told him everything that had just happened.

"Well, that's a wrap on her."

"Right? You can't sell baby blankets and be anti-vax. Right?" Her hands and feet were tingling.

At home, she got herself and Hank inside and then immediately pulled up the blog post. But what she found was much less straightforward than what had existed in her mind. The entire thing centered on a "friend" whose baby had been "vaccine injured," and how we need to respect parents' decisions to keep their babies "healthy." At no point did Regina say one way or another if Ursa was vaccinated. Leanne wished she could talk to her dad—actually, physically.

She had never heard this term *vaccine injured*. And so she kept scrolling, anticipating the comments to validate this.

But as she read them, her stomach fell, as if she'd swallowed dry ice.

Preach mamma! Vaccines are poison!

THANK YOU SO MUCH. We all want to protect our babies, and there are simply not enough studies on the side effects of the mandated vaccine schedule.

Say it again! Louder! People are in hysteria over the freaking measles. If people trust their vaccines so much then why be concerned about those who don't vaccinate?

Only one commenter had pushed back, implying that Regina must be watching too much Fox News.

What the fuck was happening? She hated to do it, but she had to. She called her mom.

With the phone clenched to her ear, she moved Hank, who had crawled himself into the closet and begun to panic, to the jumper. That should buy her six or seven minutes.

"Well, isn't this a nice surprise," her mother answered with her familiar singsong.

"Hey, everything is fine, but I need some medical advice."

"Oh. Okay." She sounded scared.

"Not advice. I just have some friends who aren't vaccinating their babies, and they're talking about how some babies get vaccine injured, and I'd never heard of that before."

"Oh, god," she said. And then: "Yeah, Janice. I'll be right in! Yeah, that bike. Thanks. I'm here at the gym about to spin. Uhm, yeah, sweetie. I don't want to be rude, but your friends sound like idiots. 'Vaccine injury' is a mostly made-up term."

"Okay, yeah, that's what I thought."

"Some kids can get a rash and soreness at the injection site obviously," she conceded. "But it's much, much riskier *not* to vaccinate."

"What about the mercury?" Leanne asked. It was something she had picked up when she briefly Googled about reasons people don't vaccinate.

"They took it out! It used to act as a preservative."

"Okay. Okay, thanks. Go spin."

"Okay. Thank you for calling! I miss you."

26

That night Leanne created a new gmail account: OliviaHatfield@gmail.com. Then, logged in as Olivia, she went to RMarksthespot.com, found the blog post, and began writing a comment in the comment box:

Roses are red.
Violets are blue.
Vaccines ARE a kind of poison.
But guess what? So are you.

She double-checked she was logged in as Olivia. She was. She clicked the *Comment* button.

27

J ulianna had really wanted Leanne to meet her friend Mona, so the three of them went to lunch. Mona was wearing the same style of gigantic circular sunglasses Regina often wore, the kind that if worn in the Midwest, Leanne believed, would evoke much more of an Elton John–impersonation vibe than what they evoked in Los Angeles, which was essentially "woman with money." Leanne also thought Mona waited way too long to take them off. It wasn't until they'd sat down on the outside patio that she slipped them from her face and Leanne could actually see who she was talking to. And by this point, she was already telling Leanne about one of the ways Regina had wronged her. Leanne listened and continued to study her. She reminded her of a specific type of woman she'd gotten used to helping at the store. A woman unafraid of asking for exactly what she wants.

As the story went, Mona had *lent* Regina a pair of vintage Prada shoes—yes, one of the shoes had an oil stain—and Regina had quite carelessly given these shoes to her housekeeper.

Leanne focused on her face muscles, trying to keep them still as she nodded and feigned a quiet understanding.

"I *knew* you would get it," Mona said, and then continued, hardly pausing to take a breath. "Aren't you sick of Regina's influence? The way she has her claws in everything?"

"Of course," Leanne said. "And now she's taking on science."

The women looked confused.

"Hmm?"

"What?"

Does no one actually read Regina's blog? Leanne had been waiting for days now for some kind of update, some kind of consequence to Regina's reckless public musings. But it hadn't come. She'd even sent the link to her group of college friends, two of whom were pregnant. Why wasn't everyone up in arms? And to think that she'd been holding on to a screenshot image of Regina *liking* an anti-vax Instagram post. To think that she thought that might get Regina in trouble somehow. Her naivete knew no bounds.

"You don't have kids?" she said to Mona.

"Oh, no. No," Mona said, shaking her head.

"Well, Regina wrote a post against vaccines. It's really upsetting, because she's essentially just spreading misinformation. And the fewer people who vaccinate, you know, the bigger the chance for an outbreak."

"Oh, dear," Mona said. She made a face with her lips turned downward. Julianna did the same so that they momentarily looked like twin muppets. "Oh, but that does remind me. Do you know Elspeth Gluck?" She pulled out her phone. "I'm going to email her about you. She's an editor at *Madre* magazine, and they're doing this new series called Mothers Who Make—basically featuring moms who make things. You'd be a breath of fresh air for them," she said, already typing away on her phone.

"Oh, okay. Thank you," Leanne said, a bit surprised. Julianna nodded at her as if to say: *I told you.*

"You know what else would be great?" Mona said, briefly looking up from her device. "You could teach a cooking class at Holly's!" She looked to Julianna and nodded with a conviction that bordered on insanity.

Leanne shrugged, again surprised. "Okay?"

28

From: Earl Swanson
To: Leanne
Subject: Two questions about the Fiction-writing class starting July 17th

Sun July 3 at 9:32am

Hello,

My name is Earl Swanson, and I've signed up for your fiction-writing class. I'm very much looking forward to it. Ever since I retired two years ago, I've been working on a fantasy-humor project. I sent it out to literary agents, one of whom sent me what was ultimately a rejection though with a great deal of notes. Very interesting! I've now revised the entire manuscript. I emailed the agent back but haven't heard anything. My first question is: Should I make copies of the manuscript for the entire class? It is 155 pages.

My second question is logistical. I am planning on making a dry run to your house today or tomorrow. I'll be coming from Sierra Madre. It looks like I can take the 210 to the 134 to the 2. Does this sound like a viable route? I am most concerned about what looks like a dicey left turn from Silver Lake Blvd. onto Fargo Street. If you could please advise me, I'd appreciate it.

Yours,

Earl

Leanne read it and then typed a response in her head: *Don't say "dry run."*

29

Leanne left Hank with Ofelia and headed for the coffee shop.
She ordered a quiche, found a seat on the outdoor patio, and opened up her laptop, immediately seeing an email saying that the *New York Times* editor had passed on the essay. "I really loved the parts about trying to acquire a portion of your father's ashes, but the verisimilitude of his spirit appearing isn't coming through for us." The rejection felt like someone had clamped her heart with a thick binder clip. *Verisimilitude.* The word taunted her. What did they want—a photo of her dad's ghost? It was a *feeling.* You can't prove a feeling.

She closed out of the browser and then almost reflexively, as if to stop the dejectedness, she opened up Maxine's Instagram account. The latest post showed her holding what looked to be a copy of the French version of her book (*La Vie Koala*). You couldn't see her face: only from her waist to her chin. She wore a plaid button-down shirt, which she'd buttoned all the way up, even the very top button. Her neck looked so small and her shoulders so bony. The caption read: "Thank you, Paris!"

She pulled up her email and began a new one.

From: Leanne
To: Maxine
Subject: La Vie Koala indeed

Thur July 7 at 10:02am

I just saw your post. You didn't tell me you were going to Paris! That's a destination that requires more specificity. And here I sit getting an essay rejected from the *New York Times*. What different lives we lead! Bring me back a crepe?

She pressed *Send* and then moved back to the task at hand. She and James had been working together on the text of the email announcement for her book. It was all but ready. She just wanted to double-check for typos and that the information was correct. It was.

Her finger hovered over the *Send* button, imagining all the people potentially about to see it in their in-box. Regina was on there. Maxine. Beth. Her mother. This editor who had just rejected her. Her college boyfriend. Her ex-bosses, old teachers, ex-crushes. Her students. She'd noticed that her dad's email was even on there. She could've unchecked it but she didn't.

She pressed *Send*.

The clamp on her heart tightened. She felt light-headed.

She checked her own in-box to see that it had arrived. It had.

She went to RMarksthespot.com to see if anyone had responded to Olivia's comment. She scrolled down the page quickly but didn't see it. She scrolled back slowly. Olivia's comment was no longer there. *You censorial B*, she thought. She looked for the other lone dissenting comment but couldn't find it either. She shook her head. In three more seconds, she'd logged out of her email and into Olivia Hatfield's. She went back to Regina's blog and straight to the comment section.

Roses are red
Violets are blue
You don't understand how vaccination works!
I feel sorry for you!*
*and your daughter.

Again, she checked to make sure she was logged in as Olivia. She was. She looked up from her computer and scanned the room.

Her heart was acting as if she were on the front lines of some kind of war. Was she? Everyone on this patio was on a device. Did any of them also have alias email accounts they used for trolling people? She breathed in through her nose. She closed her laptop.

She toggled her phone awake and tapped on Instagram. A notification popped up to tell her she had one new follower since she'd last logged in. She clicked on the little red dot, which opened the screen that would tell her the username of the new follower.

It was *maxinehunter.*

She looked up from her phone, smiling. A news headline ran across the ticker tape of her brain: *Literary Celebrity Befriends Meek Girl from Small Town.*

The image of Carmen pulling open the heavy glass door to the coffee shop snapped her back to reality. Leanne smiled and waved.

"Oh!" she said, letting the door close and walking right toward her.

Leanne hadn't seen her since the 120th-day ceremony when her pregnancy was barely showing. Now she was clearly, extremely with child. "Hi, love!" she said.

Leanne stood up and opened her arms for a hug. "Hi! Oh my god. How can you look so pretty?" As she said it, she hated herself. She was so dumb, so pandering. And yet Carmen's prettiness couldn't be overlooked.

"Ah, thank you. I'm good. I'm shopping for a client today but needed a snack." She rested her hand momentarily on her round stomach. "But what about you? I just saw your email." She held up her phone. "I want to come to your event. It's twelve days before my due date!"

"Oh, really? Wow."

"Yes, but I'm sure she's going to be late. I had a dream about the number twenty, and I woke up knowing that's when she would come."

"Oh, so it's a girl!"

She nodded. "Yes! Augustina."

"Amazing, congratulations."

She smiled. "I definitely want to come to the launch. It's very exciting."

"I've actually been thinking of you," Leanne said. "I wanted your opinion on what to wear to it—if you don't mind. I have a photo." She swiped at her phone and then angled it toward Carmen, revealing a picture of herself she'd taken in a dressing room. Hank was in it too, off to the side in his stroller. A twelve-pack of toilet paper balanced atop the sunshade.

"Hmm. Something more tailored?" She made a gesture with her thumb and forefinger, suggesting something rectangular and rigid. "With your hair pulled back and maybe a red lip."

Leanne nodded.

"Love, I've got to grab something to eat, but I will text you some ideas."

"Okay, yeah. That'd be great."

She leaned in to give her another kiss on the cheek. "I have lots of ideas already," she said, before turning toward the entrance.

Leanne nodded. "Good. I need them!"

She winked. "I got you."

* * *

From: Maxine

To: Leanne

Subject: Re: La Vie Koala indeed

Thur July 7 at 11:12am

Well, the NYT can go fuck themselves. I'll bring you the crepe in my carry-on.

30

I t was the first day of class.

The doorbell rang fifteen minutes early. All morning June had known something was up, so when the thing finally happened, she barked as if possessed, as if screaming.

Hank and James had yet to leave the house. Leanne opened the door to find a short older man standing there—he looked to be in his late sixties or maybe even early seventies. He wore pleated shorts, a long-sleeved Oxford, a sweater vest, and sneakers. His white socks went up to mid-calf. Under his arm, he clutched a sizable Kinko's box. This had to be Earl. His appearance matched that of the overly organized email she'd been sent two weeks ago.

"Oh, dear," he said, bending down and trying to make friends with the barking June.

"Sorry. She's an anxious dog. Hi. I'm Leanne."

He stood back up and looked past her. "You have a baby!"

"Yes," Leanne said, turning around to see what he was seeing. "Just getting him and my husband out the door."

James waved and said hello with a frustrated smile as he struggled to simultaneously hold Hank and fill a Ziploc bag with Cheerios.

"I'm Earl," he said.

"Yes. Come in. Come in. Have a seat. I'll be right back."

Leanne collected Hank and helped James out via the backdoor. When she kissed him good-bye, his upper lip was all sweaty.

Returning to the living room, some five minutes later, she found Earl standing up, peering at one of the framed prints on the wall. It was of a woman swimming. It was actually a page Leanne had sliced out of an art book with an X-Acto knife.

"Hi," she said. "Sorry about that."

"Ah, no trouble."

"Would you like a water or some coffee?"

"Water please."

Leanne nodded and turned around on her heels.

"You're slender for having so recently had a baby," Earl said.

Leanne hated him for feeling like he could comment on her body, but then mostly forgave him because it was the compliment she always wanted to hear. "Well," she said, "he's not exactly a new-born. He's eight months old."

"Oh. He looks pretty new to me."

"Yes. He's new, but not *that* new."

"Ah," he said, sitting down on the available armchair.

"Did you have trouble finding the house?"

"No, no. Not today. I did a drive-by on the Fourth just to be sure."

"Right." Leanne nodded, mildly unsettled.

Everyone else showed up either right on time or ten minutes late: six women and two men.

The rules of the class were simple, and Leanne had already sent them via email prior to the first class: they were to bring in eight copies of up to four double-spaced pages of what they were currently working on. In class, they would read the work together and then give their comments—positive ones first followed by constructive criticism.

The whole point of the class was to get these students writing, talking about writing, and sharing their work.

Leanne began by introducing herself. Then she had her students introduce themselves. When it was Earl's turn, he described his project as "a bird fantasy novel for adults."

"Bird fantasy!" Leanne said, genuinely interested.

"Yes, all of the characters are birds." He said it so seriously and with such eye contact that Leanne couldn't help but think of a bird—the way they could look right at you unsmilingly.

Later, when it was his turn, he passed out a twenty-page booklet. Leanne reminded him of the four-page limit, at which point he got extremely flustered. He wasn't sure which four pages to pick. He flipped through the papers quickly, almost desperately.

Once he'd finally chosen them, he offered to read the text aloud. Even though they'd read everyone else's silently to themselves, Leanne acquiesced. But immediately upon hearing his dramatic, slow, storytelling voice, she wished she hadn't. It took so long, and then he didn't stop after four pages. At the four-and-a-half-page mark, she interrupted: "Okay, we're going to have to stop there."

His head popped up, and he bird-stared hard at her. "I was about to finish."

"It's important to keep to the four-page limit," she said, already looking forward to the outrage she would express later while relaying this whole story to James.

31

Maxine had emailed yesterday saying that she'd just gotten back and had the crepe for her but that it wouldn't "keep forever." Leanne responded that she should swing by her house and drop it off. They were both joking, right? But then Maxine wrote: "Okay. What's your address?"

And *now* Maxine Hunter was on her way over.

It was so unexpected that Leanne didn't even know how to explain it to James, how to catch him up. She'd told him about Maxine's initial response to her email back in March, but he hadn't read *Koala Life*, and so he didn't really get the significance, or how cool Leanne thought she was. And then she simply hadn't told him about her encounter with Maxine at the Korean spa—it had felt too complicated to explain. So now, when he called from work just to check in like he often did, she tried to fill him in: "This is a tad weird," she said, "but Maxine Hunter—the writer I told you about a while ago—I'd emailed her and she emailed me back? Well, we've kind of struck up a friendship over email and now she's coming here to hang out with me and Hank."

"Today?"

"Yeah. It was too hard to make plans around Hank's nap schedule, so she's just gonna stop by."

"Too bad it's too late for her to blurb your book."

"Ain't that the truth."

* * *

Ten minutes later, she heard a car door shut right outside their house, and from the living room window she could see the top of Maxine's head as she made her way from the car, which was surprisingly a not-very-new-looking burgundy Toyota Corolla, to her front door.

She scooped up June, holding her under her arm, and opened the door. "Hey," Leanne said. "June gave you away."

"Ah, so you're a dog person." It was such a surprise to see her pore-less, well-moisturized face again. She'd gotten used to seeing it via her phone's screen. Leanne stepped backward, allowing her the space to come inside. She wore a sleeveless white t-shirt tucked into cutoff jean shorts, but not the short and loose variety. The shorts reminded her of the kind Baby wore in *Dirty Dancing*—slim fitting and cut off just above the knee. For a purse, she had a canvas tote bag. Leanne set June down. The dog rushed her ankles and barked.

"Well, I'd say my husband is the dog person."

Maxine bent over to pet her.

"Hank's still asleep, but he'll probably wake up any second." For some background noise, Leanne had put on a mix James had made years ago for dinner parties. U2's "Who's Gonna Ride Your Wild Horses" played quietly.

"She probably smells this crepe," Maxine said, standing back up and reaching inside her tote bag. She pronounced the word the French way—rhyming with *step*.

"I can't believe you really brought one."

"Well, the vendor who sold it to me promised it would be no problem." She unwrapped it from its foil. "Let's take a look."

Leanne leaned in to see. She imagined its journey from the streets of Paris to Charles de Gaulle to LAX and on that long, endless drive from the west side of town to the east.

"It looks normal-ish," Leanne said. She peered up from the mottled brown rectangle and so did Maxine.

Maxine shrugged. "Bon appétit?"

Leanne smiled. This whole thing should have been much more uncomfortable—Maxine Hunter, in her house, feeding her a crepe—and yet she felt at ease, secure. And though Leanne wasn't someone who loved the idea of street food nor one who typically embraced ingesting something so travel-worn, she realized that this was obviously different. This was something from *Paris*. She reached for the crepe, tore off a piece, and placed it in her mouth. Maxine watched her. "It's good," Leanne said, nodding and chewing. "Try it."

Maxine peeled back the foil and took a bite straight from it. "Yeah. Not bad," she said. They stood there smiling and chewing for another few seconds.

"Did you have trouble finding the place?"

Maxine shook her head. "This is nice." She scanned the living room as she chewed.

"Oh, thanks." Leanne looked around and took in her own living room. "The sunlight is the best feature." She looked back to Maxine. Why was this woman here? Did she not have friends of her own? Or did she simply like Leanne? "Where did you stay in Paris—a hotel?"

Maxine shook her head again. "With a friend. She has a baby too, actually. A bit older than yours." As she said this, they heard a loud whimpering sound.

"Ah, speaking of," Leanne said, brushing her hands quickly on her pants. "Do you want to come get him with me?"

Maxine paused for a moment before shrugging. "Okay."

"He's very soft and sweet when he first wakes up."

Maxine nodded and then bent down to slip off her shoes. (Leanne herself was barefoot.)

Leanne grabbed the crepe from Maxine and placed it on the kitchen counter. She passed through the kitchen, looking back and waving for Maxine to follow.

Just outside Hank's door, she paused. She slid the door open slowly. It was cool and dark inside except for the light coming in from the now opened door. The white noise machine churned.

Hank lay on his back, his head and back resting on top of his stuffed bunny. He smiled up at Leanne. How exhilarating—to share this with Maxine, for Maxine to bear witness. The women sort of sunk to the floor of Hank's room. Leanne pressed her face against the wooden slats. "He thinks this is really funny." And sure enough, Hank lifted his head and smiled a full-dimpled smile. Leanne looked over at Maxine. Could she feel what Leanne felt? It was so pure and so good. Maxine smiled back and then turned her attention to the nearby bookshelf, which held a mixture of children's books and non-children's books. "Does he like poetry?" She reached for a book—one that Leanne remembered but hadn't picked up in a million years.

Maxine said the book reminded her of that movie—what was it called?—with Diane Lane where she goes to Italy after a divorce, because at one point Diane Lane holds up a book by Czesław Miłosz (who was the editor of the anthology Maxine held in her hands) to one of the Polish workers working on her dilapidated house and tells him she's a fan of his work.

"*Under the Tuscan Sun*?" Leanne said.

"Yeah, that's it!"

"Don't tell Czesław that." Leanne pronounced the name the same way Maxine had—assuming that was right. She pulled Hank out of the crib and set him on her lap. "So you're a big *Under the Tuscan Sun* fan?"

Maxine smiled. "I got on a Diane Lane kick."

"I can't even remember when I bought that book," Leanne said, pulling up her shirt to breast-feed. "It might've been college."

"What about this one? Any good?" She held up one of Hank's books: *The Pout Pout Fish*.

"The ending's a bit fucked up."

Maxine nodded. "Ah."

"It was a gift. Almost everything in here was."

Maxine looked around. Leanne watched her reach for the wooden phone, the one her dad had sent her. She picked up the receiver.

"Hello?" she said into it. And then to Leanne: "This is actually really beautiful."

"Yeah," she said, and then paused, thinking of her dad. "It's something I liked the look of and put on our baby registry."

"It looks Japanese."

"It is. How'd you know?"

"My grandma's Japanese. She still lives there. I've visited a few times and always leave with things like this."

"Oh, so you're a quarter Japanese?"

"Yeah."

"Well, that phone has a pretty interesting story. My dad sent it, which was surprising because . . ." She paused, feeling self-conscious.

"What?"

She looked up again. "Are you into myths and legends?" She was kidding. Sort of.

"I am." Maxine nodded.

Leanne considered waving it off, saying, "Never mind, it's too long of a story," but Maxine Hunter was here, at her house. She took a breath before briefly explaining the type of person her father was, and then the registry, and then the package in the mail after his death and the accompanying note saying he would be "on call."

As she spoke, she pulled Hank off the one breast and put him on the other.

"Wow. Have you . . ." Maxine said, motioning toward the phone.

"Called him?" Leanne's voice came out very high-pitched. Hank's eyes opened wide, looking up at her somewhat startled. "Kind of," she said more quietly.

"My grandma—the Japanese one—is Buddhist, and she has this altar to people in our family who've died. It's in her living room, and it mostly consists of photos of the people, but each morning she leaves them rice and fruit and rings a bell for them. It's always a bit strange for me at first, but then by the end of the trip, it feels very normal—like small talk with the dead."

"Interesting," Leanne said, and meant it.

A gentle silence took over the room.

"Were you able to make it to the funeral? Since you were so pregnant?"

"No. I really wanted to." Quickly, all at once, she felt very exposed. "What about you? Are your parents still alive?"

Maxine nodded. "Yeah. But don't worry. They still haunt me."

Leanne smiled.

Slowly, they spilled back into the kitchen. James's mix was still playing. Hank noticed the music instantly and began bobbing his head. Leanne told her how when he was a newborn, he would stop crying whenever they played Sinéad O'Connor's "The Emperor's New Clothes." Maxine pulled it up on YouTube, and they listened to it while watching Hank smile widely. They finished the crepe, giving little pieces to Hank. They made jokes about his French palate. They were still hungry.

Leanne sliced some pieces of bread and scrambled a few eggs, topping them off with crème fraîche and hot sauce. Maxine wandered around the living room, looking at things. Hank crawled around the kitchen floor.

"I don't see your book anywhere," Maxine said, appearing at her side.

"They just came." Leanne opened a low cabinet on the other side of the kitchen and retrieved a copy for her from the box the publisher had just sent her. It still very much thrilled her to see it, to hold a bound copy in her hands.

"Oh, so it hasn't even come out yet? I didn't realize."

"Not 'til August second," Leanne said. Hank had followed them, trying to pull himself to a stand using Leanne's crouched leg for leverage. She picked him up and carried him to his high chair. The three of them ate lunch while Maxine flipped through Leanne's book. "Can I have it?"

"Of course," Leanne said, almost laughing.

"What?"

"You're basically one of my favorite writers. So it's just pretty funny and sort of embarrassing to have you here, flipping through my book."

"Embarrassing?"

"I don't know. It's no *Koala Life*."

"Would be weird if it were." Maxine smiled.

They ate their eggs. Hank didn't eat his. Maxine asked about the rejected piece she'd written for the *New York Times*. Somehow, her answer wandered into explaining how she was teaching a writing class and then about Earl and his pleated shorts and his bird fantasy novel. Maxine laughed so much that Leanne felt victorious—to make someone she admired so much laugh.

By the time Maxine left, she'd signed Leanne's copy of *Koala Life*, and Leanne had signed her copy of her book. When the door closed, Leanne reached for the book and opened it. She read the large, swooping inscription and felt something, something beyond uplifting, something propelling.

> *YOUR FAN,*
> *Maxine*

32

Leanne had just gotten Hank and James out the door when Earl showed up and June started in on her barking session.

"June, that's enough!" Leanne said loudly, and sprayed her with a squirt bottle; it was a new tactic she was trying out, suggested by James after she had complained to him about how June had to bark at each student with the same high-pitched level of intensity. June blinked, confused for half a second before she continued barking. "Sorry about her," Leanne said.

"Oh," Earl cooed, bending down with an open palm. "She's just a little pooch." June jumped up and, since he was wearing shorts, was scratching at the tops of his bare knees. "Oh, okay. That does smart." He winced.

Leanne scooped the dog up. "I'm going to put her on the deck. I'll be right back."

When she re-entered the living room, she found him comfortably sitting on the armchair he'd chosen as his seat at the last class. She cleared her throat. "Would you like a glass of water, or I have some tea?"

"Water would be great. Thank you. See," he said, "I've got a compressed disc." He took out a number of pills from a Ziploc bag and placed them on the sideboard.

"That sounds painful."

"It is," he said. "It didn't help that I had a jewelry showcase Thursday morning, so I was running around on my feet all day."

"A jewelry showcase?"

"Yes, I make jewelry."

"Oh. I did notice your ring. It's lovely." She wasn't lying. The stone was a large, flat, polished seafoam green—a kind of turquoise?—and it was set in a delicate rose gold band. "Did you make that?"

He glanced at his finger. "Oh, no. No." He shook his head. "I make *women's* jewelry."

Leanne nodded. "Ah."

He didn't immediately respond, so Leanne took the opportunity to excuse herself. "I've got to print a few things. I'll be right back." She *did* have to print a few things, but she also had to pee before class started.

As she waited for the pages to print, she sent a quick text to Maxine: *UPDATE. My adult bird fantasy novelist just took some pills (opiates?) for his compressed disc, which he aggravated at a recent women's jewelry showcase.*

33

Hank was asleep. James was cleaning up after dinner. The sun was making its slow descent. The heat of the day finally fading. And Leanne sat outside with a beer in one hand and a hand-rolled (by James) cigarette in the other. Her book would come out in one week. She didn't feel anxious or worried about her impending dream come true. Neither did she feel unprepared or unworthy.

For a few nicotine-fueled moments, she didn't doubt her book, her voice, her life. She didn't trivialize it or feel the need to apologize for it not being something else. For a sustained minute, she felt in charge of her own life. A grown-up at last.

She was glad she hadn't left that second comment by Olivia Hatfield on Regina's blog. Instead, she'd Googled to find the percentage of people who vaccinated their kids. She reminded herself that anti-vaxxers were the minority, that most people vaccinated, that she was *not* delusional.

She had a few unanswered emails in her in-box from Mona, who was trying to set up a date for the cooking class. On Instagram, Leanne had looked up the woman who hosted the classes at her house. Her name was Holly Woodcock. She had about thirty thousand followers, and after about ten minutes of scrolling, Leanne gathered that she was a sometime actress who was married to the guy who'd played Liz Lemon's bad boyfriend in *30 Rock*. Leanne would probably take the job, mostly because the money was good, but also because she was grateful to Mona for the introduction to the *Madre* magazine contact.

But what she really wanted to do was surrender. To finally delete Regina's Instagram account from her phone. (Why hadn't she yet?) She wanted to forget about her father's ashes. To be able to see that Beth was simply another woman who'd been beaten down by life and was holding on to the little power she had.

With the sunset's golden light all around her, she took a few selfies with the cigarette in her mouth. She looked pretty. But not necessarily soft, and also not lacking a sense of humor. She felt a new understanding of *the selfie*—the desire to show someone else your face. She texted one to Maxine. *I'm doing it,* she wrote. She had previously told her how she'd been looking forward to having a cigarette, something she hadn't done since she'd found out she was pregnant.

Proud of you, Maxine wrote back right away.

She placed the cigarette by her side and used both hands to text quickly back: *It didn't taste great at first, but I just kept going and now it's lovely.*

Potential new ad copy for American Spirit?

Smiling, Leanne stubbed out the cigarette on the concrete driveway. She took a deep breath of fresh air.

She would beat Regina and Beth—all of them—the old-fashioned way. She would forget about them.

34

Leanne woke up before everyone else, grabbed her phone from the bedside table, and turned it on. With her eyes squinting—still protecting themselves from the light of the screen—she saw she'd gotten an email from Brittany. The subject line was *You've lost a fan.* Her stomach swarmed, the feeling rushing up her throat. She opened it.

Hello,
My mom just sent me a review of your book where she is described as a "mistress" and I'm a secret "extramarital" baby. Wow. Dad had been living with my mom for over a year when I was born. And if your mom didn't know about me, it's because she was in denial. It's sad that you had to twist things around to make my mom a villain, and sad for me to have to deal with it on top of taking care of an eight-month-old with constant health issues. I just wanted you to know that I always looked up to you, but I don't anymore. I can see right through your fake kindness toward me online. You obviously feel guilty about what you've written. If Dad were alive, I know he would be ashamed of you for telling this "story." Hope you enjoy your fifteen minutes of fame.

Brittany

She put the phone down and stared into the quiet darkness.

She could hear her own heartbeat, like someone methodically banging against a door with the side of their fist.

Two thoughts came to her. The first: that everything she had written in the book was true. She had a copy of her parents' divorce papers, which were dated two months after Brittany's day of birth. And before her dad had died, while she was writing those early chapters, she'd asked him why he'd kept Beth's pregnancy a secret from her mom. He'd responded jokingly: "It seemed like a good idea at the time." But Leanne had heard the shame in his voice.

The second: that after his death, she'd gone to some lengths to acquire a copy of these documents, to have proof of the timeline. She hadn't allowed herself to analyze it at the time, but now she understood exactly why she'd done it. Because she'd been a kid at the time. She remembered the general mood of that year or years: the tension around baby Brittany, her mother's constant crying, the ping-ponging between houses. But kids were so powerless.

She realized now that she'd tracked down the divorce papers as ballast against any competing narratives. She'd tracked them down because she understood that her version, once out in the world, might sting.

35

Carmen had sent her, via text, images of women in high-waisted pants, trench coats, and blazers. *I love these looks for you*, she'd written. *Go to En Garde.* 😊 🐚 *And send me photos from the dressing room!*

Leanne was very good at following directions. So here she was at En Garde, having left Hank with Ofelia. She ducked behind the dressing-room curtain. She hadn't seen any trench coats to try on but probably wouldn't have grabbed one anyway. It was the end of July in Los Angeles; she had started to sweat in the time it took her to walk the two minutes from her car to the air-conditioned store.

She inspected the price tags. Each piece cost about $200 more than she was willing to spend. But she was already here. She should at least try some of these pieces on in order to text photos back to Carmen.

Leanne pulled on the $395 high-waisted pants, tucked in the $120 t-shirt, and glanced up at the mirror, immediately surprised by the angles of her own body. Carmen had known what would flatter her. She looked thin, even to herself. Her hip bones protruded a bit. When she added the blazer, she felt both ridiculous and amazing. She was never one to step outside of the dressing room—especially not for a salesperson—but it was almost as if she needed someone else to tell her that what she was seeing was not a lie.

"Oh, that's great," one of the salespeople said. Leanne studied her. She looked to be about nineteen and had a slight French accent. "You should add these." She turned around, whisked some beige, heeled leather mules off a shelf, and placed them at her feet.

"Thanks," Leanne said, and slipped them on. She peered into the mirror, pulled her hair back and tucked it under the collar of the jacket. She felt so clean and crisp. She understood the power of money then, how it could fix *some* things, could make you feel like less of an impostor, less available to scrutiny. She slipped off the shoes and then retreated back to the dressing room. She stood on the balls of her feet and took a photo. She texted it to Carmen along with two question marks. She considered sending it to Maxine too but didn't. Was it still a selfie if one didn't look like oneself?

She undressed and put on the next outfit: a structured white blouse with a pussy bow at the collar and another pair of high-waisted pants. Again, she looked so put together, serious, rich.

She pulled back the curtain and stepped out once more into the store, announcing: "I think this is it."

The possibly French girl nodded. "Classic. Try the shoes again." She gestured to the mules.

Leanne stepped into them and stood in front of the mirror. She nodded. "I like it."

Back inside the dressing room, she took another photo, this time texting it right away to Carmen along with the message *I like this one.*

This time, Carmen wrote back immediately. *YES.* 👟👟👟

Minutes later, the shopgirl rang her up. The total came to $774.30. The number hit her as if someone had just doused her face with cold water. The number was not of sound mind. It was half of the total she would make teaching. It was a number that didn't even include the childcare fees because she was technically paying someone in order to shop right now. It was a number she was positive her own mother, a doctor and consumer extraordinaire, hadn't spent on an outfit in one transaction. What was she doing? Who did she think she was?

At the homewares store, she'd rung up totals for this amount on a daily basis. So many times she'd wondered how these people could casually spend so much. She'd cast them into another realm, a different class, indeed. But now here she was on the other side. Maybe it wasn't casual for them after all, she thought. Maybe they were faking it, too.

36

Leanne took the first pass. James edited it and sent it back to her. And then Leanne took one more pass.

Dear Brittany,

I'm very sorry that you got the news about what I included in the book the way that you did. I'd been meaning to email you about it, but obviously, I was too late. That said, I want you to know that I did talk with Dad about our shared history before he died. And I'm pretty sure he understood that I was asking because I was planning to write about it all. Specifically, he was worried about this—that we'd grown up with very different stories about our parents. And maybe they're both true? But I do think that Dad comes off badly in both versions. And it's upsetting to me that the women he hurt are left to fight among ourselves. Although at least we're communicating?

I do feel bad about our relationship. At the same time, I don't think the circumstances within our family ever allowed us to be sisters, to feel a true camaraderie or kinship. I hadn't pestered you about this, but as you know I wasn't able to make it to the memorial service, and it would have meant a lot to me to have had some of Dad's ashes. I've emailed your mom about this three times with no response.

Yours,
Leanne

She reread it. She wanted to reference the *fifteen minutes of fame* line that had particularly hurt, but there was no graceful way to do it. She pressed *Send*.

She closed her laptop and walked into Hank's room. She picked up the wooden phone.

She waited for something, anything, but heard nothing.

She wanted to yell, to scream at him, but that had never worked in real life. In *living* life, her dad had always shut down when confronted. Her brother was the same. It made her think of Hank—specifically, of sleep training.

Leanne had trusted her mother's pediatric advice on the topic. She'd believed her when her mother said that letting him "cry it out" taught the baby how to fall asleep on his own, how to console himself, but now Leanne wondered if she'd also unwittingly taught him how to shut up; how to give up; how to be alone in his suffering. The last thing she wanted was to raise another person in the WASP tradition of suppressed emotions and self-sufficiency to the point of martyrdom.

She thought of Regina and the way she'd handled the news that Leanne's dad had died. She'd sent flowers. Tasteful, understated sweet peas and a handwritten card.

Regina and her mother were the same in that way. Their preferred manner of coping with problems was with a purchase or transaction. It seemed to Leanne now a potential flaw in the high-road strategy. If you had enough money, you could probably always rise above. No one *volunteered* to go down into the shit. To meet a grieving person at their level. But then she thought of giving birth. She'd heard a midwife describe labor as a descent. She thought of the women she knew who had had their babies at home or bypassed the option of an epidural. But no, that kind of descent seemed different from the one she was thinking about. That kind of surrender was still wrapped up in control, in *Look at what my body can do!* At least, that had been part of the allure of childbirth for Leanne.

But no one wanted to go *really* down, she thought. There were no birth plans that read: I want to arrive at the pushing phase of labor and then get horrifically, painfully stuck. No one *wanted* an emergency C-section. No one wanted to hemorrhage uncontrollably. No one wanted to stare into the void of their own powerlessness. That was good fodder for a poetry collection maybe, but it wouldn't help you land a *Vogue* Q&A.

No one wanted to change incontrovertibly on someone else's terms. But no matter if you birthed your baby alone in the woods or in a hospital surrounded by seven medical professionals, that *was* motherhood.

Wasn't it?

37

This morning with Earl, she aimed to keep things as professional as possible. When she opened the door, she didn't yell at June to stop barking. She simply waited for her to calm down. Once June had, she asked him, "Did you get my email?" Since Earl seemed incapable of sticking to the page limit, Leanne had sent him an email recommending that he take the novel-writing class next session.

"Yes," he said, clutching his jumbo Kinko's box. "The thing is I quite like the format of this class. I like the writing group aspect."

Leanne nodded. "Totally. But even if the novel class isn't specifically labeled a writing group, the people in your class would naturally become your writing group and you'd get to turn in more pages."

"Mm-hmm," he said vacantly, before sitting down on his armchair and requesting a water so that he could take his pills.

The rest of the students arrived right on time or five to ten minutes late.

After each student had workshopped their piece, forty-five minutes remained. Leanne pulled out a section of a short story she'd photocopied and planned to discuss. It was one of Leanne's favorites. It took place at a dinner party and introduced many characters in a matter of paragraphs. She'd picked it especially because Earl's story introduced so many birds right at the beginning, and everyone in the class, including Leanne, had trouble telling them apart. The birds were bleeding into one another. Which bird should they care about? Who was the hero bird, the villain bird? Would a bird find some redemption?

After reading and discussing the story, Leanne looked at her watch. They had about five minutes. "Does anyone have any general writing questions or questions about the class so far?"

A classic writerly silence pervaded the room.

After a solid thirty seconds, Earl and Kathleen spoke up at the exact same moment. Kathleen shook her head: "Go ahead. You go."

Earl shrugged his shoulders. "I was just going to say that if we had time, I have four more pages to share." As he said this, he reached down to the Kinko's box.

"No!" It came out panicked—like she'd shout-say to Hank as he went to put a small rock in his mouth. "Thank you, Earl, but this time of the class is dedicated to more general writing topics. Kathleen, did you have a question?"

"I, uh," she said, looking away from Earl. "I was just wondering if you could tell us about how you got your book published? Did you find an agent first?"

Leanne relaxed. She loved talking about herself and her long and winding writing journey. They didn't have much time, though. She kept it short, finishing by announcing that her book hadn't technically been published yet. It was being released on Tuesday, and she would absolutely love to see them at her reading and launch event that Thursday at Kipling's.

"But it's a cookbook, right?" Earl asked, looking around the room, seemingly for some kind of confirmation from one of his classmates.

"No," Leanne said. "It's a memoir. There are recipes, yes."

He nodded, his bottom lip rolling downward, unimpressed.

38

Tuesday morning, she awoke with a feeling of weightlessness and hope. It was the day she had marked on her calendar for eighteen months now. Her book was finally published. Still in bed, she toggled her phone awake and checked her email.

She immediately saw one from Erika—her publicist—with the subject line: *Bad review.* Leanne opened it, absorbing the information that it was from the *L.A. Times.* She clicked on the link and saw the headline: "Food Blogger Writes Bland Book." She didn't read any further.

She tapped James awake.

"Fuck him," he eventually said, still rubbing his eyes, trying to take in the light from the phone. "He clearly didn't get the book."

"Yeah," she said, not so sure.

"It's a great book, Swee," he said, propping himself up on his side and reaching over her body to put the phone down on the bedside table.

Leanne lay on her back, staring at the ceiling. She remembered a friend of hers complaining about a bad review in a national newspaper, and how she'd wanted to take her by the shoulders and say: *You published a book, and somebody wrote about it! This is not a tragedy.* But now she understood how everyone always wanted more, that one dream realized only opened up another and another, the ego just like that Hungry Caterpillar. On Wednesday, she ate through three plums. But she was still hungry. On Thursday, she ate through four strawberries. . . .

"Do you have anything planned for today? I mean, I know you have Hank."

She shook her head.

"You should do something special—to celebrate. Go to the beach or something. It's supposed to be super hot today."

"He'll just eat sand."

"What about LACMA or the Getty Center?"

She took a breath. "Yeah, maybe. The Getty is so far, though, and I've got that interview in Santa Monica tomorrow."

"Oh, right. Well, do what you want, but if I were you, I'd try and spend the day celebrating. This is a good day."

"Yeah," she said. "I know."

He squeezed her into him and she breathed him in.

39

t took resolve, fortitude, and long-term planning, but she'd done it. She'd packed a day bag full of everything she would need for herself and Hank and was now driving at a slow crawl on the 10 West to the Getty Center, her favorite museum in Los Angeles. Each time Hank cried, she took the steering wheel with her left hand and reached around with her right, stretching her torso and arm to their limits, and tried to place a pacifier in his mouth.

She listened to the country station for the majority of the one-hour trip. One song in particular—"Raise 'Em Up"—embarrassingly made her eyes fill with tears. Even the blatant references to the Christian male god Leanne had come so much to resent weren't jarring enough to keep her from imagining Hank growing up, becoming angular and inaccessible. Her tiny baby! Wearing underwear and getting haircuts!

Anytime the bad review popped into her head (bland!) she counteracted it by reminding herself that *she* was going to be on NPR—on the popular Saturday-morning food show *Full Plate*. At a previous ad agency job, James had trained spokespeople on how to interact with the media and had been encouraging Leanne to practice for the interview by speaking aloud about her book.

And so during each radio commercial, she turned down the

volume and talked to herself: "Thanks for having me! And yes, I started my blog back in 2009. It began as a simple outlet. I was frustrated with my writing career, and I didn't know how to cook. I was simply hungry and tired of eating heated-up, previously frozen pizza bites."

It had been at least two years since she'd been to the Getty, but once there, she remembered everything: the parking structure, the white futuristic tram ride to the top, and the way the doors opened and people spilled out into an expansive green space. She found the building, grounds, and blue sky itself to be the art, with the indoor exhibitions always a letdown in comparison.

Hank seemed to feel the same way. He leaned forward in his stroller, wanting *out out out*. He was officially nine months old and horribly, intensely committed to learning how to walk. Even though it was ninety degrees outside, she made sure to dress him in long pants since anytime he was not in the stroller, he was crawling toward the closest bench or chair, which he would use to pull himself up to a stand, and then he'd bob triumphantly before falling again.

She was taking an unsustainable number of photos with her phone—the entire time formulating an Instagram post and caption that would do the work of showing how beautiful her life was and also: "Did you know my book is officially in the world today? #linkinprofile." So that when she pulled her phone from her pocket to take another one of Hank as he crawled across the pristine, manicured circular lawn, she saw she had five new text messages.

Hey! It's Mona.
Julianna gave me your number. I saw the
review in the paper. It's bullshit. You know
that RM is good friends with Gretchen
Dunlop, right?

Gretchen is the L.A. Times arts and en-
tertainment editor.

I'm not saying RM got her to run that review of your book—she probably just said
something in passing about not liking it.

She sets a tone, puts things into motion—
like a Rube Goldberg machine.

Oh and Elspeth told me you guys scheduled a day for the Madre shoot! Excited.

You weren't supposed to shoot the messenger, but in that moment, as she put her phone back in her pocket and jogged off to
chase down Hank, she wanted to. She'd been having fun. She'd
forgotten for an hour that her book was bland, that she had an arch-
nemesis. She'd forgotten that she'd agreed to a photoshoot of herself and Hank in their house and that, because of it, she had to turn
their house into a museum. She had to clean the bathrooms and buy
a new rug. She needed to buy some sort of gender-neutral jumpsuit
for Hank, to shove all of his plastic toys into a fair-trade basket.
She should get her highlights redone and a manicure too. Then and
only then, she could play the role of a capable, fashionable, writer/
mother. Only then could she beat Regina at her own game.

40

F*ull Plate* recorded in a building at Santa Monica College, which meant she would be back on the 10 West, just like yesterday. And just like yesterday, the drive could easily take an hour. Plus, the producer, Yasmin, had warned her over email that parking could be tricky—especially since summer session had just started back up. In the interest of being safe rather than sorry, Leanne gave herself an hour and thirty minutes to get there and to park.

And since they had booked her on a Wednesday and Ofelia was with another family on Wednesdays, she left Hank with James, who'd managed to take the morning off.

When she got in her car, she noted that it was the first time she'd done that—left her child like an actual working mother and not one who went to coffee shops to do spec writing for editors who might or might not (usually *not*) pay her. No. Today she had a business meeting. Today she was a professional interacting with other professionals.

She got in the car and reversed down the driveway.

At the bottom of the street, she got a phone call. She looked at the number popping up on her dashboard—it was a New York City area code. Her editor? She toggled the button on her steering wheel to receive it.

"Hello," Leanne said into the nothingness.

"Leanne?"

"Yeah."

"It's me. Erika. I'm glad I caught you. The producer at *Full Plate* called me just now. They had to close the entire campus because of a measles outbreak."

"What?"

"Yeah, I guess it's all over the local news. A few students have come down with it, and they need to contain it. Apparently, the virus can live in the air for up to two hours after a sick person coughs or sneezes!"

"Jesus."

"So they're not letting anyone on campus. I'm sorry. Yasmin said she loved the book and will find some new times in order to reschedule."

Leanne pulled over. She wished she'd gotten on the highway at least. She didn't want to go back home. She didn't want to be with her beautiful family.

41

The following morning was an Ofelia day. With her book newly out and her launch event that night, she found that checking and responding to her social media accounts had become a thrilling yet Sisyphean activity; the more she interacted, the more there was to interact with.

But she'd barely gotten settled at the coffee shop when she purposefully missed a phone call from an unknown number. When the voice mail notice popped up, she clicked on it out of curiosity. She was only half paying attention at first, until she realized it wasn't a robocall from the California Democrats. No, it was a real live woman from the CDC issuing a warning about a recent measles outbreak to all people who might have attended the Getty Center on Tuesday, August 2.

Leanne stepped outside the café and called the number the woman had left. She felt shoved into a different gear, like the time she had almost sliced the tip of her pointer finger straight off. She couldn't panic or flail about. Panicking wouldn't help stop the bleeding.

Soon she was talking to a human and learning the following: that two members of a family who had visited Switzerland had contracted the measles while there, but as symptoms don't show up for a few days, the family had flown back home to Los

Angeles, bringing the virus with them. Everyone on the plane had been exposed because it's a highly contagious disease. One unvaccinated child who had been on the plane had gone to the Getty Center on Tuesday and had since been diagnosed with the measles. And so now the CDC was calling every single person who had gone to the museum on Tuesday to ask them if they had been vaccinated and, if not, to get vaccinated within forty-eight hours.

"But my baby is only nine months old. I thought he was too young to get that vaccine."

"Yes, that's the recommendation because there's a chance that before that, the infant may still hold some passive immunity from the mother and the vaccine won't be as effective. However, the recommendation for an exposed infant between six and eleven months is to get the vaccine within seventy-two hours, and then you should begin active surveillance."

"Active surveillance?"

"For symptoms."

Passive immunity and active surveillance. She breathed through her nose. The pain was hitting her now, but she couldn't give in to it. She had more questions. "Like what?"

"Fever, dry cough, runny nose."

"That sounds like a cold!"

"I'm sorry, ma'am. If I were you, I would call your doctor and explain that your child needs an emergency MMR vaccine due to potential exposure."

At this point, she had gathered up her laptop and notebook and was walking toward the car. "Okay, okay. I'm going home right now to tell my babysitter. Wait. What if she isn't vaccinated?" Her throat was closing as she spoke.

"Then she should get vaccinated as soon as possible."

"I don't even understand how you got my phone number."

"We checked the license plates of everyone who parked at the Getty Center on Tuesday."

"Holy shit."

"It's a very serious illness, ma'am."

Inside the car, the heat was stifling. She could barely touch the steering wheel. "I know, I know," she said.

PART

III

42

n a mix of English and Spanish, she explained to Ofelia what was going on, that Hank might have been exposed to measles. Was she vaccinated against that disease? She pointed at her arm and mimed a shot. But Ofelia didn't know if she'd been vaccinated. She *thought* so, but she couldn't be sure. Leanne apologized and explained the best that she could everything she'd just been told by the woman at the CDC. She Googled the Spanish word for *vaccination* and *surveillance*. She mostly kept saying, "Muy grave."

After that, she called her mom, who answered the phone by saying, "To what do I owe this pleasure?"

To which Leanne explained as quickly as possible what was happening.

To which her mom gasped.

"Don't gasp!" Leanne said.

"I'm sorry," her mother said. "It's just such a horrible virus, Leela."

Next, she called her pediatrician. Their policy in these cases was to give the shot after hours—right before the staff went home—at five-thirty p.m. Her reading was at seven. With traffic and parking, she realized she could be late to her own event. She called James. He said it was going to be okay, that he was coming home now and he would take Hank. She hated the rush of all the decisions, how everything had to happen quickly, quickly.

She told James she would skip the reading or maybe she could just postpone it? But James said no. He said that she'd already done all of the publicity. He said it would be hard to get the same number of people there on a different day.

She wasn't thinking straight. She ended up going by herself. She felt split in two. She stupidly thought of Julia Child making crepes, how she'd said that one side was always the public side—the nicely mottled brown side—and the other, the pale and less appealing side, the private one. Her nicely mottled public side is what showed up to the reading. This same side told her that Hank was going to be fine, that he was healthy, that he might have been exposed but he wasn't *sick*. At the same time her private side imagined him hooked up to an IV, tucked into a hospital bed like that baby she'd seen in a documentary about pregnancy and birth. The baby was being wheeled into surgery to correct a cleft palate. She'd grabbed James's arm as they watched, squeezing it until the scene was over.

Later that same night, she saw photos of herself from the event that people had posted on Instagram. She saw herself smiling. If her baby ended up dying of measles and there was a record of her smiling beforehand, she would never forgive herself.

Perhaps she'd smiled because Maxine had showed up. She remembered that. And some of her ex-coworkers from the homewares store. And even Carmen.

43

Surveillance, Leanne learned, came from the French words *sur* and *veiller*: *over* and *watch,* respectively. During the next few days, she played the words in various combinations in her head. She was watching over him, all the time looking for symptoms. *Does he feel warm? Is that a sick sneeze or a regular sneeze?*

She was watching over her thoughts, which were dark and circular: If her baby had measles, she would go to Regina's house and hand her Hank and make her look him in the eyes; if her baby had measles, then Ursa better fucking get measles.

How could you wish for a baby to get measles?

Does he feel warm?

She called her mom on FaceTime throughout the day so that she could watch over him too, could assess him visually.

And then at night, she *over*-watched. She put him to bed in his crib and then lay down in the dark on the floor next to it. She brought her phone for company, and from the ground, she watched over the outbreak itself, reading articles on CNN and the *L.A. Times.* She tried to find the names attached to the "confirmed cases," but the articles never said. So she took her search to social media. She could see all the people who had posted from the Getty Center on Tuesday. If the image was of a child, she clicked on the username, looking for more information. Was the child vaccinated?

Were the parents worried? Was anyone going through what Leanne was going through?

She surveilled Regina's profile. She was waiting for her to comment on the outbreak, but Regina hadn't posted anything yet. So Leanne logged in to her account. Sure enough, behind the scenes, Regina was trying to slip into the DMs of a well-known nineties actress who'd since pivoted to authoring cookbooks centered on veganism and wellness. Her name was Annalise Hart. Leanne clicked on her profile and read her bio: "That actress from the nineties / human rights activist / animal rights activist / vaccine risk aware." This was a distinction she'd been noticing: "vaccine risk aware" in lieu of "anti-vax." Because, Leanne was realizing, most of these people wouldn't denounce vaccines outright. Instead, they criticized the "rigorous scheduling" or what they characterized as the "one-size-fits-all" nature of vaccines, and in turn, promoted "boosting" one's immunity. The language was coded and dumb, and it made Leanne's face go hot.

Because she'd also recently purchased the vaccine book—the one that had garnered the long review in the *New Yorker*—and she'd begun to get an idea of the larger debate. She'd suddenly begun to reconsider the word *public*. As in public health and public schools. These things worked best when everyone bought in. When people bought a house in the non-trending neighborhood and sent their kids to the school in that same neighborhood. When people didn't consider themselves *exceptional* and *exempt*.

But people like this ex-actress avoided this argument altogether. They treated vaccines like that whirlpool of plastic in the Pacific Ocean. They worshipped at the altar of the "natural" but had seemingly missed that episode of the BBC docuseries where the baby elephant starves to death (because of *natural* conditions) and the mother elephant stands there impotent and devastated.

According to Annalise's last post, she'd recently met with a prominent anti-vax activist at the California State Assembly to lobby against a proposed new bill that would make it harder for people to acquire vaccine exemptions. And Regina, less than twelve hours ago, had sent her the following:

> *Hi Annalise! I'm a mom (and business owner) here in Los Angeles and just wanted to say: I support you. If you need help organizing or fundraising, let's chat. I have a wide network of like-minded mamas ready to help. Xoxx Regina Mark*

At this, Leanne shoved her phone across the floor and buried her face in her hands.

She didn't know how long she'd been in that same position when she heard James slide the door open and ask her to come to bed.

"No," she said. "Not yet."

She retrieved her phone, went to the CDC's website, and learned everything there was to know about measles. She looked at photos of infected children, red faced with watery eyes. She learned that most people didn't die from measles anymore, but that it hit babies and old people the hardest. She learned that the virus was an interesting one, that it wiped out all of your built-up immunity, so that survivors remained *sickly* for years after. The word stayed with her. Sickly. It sounded so old-fashioned. She heard her dad's voice. *Wasn't Proust sickly?* It had been so long since he'd last chimed in. All she felt toward him was anger.

Shut up, she said back. *You're not funny. You're dead.*

She uploaded photos of Hank onto her own Instagram, writing long captions about what was happening, apologizing about possibly acting strange at her reading on Thursday, typing that her nine-month-old had been exposed to measles and she hadn't been able to be fully present. Then she would reread what she'd written and see her own melodrama. She would roll her eyes and delete it.

On Saturday, she emailed all her students and asked them if they were vaccinated against the measles. Both James and her mother thought this step wasn't necessary, but Leanne wanted to do it. She wanted to distribute her pain. And at the same time, she wanted to wallow in it and to make it worse for herself. She was in-volved in a strange math where if she hadn't written the book, then she wouldn't have gotten the bad review, and then she wouldn't have needed to make herself feel better, and then she wouldn't have gone to the museum, and then she wouldn't have put Hank in danger.

But that doesn't make any sense! she heard her dad say.

What doesn't make sense is you. She marched across her house, picked up that wooden phone in Hank's room, and shouted into it, "Leave me alone! I don't need you."

44

When Earl appeared at the front door his standard fifteen minutes early for class, he had another box stacked on top of his usual Kinko's one. "I brought something to show you," he said.

"Okay," Leanne said. "One second. I'll be right back." She had nothing to do; Hank and James were in the backyard where she hoped they would be able to stay for the duration of the class. It was simply a power play—to show Earl that this was still *her* time.

When she returned, she saw that he had turned the kitchen table into a makeshift display case for his jewelry.

"Sorry about your baby by the way. He's okay?"

She nodded, suddenly feeling heat behind her eyes. "We think so," she said.

"I actually had the measles. I was very young, but I do remember some of it. Awful. Just awful." He was shaking his head.

"I'm sorry."

"Anyway," he said, as if pressing a reset button. "These are a few of my pieces."

Leanne feigned interest the best she could. "Wow. These are great." As the words came out of her mouth, she could hear her own lack of enthusiasm. The first one consisted of what looked like brown pearls intermixed with silver charms in the shape of musical notes. Another was made of a stone that appeared to be plastic—it was white with pink sparkles. If the third one had any sort of consistent theme, it was tutti-frutti.

Earl looked up. "I was thinking it might be fun to do a bit of market research."

Leanne said nothing.

"You could choose one of these to wear during class. We won't say anything about it, and then I can see what the other women think of it." He smiled so widely. He reminded her of Vizzini in *The Princess Bride* right before he keels over from that fatal dose of iocane powder.

She took a deep breath. She was so intensely offended. What did he see when he looked at her? A mannequin? A blank repository for his extremely unstylish jewelry? Was she not his teacher? She wanted to reprimand him, to yell. She said: "This is a writing class, Earl. I don't think that would be appropriate."

45

Without telling James, she did two things that really upset him.

1. She canceled her second (and last) scheduled reading at the bookstore in Santa Monica (on the west side of town, where she vowed never to return). It was supposed to have been on Wednesday night.

2. She texted Ofelia that she didn't need her that week, that she would pay her the sick time plus whatever the cost of the vaccination was, but that she was still concerned about Hank's health and that she wanted to be with him.

"You're sabotaging yourself!" he said.

"I taught my writing class!"

"Sure, but I don't know why you would cancel the reading. You've been looking forward to this part of the process for months and months. For a year!"

"I hate the west side. All of the west side moms can fuck themselves."

"And you can't just cancel on Ofelia. It's her job."

"It's *my* job! And I said I would pay her. I am paying her. Plus, I don't have any work to do. The book is out. I have no more planned publicity that I know of."

"What about rescheduling NPR?"

Leanne shrugged. "I don't know. They haven't emailed."

"What about starting something new?"

"I don't have any ideas!"

"But you will, eventually. And what about my shoot in Atlanta? Who is going to watch him while you teach those Sundays? You're still going to need help."

She shrugged. "I'll ask my mom to come then."

He stared at her. "Really?"

"She's been really helpful already."

"On the *phone*. If she comes, she'll have to stay for over a week. *Here*, in the house, eating creamy things."

She denied James a smile at his joke. "I'll make her get an Airbnb."

James just shook his head, resigned.

But she herself didn't understand what she was doing, so how could she possibly explain it to someone else?

46

onversation via text message:

Maxine: Haven't heard from you in a bit. How's life with a published book?

> **Leanne:** Do you know the fourth Ferrante book—*The Story of the Lost Child*?

Maxine: Yeah?

> **Leanne:** It's about me.

Maxine: Oh! Wow.

Maxine: Are you still lost?

> **Leanne:** Probably. Hank got exposed to measles at the Getty Center. He's okay now, we think. He got an emergency vaccine.

Maxine: Oh god. I'm sorry.

Leanne: Thanks.

Maxine: Do you want to hang out?

Leanne: Sure. As long as you've been vaccinated.

Maxine arrived at Leanne's with groceries. She had a plan to make a Japanese dish with chicken and eggs called *oyakodon*, which meant "parent-and-child rice bowl."

She'd asked for a cutting board and a knife. Leanne had supplied them, and now she stood near the kitchen counter, a place where she could watch both Maxine and Hank, the latter of whom had pulled himself to a stand with the help of the sofa and now slapped at the cushion with glee.

"Do you think it's weird how we've become friends?"

Maxine shrugged. "You *asked* for the crepe."

"Yeah," Leanne said, watching as Maxine sliced through an onion. "But I didn't think you'd actually bring it."

"You don't usually get what you ask for?"

"No," she said right away, but then looked at Hank. He squealed, and a string of drool pooled on the front of his onesie. "I don't know. Hank's not sick." She slunk into one of the chairs that surrounded the kitchen table.

"What else do you want?"

She thought of Ursa with the measles. *No,* she told herself. Then what? For the longest time it had been success. Always success. She'd wanted her book to become a best seller. She'd wanted it to become unavoidable to everyone who had doubted her, who hadn't supported her. She'd wanted Beth to see it written up in *People* magazine. And for Regina to have to bear it—the *weight* of her success. She'd wanted to take up space in their brains the way they'd taken up space in hers.

But now she couldn't access that desire. Something had squashed it.

"After I had Hank—like immediately after, still in the delivery room—I was so happy. I was so impressed with myself and what I'd done. It was crazy. I actually shouted, 'I love my life!'"

"That's amazing."

"It was. But it didn't last. I mean, a feeling like that can't." Leanne looked at Maxine and then to Hank. Her eyes were starting that familiar burn. Her throat ached. "What do *you* want?" She said it quickly, trying to get the words out before they caught. "And I mean this in an honestly curious way, but: What do you want from *this*?" She motioned to the space they were in, to her and herself and Hank.

"You people are funny."

Leanne tilted her head. "What people?"

"People like you," she said, turning and looking directly at Leanne, but she didn't say anything else.

Leanne looked down. Hank had crawled over to the chair where she was sitting and was pulling himself up to a stand. "Hi, baby," she said, lifting him up onto her lap. He reached for her breasts. "I just fed you," she said. But he reached again. She was wearing a short-sleeved button-down shirt. She began to unbutton it. She pulled him closer to her and unlatched the flap of the nursing bra, took the breast pad that was there and placed it on the kitchen table. The last time she'd breast-fed in front of Maxine, she'd hidden this part from her, had tucked the breast pad deeper into the bra. But the truth was that the body didn't always do exactly what you wanted. The truth was that when he began sucking from one nipple, the other breast let down too. This was the purpose of the breast pad—to absorb the extra milk.

For a brief moment, she felt the cool air on her white breast and pale nipple right before Hank took it in his mouth. Once he had, she looked up again, seeing that Maxine had watched the whole thing.

She felt something then. She imagined Maxine rushing toward her, taking the other breast in her mouth. She imagined leaning her head back and not just letting it happen but relishing it. *Ask me again*, she thought. *Ask me again what I want.*

But she didn't. And she wouldn't. And after another moment, with Hank curled into her body, Leanne said: "On Instagram, I found this mom who was at the Getty Center too that day but whose ten-month-old baby did get measles." She'd discovered this last night during her nightly search, after James had fallen asleep. The woman's name was Gelina Kramer. "It's so sad. She posted an image of the baby girl's IV and said that she was so dehydrated that her veins had collapsed. And it apparently took an hour and four nurses to get the needle in. And the baby—I think her name is Pia—was screaming the whole time."

Maxine stopped stirring. She turned and looked at Leanne. She said nothing, but in the nothingness, Leanne felt heard.

"Anyway," Leanne said after a long moment. "How's your book coming along? What's your main character up to?"

"Ohhh," Maxine said, as if singing. "She's living in her head mostly. Going back and forth, back and forth." She put the wooden spoon down on the countertop and moved away from the stove. She pulled up a chair next to Leanne and Hank. "Sometimes, she thinks there's a way to be a mother without actually becoming pregnant. And sometimes it feels completely inaccessible."

Hank was done breast-feeding. Leanne sat him upright and then handed him to Maxine so she could readjust her bra and button up her shirt. "I like that. Sometimes it feels inaccessible to me too. Not being Hank's mother. But this universal 'mother.' I can't be that."

"So we're just alike," Maxine said, though she was looking at Hank.

And then much later, after Leanne had put Hank down for his second nap of the day, the women sat down at that same table to eat. This time with bowls of rice, chicken, and egg. Leanne was about to take a bite when Maxine said, "Wait a second!" She retrieved her phone from her pocket and held it up, taking a picture of Leanne.

That night, on Instagram, the caption would read: "The Lost Child Eats."

47

It was nine-thirty. Hank and James were asleep, but Leanne was still up, reading the Wikipedia page for *A Room with a View* on her phone when a text from Regina appeared: *Oh hey! I've been meaning to text you for days now when I just saw Maxine Hunter's post and it reminded me. I didn't realize you knew her. She's so rad. Anyway! Congratulations on your book finally being out! I'm sorry I couldn't make the reading. Carmen told me you were great.*

Leanne held her phone steady but felt something cold run through her chest. She'd actually already considered this happening: that Maxine's post would show up in Regina's feed or on her search page in the same way that Regina and her circle still showed up on Leanne's. She'd briefly imagined the image sending a competitive panic through her ex-friend, followed by a need to *touch base*. After all, Regina would never let a good connection go to waste.

Leanne took a breath in. She needed to think this through. Needed to think *like* Regina. How could she use this to her advantage?

She wanted to know where things stood with Annalise. Over DMs, Leanne had seen that they'd exchanged emails and were planning some kind of fund-raiser. Leanne wanted to know when it was happening and who from within Regina's circle was involved.

She formulated a response in her head, and soon enough was typing it on her phone: *OH, thanks. And that's funny because I'd been meaning to text you too. I made a new mom friend at baby and me yoga. Her kid is almost one, and she's worried about the MMR shot coming up. I tried to talk her down. (My pediatrician mom says they're safe!) BUT she's not budging and really wants to delay it until he's at least two. Anyway, I thought of you. I know you're not a huge MMR fan. Ha. Do you have a pediatrician recommendation for her or any info that could help her navigate?*

Regina wrote back right away: *Do you have your friend's email? If you send it to me, I can forward her some information. Actually, a friend of mine is planning a kind of info-session event for the 24th . . .*

The women went back and forth until Leanne got Regina to email her the information directly. Leanne opened the message and read through it. They were calling it a fund-raiser in support of "parental choice." She recognized the address as Lila's house. They must have been done with their renovation.

Did Leanne have a plan beyond that? No. What she had was a desire to make things uncomfortable for Regina. She wanted to inconvenience her. To be a rock in her shoe. No. A boulder in her *private*, wooded pathway.

48

She hadn't left their property line with Hank since the trip to the museum over a week ago now. When they'd needed groceries, she'd waited until James came home from work and then left. She still wasn't ready to reenter the world with him exactly, but she did want to go for a walk. It was too hot for the carrier—they sweated on each other until her shirt was soaked through. And her neighborhood was too hilly for the stroller.

In the end, she decided on the reservoir. It was never crowded on a weekday, and the loop around it was flat and wide enough for the stroller.

She had probably been walking for twenty minutes when she felt the buzz of her phone in her pocket. She pulled it out to find a text from Mona.

> *Pretty sure I'm looking at a photo of you*
> *in this month's À la Table—from Regina's*
> *party in Palm Springs.*

She stopped walking and looked around briefly to see if anyone was nearby. No one was. She pressed the little microphone button in order to dictate a text message back: "It doesn't say my name, question mark. I'm on a walk with Hank, period. Can you send me a photo of it, question mark. I haven't seen it yet, period."

A picture text arrived, and she used her thumb and forefinger to zoom in on the image of herself. Sure enough, there she was: her eyes closed and mouth open in a kind of smile. In one hand, she held a plate of half-eaten cake, and in the other hand was a forked piece of cake approaching her mouth. She looked like she was about to blindly feed herself. The succinct caption read: *Partygoer eating cake.*

A familiar rage spun through her bloodstream along with a dire need to see the whole feature, to see the magazine version itself. But she was essentially halfway around the loop with no shortcut to get back to her car. She could call Mona, she thought. But phone conversations felt reserved for close friends. Mona was not a close friend. Leanne hadn't even texted her back about her proposed theory that Regina was behind the bad review in the *L.A. Times.* And since Leanne had never posted about the measles scare, no one except she, James, Ofelia, her mother, and now Maxine even knew about it.

But then, she was so curious. And she couldn't text and push the stroller at the same time. She called.

"I need more information," she said when Mona picked up. "Do you have a minute to walk me through the piece?"

"Sure, sure. Where should I start? You're one of six photos in a kind of montage section. Want me to read the captions?"

"Yes."

"Okay. So: 'Clockwise from above: Fashion designer Agnes Fass; prickly pear margaritas (recipe page ninety-eight); partygoer eating cake; interior designer Thea McManus with actor Thomas Leland; dinner is served.'"

"Was that six captions?"

"Uhm, one, two, three—well, the one photo is of an orange tree, so I guess they thought it was self-explanatory."

"Okay, well, on one hand I'm honored to be snubbed along with the orange tree. On the other, Regina can fuck herself."

Mona laughed. "Do you want me to read it?"

"I guess."

She cleared her throat before beginning:

One minute Regina Mark is dancing (and singing along) to Tay-
lor Swift. The next she's rapt in conversation with renowned street
artist Trey Madera. Later, she's stopping by the kitchen to chat with
James Beard Award–winning chef Keeley Monckton to see how the
rabbit mole is coming along. In other words, she is a woman who
wears many hats, though each hat shares a common thread: life of
the party.

Or as her husband, Val Pincher, who takes care of the business
end of their many joint ventures, puts it: "Regina works really hard to
make sure her job is fun."

"LOL," Mona said.
"Jesus."

In 2009, the duo opened up R.M. Goods, the L.A.-based store that
houses their vintage finds, private-label products, and a selection of
handpicked goods from around the world. Acclaimed interior design-
ers and their celebrity clients have flocked there for years. Then, last
year, Mark launched her eponymous line of home goods, beginning
with towels and pillows but with an eventual eye toward quilts and
rugs. Did we mention that she also has a one-year-old baby and au-
thors the award-winning blog RMarksthespot.com?

"Award-winning? It's a lifestyle blog that dabbles in misinformation! Sorry, continue."

On a cool night in early March, the couple gathered family and friends
at Native—a sprawling campus of a hotel in Palm Springs, California
(about two hours east of Los Angeles), to do just that. They'd decided
to celebrate their fourth wedding anniversary with a bang. "Why the
fourth anniversary?" I asked Mark.

"I believe in celebrating all things—big and small," she said with a wink.

"One sec. Hank's crying. I think he can hear how dumb this article is." Leanne dug around in her bag. "I gotta find the paci. Okay, here it is," she said, and placed it in his mouth. "Okay, sorry again. Please continue."

At night, the desert turns chilly, but there are giant space heaters, a fire-pit, and a bar dedicated solely to serving up various types of mezcal—an agave-based liquor meant to be sipped on and one guaranteed to warm you up from the inside out.

The guest list is a who's who of Los Angeles's food and fashion scene, including Sarah Brownstein and Johnny de Santos of León restaurant; Chad Henry, the mastermind behind Kings Creamery; fashion designer Agnes Fass and her photographer husband, Colm Fass; food writer T. J. Holmes (for indie street cred); and representing Hollywood proper: actor Thomas Leland and his longtime girlfriend, the very in-demand interior designer Thea McManus.

After dinner, there's of course cake. But it's not just any cake. It's a tres leches from Mark's favorite L.A. bakery, Las Hijas, which has been making the cake for over forty years. It's served alongside chipotle-spiked hot chocolate. And although Mark and Pincher are famous for their decadent parties, they cannot forget where they come from: patient zero of fad diets. At the end of the night, everyone is gently sent off to bed with a couple of party favors from the Gwyneth-endorsed K.O. Juice. There's a hydrating tonic to prevent hangovers, and in case that doesn't work, a pale green juice simply labeled "The Cure-All."

Guests go home happy, healthy, and hydrated. What more could you possibly ask for?

"The end," Mona said with a sigh.

"The Cure-All? I just can't. I mean, I'm annoyed not to be named, but then again Ursa is just *a one-year-old*, so."

"We should get a bunch of people to post the partygoer photo of you with captions that are like *I know this partygoer!* Or something like that?"

"Yeah." Leanne sighed. "I mean, I have an email from her saying she would mention me and my book if they used a photo of me, but no one will give a shit about that. We have to think like lawyers—like what will get us the conviction?" She stared across the reservoir as she spoke. The water didn't have even a hint of blue in it. "What is *universally* unlikable?"

"Hmm." Mona was thinking. Leanne switched the phone to her other hand.

"Nazis," Mona said.

Leanne thought of the election coverage. "No."

"What about success—too much of it, or success that's unwarranted."

Again, she thought of the election coverage. "Maybe. What else, though?"

"Animal abuse?"

"Bunny!" Leanne said, instinctively. "Do you remember Bunny?" Bunny was Regina's ex-pet dog that she'd "returned" after years of owning her. It was something that had happened a few years ago, before she and Leanne had gotten to be as close. But she still knew about it. She remembered judging her pretty hard in the moment.

"Oh yeah," Mona said. "I do remember Bunny."

"She 'returned' her, citing extreme anxiety. And now that I'm thinking about it, before that, one of her Persian cats died suddenly."

"So she's a bad pet owner."

"Yes!" Leanne said. "She is."

The women laughed.

"Okay," Leanne said, after a few more minutes. "It's so hot out here and the phone is slipping out of my hands."

"Okay, yeah, I obviously need to go look into Regina's pet history." She laughed again. "And then I'll see you at Holly's for the cooking class. Also, I think Elspeth sent you the call sheet?"

Leanne had all but forgotten about the cooking class. And she technically hadn't opened the email from Elspeth. "Yes and yes," she said. "I got the call sheet and I'll see you at Holly's."

49

Ten minutes later, Leanne had reached her car. She moved Hank from the stroller to the car seat. She buckled him in and then stared deep into his blue eyes. "I love you," she said aloud. He stared back.

She broke down the stroller, heaved it into the trunk of the car, and stood there for a moment, massaging a pinching knot in her lower back.

When she pulled into the driveway, she saw a package at the front door. Hank had been eerily quiet, and before she even looked in the rearview mirror, she knew he must've fallen asleep. Now she confirmed it. She didn't want to try to move him. Not yet. Instead, she put the windows down, turned off the engine, and got out. She wanted to see what the package was.

At her front door, she saw the label written in her mother's handwriting. She sliced it open at the seams with her car key. Inside was a stack of children's books and a note: *For my brave boy. Grandma can't wait to see you!* She grabbed the stack and brought them back to the car. Even with the windows open, it was hot and sticky inside. She turned the engine back on, closed the windows, and blasted the air-conditioning. She'd try to move him in a minute. But for now, she just wanted to sit.

She picked up her phone and pulled up Regina's Instagram profile. There it was. A few hours ago, she'd posted a picture of the magazine spread: an image of her and Val dancing at their anniversary party. *You Say Desert, I Say Dessert* ran across the page in bold white letters above their image. The caption read: "A million thank-you's to @AlaTable for so magically capturing our anniversary party in this month's issue. 💜 🐾 💜 "

It should be *thank-yous*. No apostrophe. "You're a dum-dum," she said aloud to her phone.

Leanne took a screenshot and texted it to James along with the photo Mona had sent her. *Call me when you get a chance*, she wrote.

When James didn't call, she called him.

"What's up?" he said, sounding rushed.

"Did you get my text?"

"Just now. It's Regina and Val dancing."

"And the photo of me eating cake?"

"Oh? Is that you?"

"Yes, it's me! It's *clearly* me."

"Sorry, it's super busy here today. I just glanced at it."

"Never mind. Let's just talk later."

"Okay, love you."

"Bye."

Leanne hung up and studied the photo of herself. It was definitely her. It appeared as if she was standing by herself, but she felt like she remembered the moment it must've been taken. James had been across from her. They were about to leave, but Leanne had wanted to try the cake. And of course she was smiling. Tres leches was her favorite.

She put her phone down and turned toward the stack of books, flipping through them. Her mother was famous for buying books based on the title and cover alone. For that reason, they had two copies of *Grandma Loves You*.

But one title looked like it might actually be good. It was called *J Is for Jabberwock*. She took it in her hands and flipped through the pages, quickly absorbing the theme: A was for Amoeba. B for Bird of Paradise. C for Chimera. A short description accompanied each beautifully illustrated animal. When she got to W for Wildcat, she was particularly taken by the drawing: the cat looked so charming but scary, both tame and ferocious. She read the description:

Because there are so many geographical versions of the wildcat, the species isn't technically endangered. However, the continued crossbreeding of wildcats and domestic cats should be cause for alarm. We should hate to wake up one day and find the last bit of wildness bred out of us.

It reminded her of something she'd highlighted in the vaccine book: the author described vaccines as residing in "that liminal place between humans and nature." Yes, vaccines were man-made, but they were also alive, and the antibodies they generated were "manufactured in the human body, not in factories."

Nothing was as cut-and-dried as Regina and Annalise made it seem. If you vaccinated your babies, you weren't against "nature." What was *natural* anyway? She knew Regina had gotten that test to check her fetus's chromosomes. She'd done the anatomy scan that checked for a cleft palate and/or a hole in the heart. Was that *natural*?

Leanne could feel herself spinning out. She put the book down. She twisted the keys in the ignition and turned the car off. She pushed open the door and stuck her leg out to keep the air circulating. Then she picked up her phone.

She tapped open Instagram and switched accounts to Regina's.

50

Leanne gave her students a writing prompt: *It never occurred to me . . .* The rest was up to them. They were supposed to "free-write." Sometimes she did the assignments with them. This one interested her, so she opened up her journal and began to write.

It never occurred to me that a twenty-pound baby could lose six pounds.

Every night, Leanne checked Gelina Kramer's Instagram account for an update on baby Pia, and last night she'd gotten one. Pia had lost six pounds. Gelina wouldn't post a photo of her because she said, "She doesn't look like my baby." Without overthinking it, Leanne found herself commenting: *Praying for you all.* And then put her phone down, closed her eyes, and actually prayed.

Now she kept writing.

It never occurred to me that you could fall apart and keep it together. It never occurred to me that that's what people did every day, that it was happening all around me. But of course. You idiot.

It never occurred to me that while some people could accrue wealth, others could accrue loss, that you could become rich in it. And maybe that if everything you thought had brought power had actually, eventually brought pain, then all of the pain could eventually, maybe bring you—

The air-conditioning kicked on loudly and jolted her out of her thoughts. Earl's head popped up too, and a breathy sound came out of his mouth. Leanne looked back down at her journal, trying to ignore him, but out of the corner of her eye she could see him looking around the room, panicking. After a few more moments, he blurted out: "Your air-conditioning is on."

Leanne looked up. "It's okay." She nodded.

"But the windows are open," he said.

"It's okay. It'll switch itself off in a bit."

Earl did not seem to think it was okay. He fidgeted in his seat until the air conditioner had indeed switched itself off.

At the end of class, while everyone else filed out, Earl lingered. At a snail's pace, he gathered up his papers. He waited until everyone had left before announcing, "It's really quite damaging for the air-conditioning system to be active while the windows are open."

"Well, if anything happens, it'll be me who has to deal with it."

"I don't think your husband would appreciate—"

"Earl!" She walked toward the front door and opened it. "Leave it."

He shrugged but made his way toward the door. The second he'd passed through the threshold, she swung it closed behind him.

51

On Monday, she again texted Ofelia saying she wouldn't need her that week. And again, she paid her anyway. She didn't fully understand it, but Ofelia coming and therefore Leanne having to leave Hank to go to a coffee shop to email people or answer questions about the book, essentially attempting to further sell it, felt absurd. She didn't want to pay someone to be in her house and do the physical job of mothering so that she could stare at a computer screen and feel lost, useless. If it were a *paid* opportunity, like the cooking class, fine. Or if it was her own mother watching Hank, that made sense. That was the whole point of family.

The Mothers Who Make photoshoot fell somewhere in the middle. It wasn't shapeless or abstract. It wasn't something that mostly lived in her head. Plus, she'd always wanted to be the subject of a photoshoot. She thought again about *Teen* magazine and their Great Model Search.

At the same time, it felt gross.

She'd spent some time last night clicking through the various "Mothers Who Made." The women had different names and different skin tones, but the more she clicked, the more they all felt the same, like one conglomeration of mothers.

Each one made something apart from a child. Ulla Khojasteh:

Restaurant Designer; Maura Howe: Furniture Maker; Aisha Howard: Writer; Meagan Barnes: Jewelry Designer.

Making a child alone was not enough. Of course, Leanne already knew this. She thought of her mother on call, of her sitting on the couch in matching sweatpants and sweatshirt. The TV on, the phone next to her. How many weekends did she spend like that? Talking to parent after parent and logging each call—each child and their symptoms—into that yellow-ruled notebook.

But making a child plus making a living via a nonglamorous office job didn't fit the template either. Leanne saw no accountants, no medical sales representatives, no dental hygienists, no phlebotomists. Because these kinds of jobs weren't an extension of one's personality. These kinds of jobs were jobs.

No one was fat.

No one had more than two children. Most of them had just the one, and it was a baby—impotent and drooling, perched on their hips.

None of them looked to be menopausal, so that seemingly they could continue to make children, if that's what they wanted.

Their houses were clean.

Their babies were clean, organic, nontoxic.

And these babies kept their toys in baskets. So so so so many baskets.

She wanted to think that she had said yes because she had a sliver of an idea. Now she highlighted the URL. She copied and pasted it into a text message. She sent it to Maxine with the following: *I'm worried I've bitten off more than I can chew. I've agreed to be a "Mother Who Makes."*

52

Leanne left Hank with James. She followed the directions on her phone and within seven minutes was parking in a very different, almost suburban-looking neighborhood. It was a part of Los Feliz she'd driven by countless times, giving little consideration to it apart from understanding why the public schools there were so widely acclaimed. (Money.)

She unloaded the car. She held all four of her tote bags away from her body so that the items wouldn't bang against her legs as she walked. She climbed the steps to the front door.

She rang the doorbell, and within fifteen seconds was greeted by a very petite woman with straight brown hair. "Hello. Welcome! I'm Holly," Holly said with a quick hug, which Leanne couldn't appropriately receive with all the bags she was carrying. Just then, another woman came around the corner. "And this is my friend Willa. Willa, Leanne."

"Hi," Leanne said, momentarily resting the bags on the floor and sticking out her hand to shake. Willa looked familiar, but she couldn't quite place her. "So nice to meet you."

"Nice to meet you too."

"The kitchen's this way." Holly's pint-sized body took off, leading them through the dining room and into the kitchen. Leanne quickly gathered her bags back up and followed along. The house was Spanish and sprawling, so much larger than it had appeared from the outside.

The kitchen reminded Leanne of the ceramics store. In fact, she was pretty sure she remembered Holly coming in as a customer, probably shopping for the teal three-by-nine-inch tiles that ran all along the sweeping backsplash.

Just then, from the corner of the room, a door opened and Mona emerged with a singsong "Hello!"

"Oh, hi," Leanne said, suddenly annoyed by her presence, all at once feeling like the hired help that she in fact *was*, that she had always been when around women like this.

They were all already drinking wine. Holly offered Leanne a glass.

"Sure," she said.

As Holly opened a cabinet, Leanne felt Willa's eyes on her. "You look familiar for some reason."

"I was going to say the same about you."

"You have a little boy?"

"Yeah, I do." Leanne smiled, thinking of his face.

"Mommy and me yoga?"

"No," Leanne said. "Probably not. But you have a baby?"

Willa nodded. "A little girl. Carmela."

"Cute," Leanne said as she conjured an image of Carmela Soprano.

Within ten more minutes, six more women had shown up, each one seemingly nice, seemingly older, richer, and more professional than Leanne. When the seventh woman came in, Leanne worried about having enough food. "We might be a little hungry," she said. "I brought enough for six or seven, *maybe* eight portions."

"Oh, yeah, sorry," Holly said. "Whenever I mentioned I was doing this, someone else wanted to come, but don't worry about it—if there's enough food."

There was an energy to Holly that was borderline spastic. She was nice, but so loud, lots of gesticulation. As Leanne spoke to her, trying to set up and get a lay of the land, it never looked as though she was actually listening. Her eyes darted around like a squirrel's.

Leanne had decided on making linguine and clams and a giant arugula salad. It was always a crowd-pleaser. Plus, it came together in twenty minutes, and she could make it without referring to a recipe or specific measurements.

She placed the stockpot on the stove and then turned around to address the women, all of whom were talking to one another. "So," she said to no one, almost as if it were an existential exercise, "one of the reasons I like this meal is because if you pick up some clams and parsley, the chances are pretty good that you have the rest of the ingredients at home already." At this point, two of the women had turned to look at what the noise was about. "It's just garlic, olive oil, white wine, red pepper flakes, and pasta."

"I've always got white wine," a woman named Jocelyn said, raising her glass.

A few women laughed. Leanne continued, "And the salad is just arugula, Parmesan, olive oil, and lemon."

"How bad can that be?" Mona said, giving a wink.

The women broke into chatting again for a few minutes until Mona performatively cleared her throat. "I'm sorry guys, but I just have to ask Leanne something." Leanne looked up from the sink full of clams. "Did you see Regina's latest post?" Mona held up her phone.

Leanne felt a sharp, deep-seated disgust for Mona. She responded from across the room: "You know that I didn't. I don't follow her."

"Well, it's a photo of her and a friend of yours."

"Who?"

Mona approached her with the gait of a lawyer walking the length of the juror box. "It's her and Maxine Hunter."

"What?" Leanne almost shouted. She couldn't hold back her reaction. She turned off the water and wiped her wet hands on her pants. "Can I see it?"

Mona handed her the phone. There it was: Regina and Maxine,

together, wine in hand, smiling at some fancy event Leanne didn't know about. The caption read: "Thrilled to meet this epicness tonight."

It felt like a personal attack. Like Regina had tracked Maxine down and made this photo happen just to stick it to her. Her brain worked quickly to find a way out of the pain. *Regina doesn't know her like you do*, it said. And, *They only just met*. Also, *Epicness is a very stupid word*.

Leanne realized she was flanked by women. Holly and Willa had appeared at her side, taking a look at the photo as well. "I thought you guys were all friends," Holly said.

"Who?"

"You, Regina, and Maxine."

"I'm friends with Maxine," Leanne said, holding an open palm to her chest.

"But not Regina?" Willa asked.

Leanne shook her head. "No." She looked at Mona, who looked subtly, grossly delighted. Then she turned to Willa: "Are you friends with her?" She put the phone down on the kitchen counter.

"Not really," Willa said.

Leanne nodded at her. "Good for you," she said.

"She and I get lunch from time to time," one woman said quietly.

Leanne looked at her. She was one of the plain ones, short and matronly. "So you guys are close?" Leanne said.

A few women snickered.

"I didn't say that," she said even more quietly.

"Well, what happened between you two?" Willa said. Leanne looked at her and realized why she looked so familiar. She'd been a contestant on a reality TV design show.

She walked back to her station at the kitchen counter. She could feel the room's desire. These women wanted information. At the same time, she knew they didn't want the truth—or rather, not the painful, self-incriminating version. She took in the high ceilings and the angled, setting California sun seeping in. These women had avoided the truth as much as possible. All at once, she felt like one of the birds in Earl's book—the overlooked, unassuming, but quietly plotting one. She couldn't remember its name.

She thought of Hank, of lying on the floor of his dark bedroom. She thought of Pia and her mom. She thought of her own question to Mona. *What was universally unlikable?* And even though it had felt like a joke at the time, something in her was daring her, egging her on to try it. Try it! She took a deep breath.

"I had this cat," she said. And then, "Mona, I haven't even told you this. I've told barely anyone this."

The room was silent. "He was such a great cat, but after my son was born, he—Simon was his name—was having a hard time adjusting. As cats do, you know?" As she spoke, she crushed cloves of garlic with the flat of her knife. "Regina loves cats, as you've maybe gathered from her social media. And well, she particularly loved this cat. So I had this newborn, and I was taking Simon to the vet to make sure he wasn't sick, and eventually the vet told us that it was behavioral, that this was how Simon was dealing with the new baby. I was so frustrated, you know? Taking care of a baby and then having to wash our sheets all of the time—he was spraying." She scraped the sliced garlic onto a plate and then moved on to the parsley.

"So—and I'm making a long story incredibly short here—I, you know, am talking to Regina about all of this. And Regina, who also has a new baby but has her parents nearby and a full-time nanny and is seemingly unfazed by motherhood, basically offers to take him off my hands for a bit. To see if a change of scenery might help.

"Well, if I knew then what I know *now*, I never would have done it." She placed an open palm to her chest.

"What do you know now?" Willa said.

"She's a bad pet owner!" Mona said. Leanne watched as the women's heads turned toward her. If she'd let herself, she could have laughed.

Instead, she assumed the most somber face she could and nodded.

"Yeah, unfortunately for Simon, I didn't put it together until it was too late."

"Wait? She killed your pet?" Holly shouted it.

"I'm not saying that exactly," Leanne said as she put the knife down for a moment. "I'm just saying that Simon died under her care. And all I got in terms of an explanation was a shrug. And it's basically impossible to pick a friendship up after that."

At this, the women broke into gasps and *oh-my-god*s and *how could she do that?*

"She's weird about animals, guys," Mona said, addressing the room. "You should see some of the comments she makes on this local animal shelter's Instagram. Here, I'll pull some up. Just wait 'til you see. Let me just . . ." She was looking down at her phone. "Okay, here's one. About this little brown terrier, she wrote, *Do you have this in black and white?*"

"What?" a few women said at the same time.

"And then, about this orange tabby cat, she said, *ME WANT!* in all caps."

What happened next reminded Leanne of high school chemistry—how the teacher would explain what they were going to do, and then the students had to break into small groups to execute the experiment. She could hear the women repeating the things she herself had typed into her phone. *Do you deliver to West Hollywood?* And: *I'll name this one Miss Pretty because she's a pretty kitty.* And while Leanne finished cooking dinner, a few women came up to her and offered condolences for her loss.

"Thanks," Leanne said to them. "He was a good boy."

53

Maxine and Leanne sat shoulder to shoulder on Maxine's couch in Maxine's house at nine forty-five p.m.

Leanne had left the cooking class in a semi-altered state. Her head felt dull, as if she'd been punched. And when she checked her phone to see a message from James saying he was going to sleep, she had the idea to text Maxine. She wanted to erase what she'd done with something else. She wanted to replace the Instagram image of Maxine and Regina with a new one, to reclaim her friend for herself. Maxine told her to come over, had sent her the address. And so now, here they were together, with Maxine's laptop in front of them, clicking through the *Madre* magazine website.

"In a way, these are all performance pieces," Leanne said, pausing at an image of a highly manicured woman standing in front of a fireplace with her baby in the background pushing a toy truck.

Leanne wasn't that familiar with Maxine's early work as a performance artist, most of it occurring over a decade ago, before everything was automatically recorded and uploaded. But a few months ago, Maxine had posted a series of videos on Instagram of her tripping and falling. Leanne's favorite was the one where she was dressed in high heels, a pencil skirt, white button-down shirt, and blazer. She clutched a stack of papers in her hands as she marched toward the camera in the manner of a serious businesswoman only to trip and fall and throw the papers up in the air.

This was the part of Maxine Leanne wanted to mine.

"Okay," Maxine said, angling herself toward Leanne a little bit. "Baskets," she said. "You could get a ton of baskets—we could rent them at a prop house. And then you put them everywhere around your living room, like the entire floor is covered with baskets."

"That's good," Leanne said.

"It will look like a basket store. And then," she continued, "I can go and take Hank with me, so that when they ask for the shot with the baby, you will say, 'Oh, sure, let me find him. He's usually around here somewhere. And then you start taking off lids, trying to find him.'"

Leanne laughed, and as she did, she dug her thumb into the side of her left breast. She'd noticed a tightness there at the beginning of the night, but now it was itchy and much more pronounced.

Maxine noticed. "What's going on?"

"Oh," Leanne said, rubbing at the spot. "I dropped one of Hank's nighttime feeds, and I think my body is just struggling to adjust."

"Oh."

"But wait, I love that idea. I mean, maybe it's just the baskets, though. I don't want them to call child protective services."

"Right," Maxine said. "Understandable." She looked away from the screen, brought her knuckles to her face.

"What about something religious? Like if we hung all this Christian iconography on the walls? A bunch of crucifixes?"

"Yeah! That's good," Maxine said, and Leanne watched her contemplate it. She could see the subtle smile on her face, the little lines at the corners of her mouth. What had she been doing before Leanne texted? How did she spend her downtime? What shows did she watch? Was she seeing someone? Did she work out or was she naturally lithe and sinewy? Where did she buy her clothes?

"Maxine?" Leanne heard herself saying.

Maxine turned to her. "Yeah."

"Do you have plans the night of the twenty-fourth?"

"Uhm." She picked up her phone. "I don't think so but let me check."

"It's a week from today. James will be gone on a work trip, but my mom is coming and can watch Hank," Leanne said.

"Winnie's coming? That's exciting. And yeah, I don't have anything," she said, looking up from her phone.

"Did I tell you my mom's name?" Her left hand was resting on the side of the sore breast.

"Uhm, can I get you some ice or something?" Maxine gestured at the apparent pain.

"Ice sounds lovely, actually. Thank you."

Maxine rocked herself up, placing the laptop on the coffee table. "I read your book, Leanne. I know all about Winnie." Standing up now, she turned toward Leanne and smiled.

Leanne smiled back, warm with the knowledge that Maxine had read her book.

"What's happening on the twenty-fourth?"

"Well, do you want the long version or the short one?"

Maxine stood with her hands on her hips. She was wearing sweatpants and a giant t-shirt that had been cut off at the bottom to make it hit right at her waist. "Long. But let me get the ice first."

Leanne nodded. And as Maxine walked away, she sunk deeper into the couch. Above the fireplace hung a large watercolor painting of a half-dressed woman sitting on the edge of a bed. Leanne stared at it. A feeling so unfamiliar she could barely place it suddenly overwhelmed her. Tranquility? Maxine's living room wasn't too far off aesthetically from those of the Mothers Who Made. But it felt different. It felt like somebody lived here. She put her feet up on the coffee table and pushed more deeply into her own tissue. It stung, like the prick of a thick needle. She should stop pressing on it. It hurt, but it seemed the only option.

54

Leanne couldn't sleep. Right as she was about to drift off, she'd hear herself telling the story about her pretend dead cat. She tried to rationalize it. It wasn't so bad. It wasn't a lie that would lead to any real danger. Yet she remained awake.

James was leaving in the morning for Atlanta, and her mother would arrive the following day. Gently—citing June's uncontrollable barks in the middle of the night when Winnie got up to pee—Leanne had requested that she book an Airbnb. And Winnie had done it.

At around two a.m., she booted up her computer. The clanging sound grated. It was a morning sound. It didn't belong here, but she knew she'd let her in-box go and was suddenly curious if *Full Plate* had reached out to reschedule. The screen's brightness hurt her eyes. She closed the lid. She'd do it later, when her mother was here.

What had happened to her? Why wasn't she going from bookstore to bookstore making sure they had a copy of her book? James had been right when he'd said that this was the part she'd been waiting for. Her book was *out*. She was published. But maybe it was the waiting she'd enjoyed most. Or maybe it was that these things—writing the book and anticipating its release—had happened before Hank was born. Back when she could pour herself into a single task, when she hadn't felt so torn. Splintered.

Months and months ago, she'd brought up the idea of going to

Pittsburgh for a reading, but James couldn't commit to going with her because of work. And the idea of going alone—renting a car and lugging along all of the baby gear—made her tired. Not to mention the expense. Plus, who would watch Hank during the reading?

Why was it that James's work life could go on and on undisturbed after they had had a child when Leanne's had come to a full stop? As soon as she thought it, she felt a wave of guilt. She knew it wasn't specifically true. She knew that fatherhood had changed James too. The difference was that fatherhood, the institution, expected him to work. *Outside of the house.* Motherhood expected her to love, endlessly, endlessly. What was scarier was that Leanne had expected this too. She'd bought in, without even realizing it. What other psychic transactions had she unknowingly made?

She didn't know when she'd finally fallen asleep, but she woke up groggy and to the sounds of Hank's bellows. Her immediate goal was to make her left breast as available as possible to him. The ice had helped last night, but the breast was still sore to the touch. But Hank had grown up too much to nurse for longer than five minutes. In fact, he'd begun to take his first steps. He wasn't even ten months old. It was early for a baby to walk, but he wasn't looking at the calendar.

"Okay, fine," she said in the afternoon, after the flurry of James's departure and after the baby had rolled away from her yet again. "You want to walk?" She set him down next to the coffee table, which he grabbed at to steady himself. Then she grabbed the bowl of Cheerios he'd been eating earlier. She crouched down on the floor with it, just a few paces away. "Do you want a Cheerioooo?" she called out. He made affirmative-sounding noises, slapping at the table enthusiastically, animalistically.

"Come and get it then!"

He bounced and bounced. The drool shiny on his chin. Then he let go of the table with one hand. He looked at Leanne, his eyes seeming to ask: *Can I?*

"Yeah. That's it," she said.

He let go with the other hand.

"Okay."

He took a step, his eyes glued to Leanne's, and then another.

She clapped. "You're doing it!" He seemed just as astonished as she was. And then he fell to his knees, crawling the rest of the very short distance to her.

"I saw that," she said, taking him in her arms and smashing his cheek with kisses. The pride she felt overwhelmed her. An image of Michael Phelps's parents materialized in her brain: them celebrating like maniacs in the stadium seating. Leanne understood them now, just as she understood the opposite. That two-dimensional mother, Gelina, the one whose baby was still sick. Leanne had checked in on her Instagram account last night, but there'd been no updates. When people didn't post for long stretches, Leanne assumed that either nothing exciting was happening or they were depressed.

"Here's your Cheerio," she said now.

He opened his mouth, collapsed into her for a moment, and then crawled away.

That night, without that clearly delineated marker of James coming home, the energy within the house moved steadily downward, like the rolling credits at the end of a movie. Caring for a baby all day required and emitted a certain kind of atmosphere—subdued, playful, open, unstimulating, with moments of sacredness. And James's return, beginning with June's ear-piercing welcome barks—she realized only now—disrupted this.

She felt the freedom of having one less thing to care for. She didn't need to make dinner, not a real one at least. She sliced a few pieces of cheese and laid them on a plate next to some bread and a pickle. She poured a glass of wine. She carried this into the bathroom and propped them on the sink. She noted the quiet. If James were home, he'd be telling her something. It had never bothered her—the noise of him—but she floated among the quiet. She got the bathwater running, unsnapped Hank's onesie, and pulled it over his head as he stood at the edge of the tub, reaching for the streaming faucet. She checked his diaper for poop, hooking her pointer finger around the elastic at his butt. Nothing. She pulled the plastic tabs; the diaper fell to the floor. She poured in some soap. She picked him up and put him down in the water.

She sat on the nearby stool and reached for the wine and cheese. Hank looked mesmerized by the faucet, watching the soapy water fill up around him. It suddenly looked very inviting. She dipped her hand in the water. It was so warm.

She hadn't showered all day and could feel a layer of dried sweat on her skin. She stood up, slipped her clothes off, and in the next moment was stepping into the bath. Hank looked up at her with an open-mouthed smile—a transparent sense of awe—as if she'd just crossed some previously impassable threshold. She smiled back as she sat down directly behind him, covering her breasts with her forearm. He turned to face her, thrilled and smacking at the surface of the water. He'd had no idea his mom could do that.

55

eanne spotted Winnie just a few seconds before Winnie spotted her. She stood at the curb in head-to-toe salmon—salmon-colored pants, what looked like a salmon-toned short-sleeved sweater, and salmon ballet flats.

They waved at each other through the windshield, and then Winnie took off, head down, charging toward the car with her luggage twisting behind her. But there was no immediate space along the curb for Leanne to park. She kept driving, pulling in as soon as she could, but Winnie didn't see this while barreling forward. Via the rearview mirror, Leanne watched her mother realize her mistake and turn around.

She went straight for the trunk. Leanne could see her yank on the door to open it, but it was locked. "Grandma's jumping the gun," Leanne said to Hank, who was tucked into his car seat, staring out the window. Leanne twisted the key in the ignition to shut the engine off and opened her door. She greeted her mother with: "It won't open with the engine running unless I unlock it."

"Oh," Winnie said. Leanne could see the fear behind her mom's small brown eyes. She didn't know when this shift had happened—when exactly her mother had become afraid of her—but it was so clearly part of their dynamic now.

Leanne opened the trunk. She took the suitcase from her mother and lifted it inside, nestling it next to the stroller.

"Is he asleep?" Winnie asked, pointing at the car.

"No, he's up."

She smiled, walked to the side of the car, and pulled open the rear passenger door. She stuck her head in and cooed, "There's my sweet boy! Oh my goodness. You're not sick! No, no. Look at you!" Back in the driver's seat, Leanne twisted around to see Hank's re-action via the mirror that attached to the headrest. He was looking back at his grandma carefully, scrutinizingly.

"Okay, Mom," Leanne said. "We're holding people up."

Back at the house, she watched her mother fawn over Hank. "Well, you certainly don't need to worry about his gross motor skills!"

"Yeah," Leanne said. She would barely admit it even to herself, but she'd missed her: her old-lady pixie haircut, her strange, dis-tracted, frenetic energy, the constant pursing of the lips. She wasn't the mother she'd wanted, but she was the one who'd shown up.

And now, she was digging into her gigantic shoulder bag. "I wanted . . ." Her sentence stopped, picking up a few moments later: "A couple of things." She pulled out a stack of catalogs. "They have some nice pieces in this Land of Nod and Mini Boden, and I found a few recipes I thought we could maybe try. I also saw this, and they say it's as good as any department-store brand." She handed Leanne the catalogs followed by a set of face creams produced by Target. There was a day cream, night cream, eye cream, and a cleanser.

"Don't *you* want them?" Leanne said.

"No." She shook her head a little bit. "They smell"—she hesi-tated, as if trying to find the word—"earthy."

An image of her mother's bathroom sink flashed before her. In childhood, it had been completely surrounded by creams and per-fumes. No surface area remained for more products. "Who's the *they*—the recommenders?"

"Oh, you know," she said, waving her hand in the air, "one of those daytime shows."

"*The View?*"

"No. They talk too much."

"*Dr. Phil?*"

"No."

"*Good Morning America?*"

"Yes," she said, retrieving yet another item from her monolithic bag. "Now this you can return if you want. I have the receipt, but I just saw it and thought of you."

Whatever it was had been tidily folded up in tissue paper. Leanne took it in her hands and unwrapped it, finding a dress from Anthropologie. Leanne couldn't remember the last time she'd stepped inside the store.

"I liked it," Winnie said.

Leanne didn't, but she knew this was how her mother moved through the world. "Thanks for thinking of me," she said.

The sound of the tissue paper had caught Hank's attention, and he stumble-crawled over to them to get his hands on it.

Peeking out from the stack of catalogs Winnie had brought, Leanne could see the spine of that stupid *À la Table* issue. Her mother read food magazines the same way she did almost anything that wasn't practicing medicine—with minimal attention, mostly distracted by a blaring television. She wouldn't have noticed her own daughter in the pages even if it *had been* spelled out for her.

"Are you hungry?" Leanne asked her. "I was going to cut up some avocado for Hank and then put some on toast for me."

"Oh, sure. You know me, I can't turn down a California avocado."

56

It was Sunday morning at nine-thirty a.m. Leanne had thirty minutes until class, but she was already trying to get Winnie and Hank out of the house so that she didn't have to withstand a conversation between herself, her mom, and Earl. None of it made sense to Leanne, but since Winnie was afraid to drive in Los Angeles and since she didn't want Hank at the house she was renting ("It's boring there!"), her plan had been to walk to a park with him. But after Leanne explained that the closest one was three-quarters of a mile away and up two giant hills (and it was already eighty-four degrees outside), Winnie decided to go for a walk around the neighborhood and then play in their backyard.

If they needed to come inside, Leanne told her to use the back door, which would be open, and then she hoped they could just hide out in the office until it was time for his nap.

"Okay?" Leanne said. "Are you ready?" Her mother looked scared. "It's gonna be fine. You have your phone?"

Winnie patted at her pockets. "No."

"Okay, let's get your phone and then off you go!"

They spent the next five minutes finding her phone.

They left approximately one minute before Earl arrived.

* * *

Earl felt like the notes the class was giving him revealed that no one understood what he was trying to do. "It's not a children's story!" he said. "It's a comedy!"

"We know," Leanne said. "I think what we are saying is that even children's books and comedies have something at stake. Even children's books have scary moments where characters get themselves into trouble."

"Or have love interests?" Jade said.

"Exactly," Leanne said. "Can we get a bird romance at least?"

Earl pursed his lips. "There's a marriage."

"Ah, but that doesn't necessarily imply love, now does it?"

Earl shifted in his seat and pursed his lips harder.

In that moment, it dawned on Leanne that Earl might never have been in love. From day one, she'd assumed he was gay. But he was the same age—or thereabouts—as Winnie, who managed to come out of the sixties and seventies seemingly just as repressed as her predecessors. Had it been an option for Earl—to fall in love? Was it still?

In the next moment she almost felt sorry for him. But then she remembered his jewelry request, his ever-present Kinko's bundle, his unwavering assuredness that his opinion mattered. People like Earl didn't need her pity.

They needed a taste of what automatically comes with falling in love: insecurity, vulnerability. To be crushed.

57

ee! Leelo!" her mom shouted from across the bookstore, but Leanne was hiding among the stacks, busy fielding text messages.

Ofelia had texted saying that it was okay if Leanne didn't need her to work anymore. She just wanted to say good-bye to Hank. Leanne felt both relieved and cruel. It had been so much harder than she'd thought—to have an employee. But if the measles scare had taught her anything, it was that she didn't want one; that paying someone regularly to watch her child only emphasized the stupidity, the unsustainability of what she did, of what she was. If she took care of Hank full-time—however—this self-flagellation evaporated. Her purpose, her function, and her worth became clear—no longer tangled up in numbers or worse: art. Maybe it was bigger than that, though. Maybe it was because at home, she was a mother. It meant something. In the real world, it didn't.

Leanne texted back, saying her mom was here now, but what about the week after? She knew she should look at the calendar and offer up a specific day, but the other text—from Mona—was distracting her too much:

INEZ IS APPARENTLY WRITING A
BIG PROFILE ON REGINA. One of
the staffers there just told me.

Honestly, I don't even know anymore. All
the women at the cooking class agreed that
she's horrible. Like, what more can we do????

Leanne wanted to text back: *UNSUBSCRIBE!*

INEZ was a very cool fashion/culture magazine. A publication she wished she could be featured in. Instead, she wrote: *Do you know who is writing the piece?*

"Lee! There you are! I found your book!" Leanne turned to see her mother with a copy of her book in one hand and a bunch of kids' books in the other.

"Cool," Leanne said. "Where's Hank, though?"

"Oh, he's over by the train set. There's an older kid there that he's watching."

"Okay, let's go check on him." She got on her tiptoes and looked around, trying to see where the train set was.

"Do you need an extra copy? I'll buy it for you."

"Of my own book?"

"Yeah, I bought ten already. I've just been giving them out to my friends."

"Well, thank you, but they sent me fifty copies. I don't need any. In fact, I can give you some."

Winnie shook her head as she marched forward. "Oh, if I need more, I'll just buy them."

Once she could see Hank was fine, she turned to her mom. "Can I see the books you picked out?" Her mother handed them to her, and Leanne flipped through. "I love when you buy him books, but sometimes there's no story, you know? I always like to read through them at least quickly, just to make sure it's something I actually want to read myself."

"Okay," her mother said, a bit defeated.

"See, he knows Grandma loves him," she said, putting the one titled *A Grandmother's Love* on the table.

"Oh."

"That one definitely has a story." Winnie pointed at *The Travels of Babar*. "You used to *love* Babar."

Leanne opened it up. Babar the elephant king and his new queen were on a hot-air balloon ride. The illustrations were beautiful. She turned the page. The hot-air balloon crashed. But not enough to hurt them. Now the king and queen were camping. They made themselves "an excellent rice broth." But then, oh no. Some "cannibals" appeared. The cannibals looked very dark-skinned with big red lips, toting spears. "Oh, lord. When was this written?" Leanne asked.

"Oh, a long time ago. I grew up reading them too."

She read on. "I don't know. 'Savages' attacking the king and queen." Leanne pointed at the illustrations.

"Well, I thought it was a nice adventure book," Winnie said, shrugging.

"For some white people," Leanne said, "it probably is."

58

*B*een meaning to text you all day. I had a dream about you. We were at this futuristic outdoor pool where the edges of the pool kept shifting and moving, almost like a horizontal Tetris. You were holding Hank, and you were scared you were going to fall into the deep end with him. I was scared too.

Leanne wrote Maxine back right away: *Sooooo, you dreamt about us rolling up to Annalise Hart's anti-vax fund-raiser?*

I guess so!

Speaking of, I don't have much of a plan, Leanne texted back. *Winnie's keeping me busy. Did you still want to meet her?*

Definitely.

Leanne considered the two women in the same room. Maxine: nuanced, strange, soft. Winnie: blunt, loud, dismissive. *SIGH. Okay,* she wrote back. *Come over Wednesday at 6:30? We can leave from there.*

See you then!

59

She had to deal with her emails. She also needed to invoice Holly, from whom she had never received payment. Still, she could have probably put all of this off even longer if it weren't for Winnie.

The schedule they'd fallen into was that Winnie went to a six a.m. Pilates class at a neighborhood studio, then back to her rental to shower, and then she walked over to Leanne's house, where she stayed until after dinner. During that time, the things her mother said aloud astounded her. It wasn't just the content, but also how her sentences often ended midway through. It was the pitch, shrill and thin, like a whistle. "Who wants a banana? Banana, banana, bananaaaaa!" And poor Hank didn't know enough to take offense.

Sometimes, she simply growled, and when Leanne looked over, her mom would be looking at her phone with her nostrils flared and lips curled. It took Leanne a few of these instances until she understood that her mother had received a push notification from a news site. And that's what she was doing: she was snarling at the news. Sometimes the noise came with commentary: "Did you know she spent eight thousand dollars on that pantsuit?"

"Hmm," Leanne said. "And how much did you spend on that Rolex?"

"That's jewelry!" Her mother was aggrieved.

And so Leanne had no choice but to flee to the coffee shop. Now she was without her, and she breathed it in. She went through the emails systematically, from newest to oldest.

She reviewed the call sheet for the Mothers Who Make shoot, which was happening the following Wednesday, after Winnie left. She wrote back confirming, although she and Maxine were still brainstorming ideas. (She had not looked into buying one hundred baskets.) But she couldn't really focus on that event until she'd dealt with Annalise and Regina's fund-raiser.

She reread the email Regina had forwarded her to make sure that she and Maxine could just show up. It sounded like they could. The email simply stipulated that they were accepting donations at the door. (The "suggested" amount was $500.) It was a bold step. Until then, Regina and Leanne had been fighting behind closed doors. This would put it all out in the open. *But* she would have Maxine on her side.

She felt that jagged sheet of ice reemerge in her chest. It made her sit up in her seat. And then call attention to her left breast. The tightness was back—if it had ever gone away?

She continued through the in-box. A few of the messages were from people who had read her book and loved it. One was from her father-in-law, who forwarded an email from his sister who had read it and loved it. These made her feel good. She wrote back saying thank you. She still had more to click through, but now the afflicted breast asserted itself.

She stood up and asked the young man sitting closest to her if he could keep an eye on her things while she ran to the bathroom. When he looked up to respond, she was unnerved by his face. He looked like a young Ralph Fiennes, from the *English Patient* era. She wanted to tell him so or to caress his cheek or both. But instead, he said sure, and she said thanks.

In the restroom, she pulled up her shirt and unlatched the flap of the nursing bra. This time, instead of just soreness, it was as if she could feel the extra milk. She grabbed a wad of toilet paper and held it to her left nipple as she slowly but firmly pressed on the entire breast. What came out was a thin, whitish liquid. She pressed and pressed, feeling around for the clogged duct. She couldn't quite find anything specific. As soon as she felt a bit more comfortable, she rehooked the bra, pulled her shirt back down, and peed.

As she washed her hands, she studied her chest in the mirror. The shirt looked dry. She glanced up at her face. She'd washed her hair last night before bed and gone to sleep with it wet so that this morning it was extra curly and shiny. She had a lot of pride in her hair. She believed it made her prettier than she actually was.

When she got back to her table, she sat down and looked toward the young Ralph Fiennes, who looked up at her. "Thank you," she said.

He nodded and then went right back to his computer.

What was he was working on? What was his day job? She was staring now. Had his mother been worried that his beauty would get him into trouble? Did she post photos of him on social media with that same knowing delight that Leanne did when posting ones of Hank? The subtext so obvious: *This is beauty. Take a look!* And then she thought of Gelina Kramer. She still wasn't posting anything.

As she continued to watch him, the man at the table next to his brushed his arm to get his attention. Ralph turned to him with such happiness, a lightness. They were lovers—clearly. The lover was good-looking too, but not as pretty. They spoke to each other quietly. She couldn't hear what they were saying, but she could feel the energy behind it—so playful, bright, new. She told herself to stop looking, but she couldn't turn away. When Ralph did finally move back toward his computer, he caught Leanne's eyes. She smiled, and he very subtly smiled back, before she quickly went back to her own work.

She was going back in time. Most of the emails she'd missed were missable. Even the ones from her publicist—letting her know her book had been featured in some magazine called *Houston Resort*. Who was reading *Houston Resort*? But then she saw something that made her sit straight up, made her insides squish, like a stomped grape. An email from *Beth Hazelton*. It had come in on the day after her book launch event, the day after Hank had had his emergency vaccination. She clicked on it and almost had to look away, afraid to read it.

Hello Leanne,
When your dad died, I stopped checking this email. He was the only one who emailed me. I checked it the other day because Brittany told me you had tried to contact me here.
   Anyway, Brittany and Jordan say it's fine for you to have some of what's left of the ashes. Jordan scattered some already. But I don't feel comfortable sending them through the mail. I don't think Chuck would like that anyway. You know how he wouldn't fly. Maybe on your next visit to the east coast, you can pick them up in person.

Beth

p.s. Brittany sent me the review of your book in the L.A. Times. *Life's a bitch, huh.*

Leanne covered her face with her hands. She pressed her fingers into her eyelids. She felt so dumb, stupid. She felt glad and also challenged. Beth probably assumed she wouldn't actually go to Middleton.

With her hands still on her face, she opened her eyes and peeked in between her fingers, staring at the young man. What did he think of her? Had he considered her at all?

60

Her breast was fucked. She'd Googled what else to do and was told to use a hot compress or to take a hot bath. Also that if she showed signs of a fever and/or flu-like symptoms, she probably had mastitis, in which case she should call her doctor, who could prescribe an antibiotic.

At six-fifteen p.m.—Maxine was going to be there in fifteen minutes—Leanne gave up on getting dressed. Her skin hurt; she couldn't put on clothes. She started running water in her bathroom sink. She waited until it got really hot, and then made herself a compress with a washcloth. She unhooked her bra and placed the hot cloth on the tautest part of the breast. She began to lightly massage it over the skin and shuddered. She knew she needed to text Maxine and cancel, but she couldn't pull away from the task at hand. She stared at the nipple as she pressed, watching as nothing came out. It was like pressing on a tube of glue that was sealed shut. There was something in there, but it wasn't coming out.

She could hear her mom's high-pitched voice reading *The Hungry Caterpillar* as a wave of chills ran through her.

That's when the doorbell rang, instantly followed by June's barking.

"Mom! Can you get it? I'll be right there!" she shouted.

She dug through the bathroom closet to find the old robe she knew was in there. She put it on and walked out to explain to both

Maxine and her mom what was going on. Even in her sad, primitive state, she could appreciate the strangeness of finding these two women in conversation in her own living room.

"Well, I'm going to read it!" Winnie was saying. She had Hank on her hip with her back facing Leanne so that Maxine was the one who spotted her first.

"Hey, you okay?" Maxine said. "Your face looks a bit—"

"Sweaty!" Winnie said, almost squealing.

Leanne tried to smile. "I'm pretty sure I have mastitis. My breast is all swollen, and I just started to get the chills."

Now that Winnie had turned, Hank could see his mother and began trying to wriggle out of Winnie's arms to get to her.

"Oh, sweetie. I can call you in some antibiotics." She looked around, seemingly for a place to put Hank. "Can you hold him for a second?" she said to Maxine.

Maxine opened her arms and, surprisingly, Hank went to her.

"I just need to find my phone," Winnie said. "Do you have the number for that CVS down there?"

Leanne almost laughed, looking at Maxine holding Hank while her mother jumped into doctor mode.

"I'm sorry," Leanne said. "It was bothering me all day, and then that sick feeling just came on so quickly."

"Please," said Maxine. "Don't worry about it." Hank was touching her earrings, which were small golden circles.

"You look like Diane Keaton in *Baby Boom*. When they hand her the baby and she's in her skirt suit."

"So a natural?"

Leanne nodded. "Sucks we're going to miss the fund-raiser."

From the back of the house, they heard Winnie bemoan, "Ah, it was a fund-raiser!"

In the next two minutes, Maxine and Winnie came up with a plan. Leanne would get in the bath. Maxine would find the number for the CVS. Winnie would call in the antibiotics and then put Hank to bed. Maxine would pick up the prescription.

Healthy Leanne would never have let this happen. She would never have allowed Maxine to deal with her mother without Leanne there to chaperone, to clarify, to apologize for the way she talked over people, the way she said, despite Leanne's corrections: *volleyvall* instead of volleyball, *orientals* instead of Asians. And she never would have allowed the best-selling author and visionary thinker Maxine Hunter to fetch her antibiotics at CVS on a Wednesday night.

Except that she did. Because the only thing she could concentrate on was getting that milk out of her body. Because she felt cold, and a hot bath called to her so viscerally.

And so she went to it. She ran the water as hot as she could stand. She found some bath salts and poured them in. She let her robe fall and stepped into the tub. She sat down and watched the water as it rose around her. It felt like the best idea she'd ever had. She lay back and draped the soaked washcloth on top of her poor breast.

Suddenly, there was a knock on the door. "Yeah?" she said, and her voice caught. "I'm in the bath."

"It's Maxine. Can I come in?"

Leanne looked at herself. At her stomach and pubic hair under the water. The water was cloudy because of the bath salts, but there were no bubbles. Maxine would see everything. And funny enough—remembering the Korean spa—it wouldn't be the first time. "Uhm, okay."

Maxine slid the door open. Their eyes met, and Leanne broke into a smile. "There's some gnarly shit happening in here."

"Good for you." She closed the door behind her and stood there, a modest distance away from the tub.

"My mom putting Hank down?"

"Yeah. How are you feeling?"

Leanne shrugged. "I'll be okay. I'm mostly annoyed that Annalise will be off the hook for the night."

"Well, that's why I came in here. What if, after I pick up the antibiotics, we send your mom to the event?"

"Winnie Wenderson?"

"She asked what the fund-raiser was for, and I told her—and how we were going to go as representatives for the opposition. And then she said: 'Well, can I go?'"

Leanne sank further into the water. She imagined her mom winding her way through Lila's Hollywood Hills "entertainer's dream" Spanish Colonial, stalking down hors d'oeuvres, turning down wine with the explanation that she'd rather "eat her calories."

"I mean, sure? It's better than nothing."

Maxine clasped her hands together, nodding with enthusiasm. "Okay, so: you finish up in here. Take your time. I'll talk to Winnie, go to CVS, and then we'll call her an Uber when I get back."

Leanne shook her head and smiled. "Okay then."

Maxine's eyes widened with delight. She turned to slide the door back open.

"Maxine?"

"Yeah," she said, twisting back to face Leanne.

"Thank you."

"It's gonna be great," she said, before slipping out the door.

61

Hank was asleep in his crib, and Leanne was out of the bath by the time Maxine returned with the antibiotics. She took two pills and then oversaw that Winnie understood how to use Uber to get herself to Lila's house and back.

"Are you sure I'm dressed up enough?" her mother asked, stretching her arms out and looking down to assess her white tapered jeans and silver ballet flats.

"Yeah," Leanne and Maxine said at the same time.

"Think of it less as a fund-raiser and more as a chance for rich people to casually speak in coded language about their freedom of choice," Leanne said.

"Well, of course I believe in freedom of choice."

"Yes, Mom. But you also believe in public health."

"Of course!"

Maxine stepped forward, placing her hands on Winnie's shoulders. "Just have fun, and remember that you're probably the only one there who is an actual medical doctor."

Winnie nodded.

When her Uber arrived, Leanne and Maxine waved good-bye to her like two parents sending their teen off to the big dance. "Text me when you're on your way back to your Airbnb," Leanne said.

It did feel oddly like a moment from high school. Except in the next moments, it was Leanne and Maxine who felt like the teenagers, giddy with their stunt in progress. Who knew what kind of an impact Winnie would make, if any, but the hope in the effort sustained them and brought them joy. It also made them hungry.

Leanne opened the refrigerator door, still clutching the side of her breast, and studied. "Grilled cheese?"

"I can make them," Maxine said.

Leanne's chills had passed, but she was happy to let Maxine do the cooking.

"There's some wine in the fridge if you want," Leanne said as she took a seat at the dining room table. And then: "I can't help but feel relieved. It's a lot of work—fighting a culture war."

Maxine smiled. "A lot of work and no official training." She was buttering slices of thick sourdough bread. The sun had just gone down, and the kitchen filled with a beautiful pale-orange glow.

"Oh, also, I've been meaning to tell you that I fell down an Internet rabbit hole that might be good for your project." She explained that it was JFK's mother's Wikipedia page. "Her name was Rose," she said. She'd had so many children, one every eighteen months for seventeen years, that Wikipedia used a timetable to organize them by their birth and death dates. Leanne couldn't understand how it was possible to do that and still remain a person separate enough to continue on.

"Wow," Maxine said. "I mean, that's super interesting and horrifying, but I don't know if it fits into my book. Maybe for *your* next book?"

As they ate, they continued reading Wikipedia pages, if they existed, of famous men's mothers. Maxine discovered that Reinhold Messner (Maxine was into mountaineering) had eight brothers and one sister. They thought of making breakfast for a family of eleven, if any brain space would be left after all that meal planning and cooking. But they didn't say *meal planning* back then, did they?

"So many lost thoughts," Maxine said.

"Yeah," Leanne said. "Who cares about thoughts, though? Ugh."

Maxine smiled. She'd finished eating and was wiping her hands with a paper towel.

"It makes me *think*, sadly, of the whole Mothers Who Make shoot. And how, if it weren't for you, I'd just be trying to make myself fit in among this accepted, cool way of being a mother."

Maxine had just taken a sip of wine. As she swallowed, she shook her head. "Don't be cool!"

"I've been thinking about that word. *Cool.*" She said it mockingly.

"Cool and refreshing," Maxine said.

"Cool, calm, and collected," Leanne said.

"Collected. That's a good word. What does a cool person collect?"

Leanne considered it. "Skateboards?" And then: "No. Confidence."

But Maxine didn't respond. She was looking off, thinking.

Leanne continued: "Well, the houses of these women don't show a collection of anything. Or maybe *that's* it—they're collecting space. Wide-open, dust-free space."

"Right, right," Maxine said. They sat in silence for a long moment. "Maybe the question is what is *not* cool to collect?"

Leanne took a long sip of water. She looked around the room. "This one contestant on *The Bachelor* collected stuffed animals. Like, her entire bed was covered in them. It just seemed deranged—"

"Oh my god. That's it!" Maxine almost shouted.

She had it. She explained the idea to Leanne quickly, with lots of arm motions.

Leanne loved it. It was a Maxine Hunter idea™. It was weird. It was involved. It was a commentary on the oppressive milieu of modern-day moneyed culture.

It was also terrifying. "How are we going to do it?"

"I'll take care of the logistics," Maxine said.

"Okay, but I'm not an actress."

"You won't be acting!" She quoted another performance artist, someone Leanne had never heard of. "'In theater,'" she said, "'if someone is stabbed, the wound is fake and the blood is fake. In performance art, the wound is real and the blood is real.' That said, hopefully you won't be wounded."

This is what she loved about Maxine. She allowed the irrational to be part of the conversation. She didn't cast it aside and say it had no value. She brought it closer.

It reminded her of what James had said when she'd proposed the idea of going to Middleton to retrieve her dad's ashes. He'd told her that it didn't make sense to go right now. He'd said: "Maybe over Thanksgiving?" It had annoyed her so much. Didn't he realize that sometimes you *had* to do things that didn't make sense? That you had to acknowledge the arbitrary? If not, you could begin to believe you were actually in control. She thought of Pia. Of Gelina.

She thought about Regina and Winnie and the way they made sense of their good fortune. The way they could justify their good lives with their hard work. But you could work hard *and* also be extremely lucky. Luck and its lack—that made no sense.

She looked at Maxine and shrugged. "Okay," she said.

Maxine smiled. She stood up and grabbed Leanne by the shoulders. "It's going to be great."

62

Leanne woke up feeling much better and very curious. Last night, just before eleven, her mom had sent a quick, deeply unsatisfying text with zero punctuation: *Back at the rental Nice night great view of city.*

Leanne had responded: *??? But did you accomplish your mission?*

Can't type on this thing 😑 *Take two more antibiotics in the morning Talk then.*

So when Winnie finally knocked on the front door almost twelve hours later, Leanne had been actively waiting for her. She pulled the door open and told June to be quiet.

"Hooo!" her mom exhaled with a squeal, and dabbed at the sweat that had gathered by her ears. "It's hot out there!"

"Hank's napping," Leanne said softly.

"Oh, of course. Sorry. And hello, Juney!" She crouched down and greeted the dog whose tail wagged furiously. "Oh my little Juney!"

"So," Leanne said, "what the heck happened last night? Did you speak truth to power?"

Winnie stood back up and slipped off her shoes. "See? I remembered." She gestured at her shoes.

"Thank you," Leanne said. "So?"

"Well." She paused. "Everyone there was really nice." She shrugged and made her way through the kitchen. "Nina J. Brown was there! She was one of my favorites on *Dancing with the Stars*." She opened the refrigerator and retrieved a can of Diet Coke from the stash she'd placed there at the beginning of the trip.

"Mom! We sent you there to represent medical common sense, to talk about your positive experience with vaccines over your long pediatric career!"

"Well." She cracked open the can of soda. "No one was really talking about vaccines. I didn't want to be rude. I ate the most delicious—I guess you would call it a canapé? It was so simple. Spicy chorizo with honey on top."

Leanne threw her arms in the air and made a guttural sound.

"Oh, c'mon. It's not like I wrote them a check."

"These people are dangerous!"

Winnie rolled her eyes. She looked ready for this conversation to be over. "You do realize you dress just like them. I really don't understand these jumpsuits." She gestured at Leanne. "They do nothing for your waistline. They're just like"—she searched for the right word—"like sacks." She shook her head.

Leanne dropped her face into her hands. The only thing keeping her from fully melting down was the idea of relaying the entire conversation to Maxine.

63

Leanne had one more class to teach with Winnie as the babysitter. Again, her mother's plan was to walk the neighborhood with Hank for the duration. And again, they'd left moments before Earl knocked on the door.

"Where's the pooch?" he said, entering the house.

"Oh, I put her on the deck so she wouldn't bark at everyone."

"Aw, she's just a little pooch."

Just then, someone else knocked on the door. It was Jade.

"I hope I'm not too early," she said.

"Not at all," Leanne said, and meant it. Now Jade would have to deal with Earl. "I was just making some coffee."

"There was absolutely no traffic anywhere."

"Mind if I use the restroom?" Earl asked.

"Go for it," Leanne said.

Jade and Leanne made small talk about traffic patterns as Leanne poured another round of hot water over the coffee grounds in the Chemex.

Two more students arrived at the same time. As Leanne greeted them, June caught on. Leanne could hear her frantically barking and scratching at the back door.

It was a small house. The front door opened to the living room on the left and the kitchen/dining room on the right. What separated the spaces somewhat were the walls of the bathroom, the entry to which could be found only after walking through either the living room and hanging a right, or the kitchen—bypassing Hank's bedroom—and hanging a left. The bathroom door opened into a long hallway, which led directly to the back door. It also led to Leanne and James's bedroom on the left and their office on the right.

Even though Leanne taught these classes in her living room, which lent an inherent casualness, she made every other effort to keep the atmosphere as professional as possible; she believed that it went without saying that the back half of the house was private and off-limits.

So she was both surprised and annoyed when Earl made his way back into the living room with June squirming under his arm. "You just wanted to see what was going on out here," he said into her ear as he petted the top of her head with his free hand. And then, before Leanne could even say anything—although what would she say?—he bent down to release her. She jumped out of his arms a few feet from the ground and charged, barking as she went, toward the nearest student.

Standing up again, he said, "You know, I didn't realize you were Jewish."

"June! No!" Leanne said, and snapped her fingers. And then, to Earl, "What are you talking about?"

"The photo of you and your husband. You're up in the chair during the hora."

It took her one full second before she realized he was referring to the wedding photo that hung in their bedroom. It was visible from the hallway that led to the back door, where he'd obviously gone to retrieve June. She could feel her face going red. What else had he seen? Their unmade bed, their pile of not dirty but not clean clothes, Hank's toys strewn about. "I'm not Jewish. He's Jewish."

"Ah," Earl said. "The lacework on your dress is stunning."

Leanne nodded. After this class, she was going to email her boss and openly complain about Earl.

Halfway through class, as they discussed Jade's pages, she heard Hank crying. A second later, there was a knock on the door. June began her barking spree as Leanne popped up out of her seat and went to the door. Through the small windows, she could see her mom standing there with her sweaty red face, holding a crying Hank. She opened it.

"I'm really sorry to bother you, but it's so hot, and the back door was locked." Winnie truly looked sorry. Not to mention incredibly shiny. Leanne took Hank into her arms.

"It's okay. Come in," Leanne said. "Do you have his binky?" And then she turned to Earl: "Earl, did you lock the back door when you got June?" She almost had to yell it over Hank's cries.

Earl stared back, blinkingly. "Well, naturally."

Winnie found the binky and placed it in Hank's mouth. "Well, you locked out my mom and my baby. Guys, I'm so sorry," she said to the rest of the class. "My mom is visiting, and I was trying to keep them to the back half of the house."

"Sorry!" Winnie said with hands up in the air. "We'll go to the back. It's just so hot out there."

"Aw," one of the older woman students said. "This is your son and mom?"

"Yeah," Leanne said, turning her face toward Hank's. He was sucking on the pacifier with red cheeks.

Winnie reached for him. "We'll go read a book or two."

"It's okay," Leanne said, not relinquishing him. "I'll walk you both back." She turned to the class. "I'll be right back."

Leanne carried him to the office—it was further from the living room than his bedroom—and whispered in his ear, "You're gonna play with Grandma." And then to Winnie: "He really likes these ones." She pointed to two books on the floor.

Winnie nodded, and Leanne handed him over. He reached for her, and she squeezed his hand. "I'll be right back, my love." She ducked out as quickly as possible and slid the door shut. She waited for one breath. He wasn't crying.

Standing in the hallway, she had a vision of herself punching the wall. If no one were there, she would have done it.

64

After class, Leanne walked down the hallway. "Mom?" she said softly, and slid the door open.

"Yeah?" she whispered back.

Leanne found her mother sitting on the floor, her back against the wall, phone in hand, with Hank sound asleep, his body splayed across her lap. Winnie smiled gigantically, beyond proud.

"Aww. So sweet," Leanne whispered.

Her mom had her reading glasses on. "I was just reading to him, and he kind of got heavy in my arms and then . . ." She shook her head and shrugged her shoulders.

"He must've been so tired," Leanne said. She crouched down on the floor, preparing to pick him up and take him to his crib.

Winnie nodded. "Hey, also, I wanted to tell you that as I was walking around the neighborhood, I ran into the woman who runs that day care over there." She pointed in the direction of someplace located up their street.

"What day care?"

"That day care," she said, trying to point more specifically.

Leanne thought hard. "On Alvarado?"

"Yes," Winnie said.

Though she'd passed by the place many times, it was as if she just now registered it for the first time. It wasn't a day care that had been recommended to her. It looked like a normal house with a sad kind of banner outside announcing it as Hernandez Day Care. "Oh, yeah," Leanne said. "I don't know."

"Well, I talked to the woman who runs it, and I mentioned that you were having problems since your nanny left, and she said they have space."

"My nanny didn't leave. I let her go."

"Well, you're going to need help at some point, so you can write."

"Maybe," Leanne said, shrugging. "Maybe I'll just have another baby."

"But you'll still want to work."

"Isn't that work?" Leanne said.

"Of course," Winnie said. "But I know how you get"—she paused—"when you don't write."

Leanne stared at her mother from just a few feet away. Her eyes were solidly brown, unlike her own and Hank's. Her mother stared back, unwavering. It was an odd moment. *Did* she know how she got? And had she gotten there? After all, she hadn't written anything more than a few sentences in weeks. Months?

And if her mother was right, what would that mean? Leanne had put so much stock in distancing herself from this woman. She'd moved to California. She'd started a new family—her own family. What would it mean if her mother wasn't always, completely, irredeemably wrong?

Leanne heard the buzz of a phone and looked toward the sound. It was Winnie's. She watched her mother pick it up and tap on the screen. She giggled quietly. Leanne was positioned slightly above the phone's screen so that she could see it was a political cartoon. She could see one of the candidate's faces. She leaned in to see more, but Winnie dropped the phone down to her side.

"What is it?" Leanne said.

"Oh, nothing. Just something from my friend."

"Let me see it."

Winnie made a face but then obeyed, handed over the phone.

It took Leanne a second to understand what she was looking at.

But then it hit her all at once. It was a black-and-white drawing of Jesus talking to a woman with short hair. Via a speech bubble, the woman was saying, "Black lives matter." She looked serious, a little bit angry. And Jesus, who looked white, European, kind, and calm, was responding, didactically: "*All* Lives Matter."

Leanne's body came alive, readying itself to fight. She put the phone down, shook her head, and scooped up her baby. "There are so many things wrong with that, I don't even know where to start." She stood up awkwardly, Hank's weight pulling her down, as she searched her brain for facts. But all the blood had gone to her heart. All that came to her was that scene in *Malcolm X*, an image of Denzel Washington's face calmly explaining to the chaplain that Jesus was not a "paleface." "I mean, haven't you seen *Malcolm X*? Jesus wouldn't have even looked like that."

65

From: Earl
To: Leanne
Subject: Next session

Mon Aug 29 at 8:05am

Hello Leanne,
Your next class is referred to as a Fiction Writing Workshop, and the description leads me to believe we will be reading various texts as well as sharing our own work. I'm interested in signing up, but not enthused about too many "literary fiction" assignments. Can you elaborate specifically on what we would be reading before I send my check in?

Thank you,
Earl

From: Leanne
To: Earl
Subject: re: Next session

Mon Aug 29 at 9:15am

Dear Earl,

Thank you for inquiring about the next session. I'm still working on solidifying the reading list, so I cannot give it to you at this time. I will say that of course much of it will be under the umbrella of "literary fiction."

As previously stated, for your project, I would recommend one of the classes specifically geared toward novel writing.

Also, in our final class together, I would greatly appreciate if you would leave June on the deck if I have decided to put her on the deck. Ditto with any other decisions I've made about my house, e.g., open windows. Thanks so much.

Leanne

www.diaryofahomecook.com

or the book version here!

From: Earl

To: Leanne

Subject: re: Next session

Mon Aug 29 at 10:09am

As you well know, I worked for thirty years within the field of engineering. I know firsthand the strain an open window on a hot day can put on an air-conditioning system. I was acting in your best interest. As for June, surely you realize that she was scratching at your back door. I could tell that it was doing damage to the wood. Again, this was for your benefit. I had already written the check to register for your next class, but now I think I'd rather not send it in. I don't think I could endure eight weeks worried that any of my kind actions might be interpreted as offensive to you.

Earl

From: Leanne
To: Earl
Subject: re: Next session

Mon Aug 29 at 11:01am

Hi Earl,

The good news is that there are so many other classes available to you! I would aim for the Novel Writing.

Leanne

www.diaryofahomecook.com

or the book version <u>here</u>!

PART IV

66

When she parks on the street in front of Maxine's house, it's not quite dark. She lets the car idle so that the air-conditioning doesn't shut off as she pulls down the visor and looks at her face in the mirror. She spreads her lips to make sure there's nothing in her teeth. She closes them. She considers her face. She's a bit tan. She's also a bit early. She grabs her phone from her purse. She taps it awake and opens Instagram. Her screen holds the image of a woman's unsmiling face. She looks at the username. Oh. It's Gelina. Leanne reads the long caption:

"Pia will survive. I can say that now, almost one month after she got sick. All told, she was in the hospital for five days on two separate occasions. She had a fever of 106 for three days. Ryan and I missed a month of work. Apparently, it's hard to focus on anything else when your ten-month-old could spike a fatal fever at any moment. And listen, unless you've held a sick, barely conscious baby's body in a tub of ice water, don't talk to me about your vaccine conspiracy theories. Unless you've asked a doctor what the chances are that your baby is going to come out of this alive, I don't want to hear your thoughts or opinions on the standard vaccine schedule. Dr. Sears and the like should have their medical licenses revoked. As for all the doctors and nurses at Los Angeles Children's Hospital, you're saints. You saved my baby. I will be forever grateful."

Leanne can feel Gelina's anger, as if it's shooting out of the screen and into her. She switches accounts. The other day, Regina had posted a photo of the writer profiling her for *INEZ* along with her Instagram handle. She goes to Regina's DMs now and reads through their brief exchange, which is the digital equivalent of a two-cheek air kiss. Now, within the phone's web browser, she pulls up Regina's anti-vax blog post. She copies the URL. She goes back into Regina's Instagram. She types the briefest of explanations. She pastes the URL. She presses *Send*. She logs out. She tosses her phone into her purse. She turns the car off and gets out. The hot, dead air hits her skin, and she wonders if what she just did was illegal. She pushes the thought out of her head. No. *Wait. Was it?*

She opens the back door to get Hank out. Only he's not there. Of course he's not there. He's at home with James. James had returned. And Winnie had left. Maybe she is going crazy, like someone at the beginning stages of Alzheimer's when they still have enough memory or consciousness to know that something is wrong with them. Then again, maybe she's sane and everyone else is crazy. It's something her dad would say about being color-blind. "But maybe this *is* red. Can you prove that it's not?"

At the front door, Maxine greets her. "Hello and welcome," she says, in a faux-solemn voice.

Leanne smiles. "No cloak?"

"It's at the cleaners," Maxine says, making an apologetic face, continuing the joke.

Maxine had told her they were going to do a ritual. She said it would help them get in the right frame of mind for tomorrow. And Leanne had laughed, thinking of both the Old Testament and her college sorority's initiation ceremony.

Now she steps inside. Maxine is dressed for the heat; she's wearing shorts and a billowy tank top. Leanne notices her shoulder muscles immediately. The place smells sweet and smoky. Music is playing too. It's not a present-day sound. Some band and voice from the past.

They move into the living room. The sunlight is fading fast now, the room dim. "How does one get into doing rituals?"

"Catholic school probably helped. I remember both loving and hating the smell of the incense. And the way the priest walked down the aisle with that contraption, chucking incense smoke at the people. And then I read this book about how humans crave ritual—there's a line in it I loved about life being far too complex to rely solely on intellect."

Leanne nods.

"I mean, when else in life do you get the opportunity to try and make the intangible tangible?"

Leanne thinks of Hank coming out of her body, of that wooden phone, of the digital message she'd sent as Regina five minutes ago. Could she get in trouble for that? It seemed particularly reckless, three steps beyond those dumb comments she'd left on pet store accounts. She didn't know the first thing about IP addresses or how digital data was tracked. She'd just wanted Regina to have to suffer some kind of consequence, but knowing how the world worked, it would of course be much more likely that Leanne would end up playing the fool, being held accountable for her sins.

But she doesn't say anything. She's here because she doesn't want to be the one in charge. She's here because Maxine usually silences her spinning brain. She shrugs.

"Okay, so let me explain what we're going to do. Oh, wait, do you want something to drink? Wine? Water?"

"I'll take some wine," Leanne says.

Maxine nods and moves toward the kitchen. Leanne follows a few paces behind. It's an older house, so the kitchen doesn't spill out into any other room. It reminds her of her and James's old apartment. It even has the tiled countertop and enameled cast-iron sink. "White?" Maxine says, holding up a bottle.

Leanne nods. "Do you like living by yourself?"

Maxine pulls two tumblers from the cabinet and sets them on the countertop. "For the most part. I like sleeping by myself. I like spreading out. But in each . . ." She stumbles. "Each breakup shows me the things I avoid doing. Like something is wrong with the WiFi right now, but I hate calling the cable company, so I'm just living with it only sort of working. There's a lot of stuff like that." She hands Leanne a glass and then holds up her own. "Cheers."

They clink glasses.

Leanne recognizes the voice of the singer now. It's Otis Redding. He's begging, "Pleaaase, pleaaaase." On the wall hangs a photograph of a person lying on their back sunbathing next to an ocean cliff. The person is topless but far away enough that Leanne can't tell if it's a woman wearing bikini bottoms or a man in a blue Speedo. How or if the person can access the dark-blue water below is also a mystery. There must be a way, some wooden stairs leading down.

They move back into the living room.

"Should we get started?"

Leanne takes a sip. She nods.

"Okay. The main idea is to lay something to rest," Maxine says, putting her glass down on the mantel. "But we're going to do it literally. We're going to actually lie down." She gestures to the floor. She tucks her hair behind her ears. "We'll meditate for a few moments on something we're ready to be done with. It can be anything. Anything. Then we'll sit back up and invoke the four elements. We'll *earth* it by writing the thing down on a piece of paper. We'll *air* it by saying it out loud. Then we'll burn it—*fire*, and lastly, finish with *water*—the purifier—pouring water over the flames and ashes. Sound good?"

Leanne nods. She's sitting on the edge of the couch, watching Maxine as if she were a college professor.

"The only other thing I'll say is that in my experience—in rituals or otherwise—you get back what you give, in terms of energy."

Leanne nods again, wonders how much she's willing to give. She imagines what this situation would be like if Maxine were a man. She wouldn't be here. Not alone at least. She wonders if she's in love with Maxine—if she's capable of that—or is she just blinded by her celebrity and self-possession?

"Here's a pillow for your head, or you could put it underneath your upper back, which will help open your heart. And I'm going to do it too." She grabs another pillow from the couch and puts it down next to Leanne's so that they'll be side by side. "I just want to change the record and read this short poem first."

Leanne lies down on the living room floor, adjusting her body so that her upper back rests on the pillow. She can feel the blood rush to her head. She can hear Maxine stopping the record and putting another one on. She closes her eyes, thinking about all the choices she made and didn't make to arrive right here in this very moment. She hears the music swelling and Maxine's footsteps coming back toward her.

"The poem is called 'Working Together.'" Her voice is quieter now.

At first, Leanne has trouble paying attention. The words are flying past her, over her, without landing. But then a sentence stands out; she's pulled in.

I am thinking of the way
the intangible air

traveled at speed
round a shaped wing

easily
holds our weight.

So may we, in this life
trust

to those elements
we have yet to see

or imagine.

She feels something falling away inside her.

She feels light and then heavy. She breathes in through her nose. She feels the atmosphere of the room: swishing and calm, quiet and loud. She tries to concentrate on her breath. She is trying to control herself, while at the same time she knows that she can't, like she's hanging on to the ledge of that cliff in the photograph and her grip is slipping, slipping. And then she shoots herself upward. "I'm sorry," she says. Her throat is closing. Tears are already running down her face. "I'm sorry. Please continue without me." She rocks up to her feet. She wants to be alone for this. She considers running straight to the car, but the bathroom is closer. She jog-walks to it and quickly closes the door behind her.

She sits on top of the lidded toilet and buries her face in her hands. The tears are pouring out of her. They're so hot. They feel like they're coming from her stomach, each heaving breath bringing more and more up. She grabs both hand towels and puts them to her face and cries into them. *What is happening? What is wrong with me?* At the same time, it feels good, like she is crying something much more than salt water.

She makes an exit strategy. After this sob, she tells herself, she will stand up. She will relocate this to the car. She'll thank Maxine. She'll apologize for ruining the ritual before it even got started. Maybe she is getting her period. She hasn't had one in nineteen months. *Maybe you're getting your period?* she mocks herself. *Maybe you're just sad. Maybe you're confused!* she defends herself.

"Leanne?" she hears from the other side of the door.

She covers her face with the towels. "One second," she says into them. She tells herself to take five deep breaths, but she has to inhale through her mouth because her nose is stuffed, and so the breaths don't have the same effect.

She reaches for the doorknob. She twists it and lets it crack open.

Maxine steps inside, and Leanne peeks out from under the towels for a second, but when she sees Maxine's face, it makes her heave. "Sorry," she manages to say.

"This is all part of it. I should have told you that there's usually crying."

Leanne sits up, pressing the heels of her hands into her eyes, clearing them for a short second. She looks at Maxine, who is sitting on the ledge of the bathtub. "But you're not crying."

"Not *yet*." She says it softly with a raised finger.

Leanne laughs. Or cries. It's hard to tell.

Maxine grabs Leanne's shoulder and squeezes. Leanne looks up again. She stares at her pretty, square face. "I always like your hair," she says.

"Thank you," Maxine says in a way that's both earnest and deflecting. "I'm going to tell my hairstylist you said that."

Leanne laugh-cries again. She wipes at her face *again*. "But do you spend time on it? In the mornings?"

Maxine nods. "I do. I really do."

Leanne makes a strange sound. It's not a laugh this time. "Don't worry," she says. "As soon as I can stabilize, I'm going home."

"Well, you can if you want to. But you don't have to."

"I feel so stupid," she hears herself saying. "I don't even know what I'm crying about."

She looks at Maxine, who is slowly shaking her head. "You don't have to know."

Leanne pushes her tears to the sides of her face. She stands up. "I think I just want to go. We've got a big day tomorrow."

Maxine stands up too. She opens her arms for a hug, and Leanne walks into it, inhaling that familiar pine-tree, woodsy smell of her.

"I don't even know what I was going to lay to rest."

Yes, you do.

She wraps her hand around her own opposite wrist and squeezes Maxine, surprised by how small she feels. Not fragile but almost. Have they never done this before? Surely all the times they'd greeted or said good-bye to each other, they had hugged. But no. Not like this. There is no space between them. This is the way she and James hug after having gone through something. And yet it isn't like hugging James at all. Maxine is at least an inch or two taller than Leanne, but her frame feels so much more delicate than her own. When she holds James like this, she feels *his* sturdiness. Now she feels her own. Maxine feels tiny, bony. If someone were to observe this hug, would they even see Maxine's body? Does Maxine feel this as well—enveloped by Leanne? Who will pull away first? They can't stay like this forever.

67

They don't.

On the drive home, she listens to the CD that's already in the player. It's a mix James made her for her twenty-seventh birthday—seven years ago now. He'd made it after they'd watched *Dirty Dancing.* So many of the songs from the movie are on it. She skips to the song "Stay." She loves how it starts, with that "Hey!" followed by the singer kind of moaning: *aahhhhh.* It's like it begins in the middle. *If your daddy don't mind . . .* It's not even two minutes long. When it ends, she presses the back button and listens to it again.

When she gets home, it's almost ten.

She sneaks in so quietly that June doesn't even realize it until she's in the bedroom. Then, from her perch on the bed, she barks, one piercing, surprised bark, and James turns over.

"You sleeping?" she says.

"Not yet. I thought you'd be later."

"Yeah, no." She sits down on the bed, and June growls.

She wants to have sex with him. The urge hits her that very moment. But she doesn't want to initiate the usual way—by one of them asking the other one if they want to. She wants to lean in and kiss him. She wants to press herself into his body, reach down and grab his dick. She doesn't want the ending to be predetermined. She wants the mystery. She wants desire itself. But June's protective growl means that Leanne will have to pick her up and put her on the floor. And that will be a tell. She despises June in these moments. For being one more thing in her way, one more thing she has to consider.

She lifts her up and places her on the carpet. She makes a squeaking noise, announcing her indignation.

James looks at her with a clichéd raised eyebrow.

"What?" Leanne says, trying to go back in time, to before they had a dog, a baby, a nuclear family.

"Okay," James says, pulling back the covers and slipping off his boxer shorts.

Leanne pulls her dress over her head. It's been weeks since they've done this. She grips him and pulls him into her. They stop only to unwrap a condom. But it barely slows them down. They come quickly, maybe a minute later. Afterward, Leanne feels odd. The air in the room feels so stuffy. When James gets up to clean himself off, she asks him to put the air-conditioning on.

If understanding oneself is a full-time job, Leanne hasn't been showing up to work regularly. That much is clear now. Minutes later, when he slips back into bed, she says: "I want to go to Middleton to get my dad's ashes."

"I know," he says.

"No. I don't want to wait. I want to go as soon as I finish teaching this session."

"Okay," he says. The tone is defensive but also conciliatory. "I mean, I can't go with you."

"I didn't expect you to."

68

The next morning begins like so many others. She nurses Hank while tapping at her phone's screen. Next to her, James is still sleeping. Last night, they'd gone online together and bought the plane ticket to Pennsylvania. She would take Hank. She would get a hotel. It would be an adventure. Now she opens the weather app. Yesterday had been hot, and she was holding out hope that today might be different. Alas, no—today's high reads ninety-five degrees.

When Hank is done, he rolls off her and half onto his dad. James lifts his head and begins to register his baby's body.

"There's one more thing I haven't quite told you," she says.

"Yeah?" He says it to her but he's looking at Hank, smiling.

"I'm doing something weird for the shoot. It may cause some trouble. Possibly just for myself."

"Sounds promising," James says. He's joking, but he is also distracted. He's walking his pointer finger and middle finger up Hank's leg, and Hank is responding with a gigantic smile.

"I'm telling you solely in the interest of being transparent." They'd talked about this last night. James said he hadn't realized that going to Middleton had been weighing on her.

"Well, be even more transparent then. What are you doing?"

She thinks about explaining it further. She imagines the words she needs to say, but then, if she says them aloud and it doesn't make sense to him, she might lose her nerve. Worse, she could hate him for not getting it. "I can't," she says. "You'll just have to wait and see how it goes."

An hour later, James is gone, and Hank is standing at the washing machine, watching the clothes spin while his mother moves from room to room, ironically trying to tidy the house in anticipation of Maxine's arrival and the chaos she'll be bringing with her.

June can sense that something is up. She keeps scratching on the back door, but when Leanne lets her out, she just sniffs around on the deck, doesn't even make it to the grass. So that when she scratches on the door yet again, Leanne yells: "What do you want?" Hank hears this and comes walk-stumbling toward them. "Okay, fine, let's all go out."

The way their house has retained the night's coolness only becomes apparent as soon as the heat from the sun hits her skin. It's not oppressive at first. In fact, it's the opposite. She stands there, holding Hank in her arms, taking in the warmth. And June, apparently comforted by their presence, ventures into the grass. Leanne watches as her back hunches and her tail curves upward in that familiar dog-shitting way. Hank, meanwhile, begins to flail. He wants down. Normally, she wouldn't let him. Maxine is about to arrive. And the photoshoot—as strange as their plans may be—is still a photoshoot. She doesn't want to play outside and get all sweaty beforehand. They should all be inside, ready and waiting.

But if last night had revealed anything, it was Leanne's general deficiency in letting go. She puts Hank down. She watches as he maneuvers himself from his knees to a crouch and then stands himself up. He hobbles toward the two steps leading to the yard. Once there, he crouches back down, scooting himself butt-first toward the step. Leanne is impressed by this, how he knows his own skill level.

When she looks up, she sees that June has moved to a new spot of grass and reclaimed the shitting position. Leanne knows exactly what this means, that for some reason June can't pinch the excrement off, and so she's trying again. It happens from time to time. Leanne sighs, very glad to be dropping her off at dog day care as soon as Maxine gets here. Just as she thinks this, she hears a car pull into the driveway. So does June. The dog takes off running toward it at the same time that Hank is standing himself up again. June hadn't seen that coming and can't adjust her direction, so she sideswipes Hank, knocks him down into the grass, and then steps on him as she continues sprinting. Leanne watches in dual horror and amusement. She rushes toward the baby, but he's already lifting his head up. He's laughing, his face asking: *What the fuck was that?* When she looks to the driveway, she sees Maxine's car, June barking at it, and a cylinder of dog shit lying on the pavement.

69

They'd needed enough cats to make a statement—a point—but once the cats were inside, was it enough? They'd decided on thirty because that was the starting number of contestants on *The Bachelor*, the show that had originally inspired Maxine to fill a house with cats.

"It *feels* like enough," Leanne says, looking at her living room. The lyrics to "Old MacDonald" run through her head. *With a meow-meow here, a meow-meow there.*

"I guess it has to be," Maxine says with her hands on her hips. "Because this is all I could get for an afternoon." She'd enlisted the help of Taffy, an animal trainer for TV and movies. Apparently, Maxine had worked with her in the past. But now Taffy is gone. She's promised to come back in three hours to retrieve them all. It reminds Leanne of working with prop stylists at the homewares store, how they'd walk around the store, tapping on the items they wanted to rent, followed by "We'll take fifty of these." They were used to excess and drama; it was always better to have more.

"The finishing touch," Leanne says now, pouring about half of a giant bag of cat food into a large metallic salad bowl, which sits in the middle of the room.

"Yes, exactly how I pictured it," Maxine says.

"He should be waking up soon." Leanne had put Hank down for his first nap when there were probably only fifteen cats inside.

"It's so funny," Leanne says, looking around her living room. "All the ways babies have no choice in their lives. If we adopted thirty cats, Hank would just grow up with thirty cats."

"And be the better for it," Maxine says from her new spot on the sofa with three cats mewing around and on top of her.

Leanne smiles and then crosses the room to sit next to her. "I'm nervous," she says.

"That sounds about right," Maxine says, shifting her legs to the left, turning toward her. "Just remember: What's real to you will be real to them." Leanne lets the words sink in.

On one hand, what they're doing is a prank. It's silly. *LOL. Look at all these cats!* But on the other, she's trying to impose a different reality. She's trying to start a conversation about what we unconsciously absorb as important and worthwhile. She's trying to show how stupid the other side is. How stupid we can all be.

"Oh, and I almost forgot, I wrote down a list of names—cat names—just in case you get stuck." She removes a piece of paper from her pocket and hands it to Leanne.

Leanne unfolds it, reaching her arms around the body of a cat who has claimed her lap. "Olga, Nadia, Svetlana, Roger, Novak, Rafa, Serena, Martina." She looks at Maxine. "Very athletic."

Maxine nods, moving the palm of her hand down the back of a calico cat.

70

Chaos, chaos, chaos. *Why hadn't she invited it in sooner?*

There's no hiding the cats, the crunching of the food in their mouths, the general sound of them. There's no hiding Maxine or Hank, the latter of whom has woken up and is sitting in his high chair with a smattering of blueberries before him.

The two slim women—Jesse and Mitsumi—can see everything. They're taking it in, trying to process it, it seems, but not saying anything, at least anything about the cats. Jesse is the photographer. She has long, wavy strawberry-blond hair, which she has pulled back in a low ponytail. Leanne thinks she must've gotten into photography as a reversal—after years of modeling. Mitsumi is the assistant. She's even tinier than Jesse. Leanne wonders how they spent the morning, while she and Maxine wrangled cats.

"Do you guys want anything to drink? Coffee, tea, water?" Leanne says.

"I'll take a water. Thanks," Jesse says. "I'm sorry, I just have to say: You're Maxine Hunter?"

Maxine is sitting next to Hank in one of the dining room table chairs. Two cats are at her feet and another two are sitting on the dining room table itself. Leanne tells herself to surrender—that she can clean up the cat hair later. "Yes," Maxine says, quickly nodding.

"Oh, wow. I'm such a fan of your work."

"Thank you," Maxine says.

"You, you live here?" she asks, her voice rising to a squeak.

"Oh, no. I'm just a friend, tagging along for the afternoon." And then: "So do you guys do most of the shoots for this site?"

"Yeah," Jesse said. "They keep us pretty busy." As she talks, she takes her foot and tries to nudge a cat's nose out of her camera bag.

"That's the most cat food I think I've ever seen in my life," Mitsumi says, her eyes focused on the overflowing bowl in the middle of the living room.

"You should see the litter box!" Leanne says.

Mitsumi nods in a way that telegraphs she probably *doesn't* want to see it.

"Do you want me to give you a quick tour so you know the lay of the land?"

"That'd be great," Jesse says.

"You got Hank?" she says to Maxine.

"Yep," Maxine says.

"Okay, follow me. It's a pretty small house." She leads Jesse through the kitchen. A trail of cats snaking behind them. "This is Hank's room," she says, sliding the pocket door open and pausing for just a moment under the doorframe. Cats cascade over her feet, curious about the newly revealed room. She moves on. "The bathroom is right there, and then down this hallway, we've got the main bedroom to the left." Again, she pauses underneath the doorframe. About four pairs of eyes stare back at them from atop the queen bed. "They like it there," Leanne says. "And then just across the way is the office slash nothing room."

When she pauses long enough to actually look at Jesse, she can see the fear in her eyes.

"You okay?" Leanne says.

"Yeah, I, I've just—I didn't account for the cats."

"Ah," Leanne says. "Right. I can say that you do eventually get used to them."

"It's just—there's kind of a template to these shoots, and I'm worried about how to apply it here."

"Hmm," Leanne says, pressing her lips together. "I'm not a photographer, but my first thought is to just add cats to the template?" Leanne frowns and shrugs, like a confused clown, and Jesse continues to scan the two rooms and the hallway, as if trying to solve a riddle. One of the cats starts scratching at the quilt, trying to dig through it. "Sveta, no," Leanne says.

"Do you mind if I just call my boss real quick?"

"Elspeth?"

"Yeah, Elspeth."

"Sure," Leanne says. "I mean, I don't mind."

They walk back to the living room. Hank is out of his high chair and sitting on Maxine's lap. "She didn't account for all the cats," Leanne says to Maxine, realizing that she is enjoying herself.

"They're fine," Jesse says, almost defensively. "I just, I just need to call my boss. I'll step outside." She points to the front door and then disappears behind it.

"Do you have cats, Mitsumi?" Maxine says.

Mitsumi shakes her head.

"You want one?" Leanne says, and then laughs. "Just kidding. They're all mine."

Hank has wormed himself off Maxine's lap and is now waddling toward the giant bowl of food. Leanne crouches down next to him. "This is for the kitties." He leans in and grabs a fistful of cat food. "No, no, no." She takes his hand in hers and pries it open, dumping the cat food back in the bowl. Hank's face crinkles. He shakes his head. "Okay," Leanne says. "You can feed it to the kitties." She takes a piece of food in her hand and extends it open palmed to a nearby cat. The cat declines.

Jesse steps back inside and holds the phone out to Leanne. "Elspeth would like to speak with you, if you don't mind?"

"Not at all," Leanne says, standing up. And then to Maxine: "Just make sure he doesn't eat any of it." Maxine nods. Leanne takes the phone in her hand and presses it to her ear. "Elspeth?"

"Yes, Leanne. Hi. So, it sounds like you have a lot of cats over there!"

"Well, I don't like to brag, but yes. Yes, I do."

"Mona never told me."

"Well, I don't think Mona's ever been here."

"Look," Elspeth said. "I'm just gonna come out and say it: we think there are too many cats."

"Too many cats?" Leanne feels the smile trying to form but represses it. She turns to Maxine, who is holding up her iPhone, possibly taking a photo or a video—Leanne can't know. "She says there are too many cats."

Maxine shakes her head. "There are less than thirty-one."

Elspeth is talking to her about the magazine's brand. "We're a lifestyle magazine, and there's just not a strong focus on animals."

"She says there's not a strong focus on animals," Leanne repeats back to Maxine, speaking away from the receiver. And then to Elspeth: "But we're technically all animals." She looks to Maxine who nods—her phone still in hand.

Leanne presses the speaker button so that now Elspeth's voice can be heard by all. She continues: "I just don't want to waste your time."

"We don't mind," Leanne says. "We're not doing anything else."

Now Maxine is aiming her phone at Hank, who is sitting in the middle of the floor, in a staring contest with one of the cats.

"I'm trying to be polite," Elspeth says. "But we don't want the cat content."

"Wow," Leanne says. She looks up at Jesse and then Mitsumi. They look so uncomfortable. What's happening before them was not part of the day's plan. She looks to Maxine, who seems pleased. "Okay," Leanne says. "So the mothers you profile don't have pets?"

"No. They have pets! They just don't have swarms of them."

"So it's just a numbers thing."

"Yeah. Exactly," Elspeth says. "Let me think. Jesse says that

Maxine Hunter is there. I wonder if you could corral some of the cats into one room and then we could take a few shots of you two together?" Leanne looks to Maxine, who shakes her head subtly.

"I'm not a 'Mother Who Makes,'" Maxine says.

Leanne is grateful for Maxine's directness. "She's not a 'Mother Who Makes,'" she repeats back to Elspeth.

"No, but I think our readers would like to see her."

"I feel like a 'Mother Who Makes' and also happens to own a lot of cats is much more in line with your brand than, what? Two women friends and a child and some cats. The message becomes muddled."

"Look, this is my fault. I should have personally scouted your house instead of trusting Mona." Later, Leanne will feel bad about this part, about throwing Mona under the bus. But in the moment, she must finish what she's started. She can apologize later.

"Yeah, I mean, what if I were poor?"

Elspeth doesn't like Leanne's tone. She hangs up a moment later. Jesse and Mitsumi pack up their things, although Jesse is moving slowly. Leanne can see that she wants more from Maxine, but Maxine isn't giving it to her. *Good-bye, Jesse!* Leanne wants to shout, but she doesn't.

71

For the first time in a long while, Leanne doesn't feel that swirling motion in her head and fingers. She doesn't feel like a helium balloon that some child has let go that is floating up into the blue.

She feels dirty, but physically—actually. She feels sweaty, too, and covered in cat hair. The rest of the afternoon is the equivalent of that scene in *The Cat in the Hat* when the cat must clean up the house before the mom comes home, except here, she and Maxine together are the cat (and at one point, Taffy, with her clipboard), and James is the mom. The women take turns between vacuuming and playing with Hank, between sweeping and scrubbing. (They find two instances of what has to be cat vomit.) They move all the furniture off the carpet. Leanne finds spots with thick layers of dust, seemingly never vacuumed.

By four in the afternoon, they can't take it anymore. They need to shower. They take turns. Leanne goes first. When she's done, while still wrapped in a towel, she slides open Hank's bedroom door to check on him. He's still asleep—nap number two. After the day of movement, of mayhem, her ears ring with the stillness and quiet of the moment. She gulps it in. She closes the door and moves back to her bedroom. She lets the towel drop, pulls on underwear and a bra. She moisturizes, and then lies down on top of the quilt.

It's not happiness. It's simpler than that. It's not exhaustion either.

The way she feels is akin to how she felt in that bathroom with Maxine, after Leanne had pulled away from the embrace and after Maxine had moved her hands to Leanne's cheeks and held her face in her palms, after they'd been inches away from each other, so close Leanne had smelled her breath.

When she'd been able to momentarily glimpse what Maxine saw in her, when she'd felt her own power, her own softness, her own appeal. When she had felt both seduced and the seducer. When she'd seemed to understand the point of it, of her relationship with (to?) Maxine. That she didn't *want* Maxine. Not like that. She'd wanted a different role for herself. She'd wanted not to be defined so singularly. Mother. She wanted *not* to feel so trapped.

And that's when she'd said, "I think I do know what I want to lay to rest."

She'd started with Regina. She'd had to. Maxine knew *of* her of course, but not in the context of Leanne. Then she told her about Palm Springs, the fallout, and how she'd hacked into her Instagram account. But was it technically hacking if you had the password? But there's more, she'd said. She told her about the dumb vaccine-injury blog post and about Lila, and then reminded her about Gelina and Pia. She told her about talking to her dead father or whatever it was she'd been doing, and then about how he'd stopped after she yelled at him. She told her about the emails to Beth about his ashes and that fucking cartoon someone had texted her mom. What had happened to her mom? She didn't understand. At that point, she had to backtrack to tell her about the cooking class and Mona showing everyone the photo of her—Maxine—with Regina, and then the story she made up about her nonexistent dead cat. She told her that she just wanted Regina to have to pay for one fucking thing. And how, because of all this, she'd done something. Then she'd opened up Instagram. She'd switched to Regina's account and showed Maxine what she'd just sent.

Maxine had taken the phone in her hands and read it. "Okay," she'd said, still looking at the phone. And then, looking up at Leanne: "That was one way to handle it."

Leanne had started crying again. And as she did, she promised to remember this response for the future, for when Hank was a teenager and did something so dumb: the acceptance. Nothing was too much for Maxine. Leanne loved that. She wanted to bury herself in it.

72

ow it's Sunday morning. Leanne looks at the clock on the microwave. For the first time all session, Earl isn't early. He hadn't replied to the last email she'd sent, and for a moment, she thinks that maybe she has defeated him altogether. She thinks: *Maybe he won't even show up!* But then, right at ten, she hears a knock and June's telltale barking.

She opens the door and there he is, as upright as ever. "Hello, Earl. Nice to see you."

"Hello," he says without smiling or making eye contact. As he steps inside, June pounces at his legs, pawing at them. "Okay, okay. That'll do," he says.

Leanne turns around and makes a face to no one but herself. Has she tamed him at long last?

He takes his regular seat without any further comment. The rest of the class arrives shortly after, and he spends the entire two hours in this subdued, almost pouting state.

Leanne loves it. Finally, she feels confident, unquestioned, in charge.

In the last five minutes, she wraps up the session. She tells her students what a pleasure it's been to teach them and feels a reciprocal energy in their responses, that they too had enjoyed themselves, had learned something.

She notices, however, that while the other students file out,

Earl has once again ducked out toward the restroom. So that she is standing at the front door, waving good-bye, when she hears the toilet flush and the bathroom door open. She makes a point to remain there, as usher, holding the door slightly ajar—letting the hot air in—while Earl reenters the living room.

"I hope you realize you've made me quite uncomfortable in your house," he says with his nose in the air, in a stance of protest. It strikes Leanne that if he were a cartoon character, he'd be a pig—but one that stands on his hind legs and is fully dressed in exactly what he's wearing now: khaki pants, dress socks, sweater vest. A nerdy, old-fashioned young-boy pig.

"That wasn't—" Leanne starts but is interrupted.

"But I also hope you realize that I can behave according to your mandates."

"Mandates? I don't know if I'd—"

"Look," he says. "If you've quite finished with reprimanding me and you can agree that there won't be any more of *this*"—at which he waves his arms in the air—"I will send this check in for the next session," at which point, he pulls out a check from his pocket and holds it in the air.

"*This?*" Leanne says. She throws her hands in the air. "If you're referring to the extremely reasonable requests to leave my house and dog alone and to act like a normal student, then you truly don't understand how to behave in a class atmosphere. There will be plenty more of *this*. Just take someone else's class!"

"I tried taking someone else's class before this one, but their house was located near the Hollywood Bowl and traffic was a nightmare. Not to mention parking."

She shakes her head. "So this is the most convenient class for you?"

"Yes."

She pulls the door wide open. "Well, so sorry to inconvenience you, but I need my house back." She gestures for him to leave.

He looks furious, shocked.

"Very well," he says, shaking his head and gathering up the eternal Kinko's box. "I'm extremely disappointed."

"Aren't we all?"

He walks out with his jaw clenched.

"Best of luck with the book," she says, and swings the door shut behind him.

She leans her back into the closed door. She feels ridiculous and good. Good. Good. Good. *Good riddance.* The two words cannot be truer. It feels so good to be rid of him.

73

The rental car doesn't have one of those mirrors attached to the headrest like she has in her own car, so that she can't actually see Hank's face—twice reflected—when she looks in the rearview mirror, but ten minutes into the drive, he has stopped crying and she can sense he's asleep. She has an image of him with his eyes closed and his fat cheeks pulsing ever so slightly as he sucks on the binky.

It's six p.m. The late-summer sun is to her left—to the west—as she drives north to Middleton.

She's been with James for so long that she can't remember the last time she drove a long stretch of highway by herself. Maybe graduate school. That was seven years ago. She thinks of Winnie and her driving phobia, and she only feels sorry for her. At some point, her mother had become very accustomed to relinquishing her own agency.

She thinks of Maxine, always doing the opposite.

Just that morning, she'd posted the video of their *cat-venture*. That's what Maxine was calling it. The video opens with Leanne—a shot of her with Hank in her arms as Maxine, off camera, asks if she's excited to be featured as a "mother who makes." Leanne nods. She says, "Yeah," and then looks out the window. "Is that her? Oh no, that's a plumbing van." A flowery title card flashes. It reads: *Behind the Scenes of Madre mag.* Next, the video moves to time-lapse footage of the cats arriving. Cat after cat after cat after cat. Slowly building classical music hums in the background. Then, abruptly, it cuts to the video Maxine took while Leanne talked to Elspeth on the phone. Maxine has added subtitles, though. And when Elspeth says the line "We don't want the cat content," the screen freezes. Next, the frame swirls around, like a moment from an eighties movie, as if the frame got sucked into a whirlpool. After that, it goes straight to Hank. He's sitting in the middle of the living room floor, flanked by cats. With a completely straight face, he rocks himself up to his knees, and then pressing on the two cats' bodies on either side of him, he pushes himself to a stand. Both cats close their eyes at the pressure but do nothing more. And then Hank, stumbling just a bit, teeters off camera. So far, it has 200K views.

74

Middleton is so small that it doesn't have any hotels. Instead, Hank and Leanne stay the night in the next town over: Elkersville. They sleep until nine a.m., though it feels like six a.m. It's so strange to be there as an adult: to be there and in need of adult things, like a cup of coffee and breakfast for your baby. At the same time, she relishes it. She likes being on her own. Having no one else to blame.

For breakfast, she settles on Perkins, a chain restaurant that shares a parking lot with the hotel. The food is generic and beige, but she feels safe, tucked in the booth with Hank in the high chair. Looking around, it cannot be clearer that they're not in Los Angeles anymore. These people aren't hiding anything. Or rather, they have different hiding spots. And some of them are very, very old. She asks for the check and then texts Beth—letting her know they'll be there shortly. As she does, her body responds as if she's just stepped outside into a wintry day. She's nervous. She inhales through her nose to calm herself and looks to Hank, so grateful he's coming with her.

She could put the address of the house where she once lived, where her dad died, and where Beth still lives, into her phone, but she's too curious about her own memory, if she can make it there without technology's assistance.

"Whaddya think, Hank?" she says as she pulls out of the parking space. "Can Mama do it?" She makes a left and then a right, each road both familiar and foreign to her. It's mid-September. The air still smells like summer even though many of the leaves on the trees have gone yellow. Soon, she's out of Elkersville entirely. And then she's passing marquee houses, the ones seared into her memory, from her old bus route: the double-wide trailer with the adjacent collapsed barn—although now a campaign sign next to an American flag stands firm in the front yard. The houses are few and far between, like blips on a heart monitor, only the heart is beating slowly, spaciously, one beat every few seconds. Next is the house with the Greek-ish columns in the front, and then, the brown single-story with all the cars in various states of disrepair in the driveway.

They drive past Middleton Elementary and Middleton High, standing alone together, surrounded by a concrete parking lot and a grassy football field. No one walks to school here, she thinks. There are no sidewalks here. She imagines what it would be like to live here as a mother. Would it even make sense to have a stroller? Where would you stroll? For the first time ever in her life, she imagines Beth not as her stepmother but as a woman with a newborn. She wonders how she spent her days with baby Brittany while her dad was at work delivering other babies. She'd had Jordan only eighteen months later. Did she have mom friends she met up with? And then she realizes she'd never once met Beth's mother. She'd never considered that Beth had a mother.

She sees the trees first: three gigantic pines mark the front yard of the dark-green house she'd lived in until she was fourteen. She slows down to make the left turn and whispers to herself, "What have you done, Leanne?"

The gravel driveway shifts and rumbles under the weight of her rental car, giving her and Hank away as it had given her dad away on those weeknights when she'd wait for him and her brother to come home from work and basketball practice. She puts the car in park and turns off the engine. She looks up and sees a campaign sign for the candidate she hates in the front window. She doesn't want to be here. But she's come this far. She's so close to getting what she thought she wanted, to what she thought she deserved.

With Hank on her hip, she walks toward the door they always used—the side door. It was part of that new construction her dad and Beth had added onto the existing house. She can barely remember the actual construction. She just remembers it being new. And she remembers when people would come to the front door and how odd it felt on the receiving end. Her stepfather had done it once, actually, when he was picking her and her brother up one Christmas morning to take them to their mom's. Her mother had never come here, or at least Leanne had no memories of it.

She knocks twice and can feel that the door isn't made of solid wood. It feels like thick plastic, hollow. A bedraggled, splotchy-haired tabby cat appears at her ankles, mewing, and when the door opens, Beth is standing there. It's been nine years since Leanne last saw her and nine years since she'd been to the house. She had calculated it this morning. Beth looks the same but shrunken. Her eyes have receded into her face and her neck into her shoulders. But her skin has the same orange tint to it. It must be makeup.

One of her feet is slightly lifted and flexed. She's looking at the cat, who is trying to come in. "Oh, no you don't," she says. And then to Leanne and Hank, "Hi, you can come in. Just not this one. She stays." The cat meows as Leanne ducks to the side and further into the room so that Beth can close the door.

The stale smell of cigarette smoke hits her right away. She can feel it on her eyeballs and worries for Hank. She doesn't want to expose him to it, but she already has. She kisses him on the cheek. When Leanne lived here, this room, just off the kitchen, was part mudroom and part playroom for Brittany and Jordan. It looks much the same now, minus the kids' shoes lined up along the wall.

Beth has already moved into the kitchen and is standing at the island, the surface of which is almost completely cluttered with food miscellany: a few Folgers coffee tin cans, a plastic Target bag filled with something, a jar with kitchen utensils, Orville Redenbacher's microwave popcorn boxes still wrapped in cellophane, and so on. "I was just portioning out the ashes," she says, looking up at Leanne for the first time.

Leanne realizes she has yet to say a single thing. "Okay," she finally says, and nods. At this, Hank grabs her face with both hands. She looks to him and says it again, sweetly: "Okay."

"Like I said, Jordan already took some, but there's still plenty. I was going to give you a cup. All I have is a Ziploc."

"A cup would be great. Ziploc too. Thank you."

Leanne watches as she sets up a plastic freezer bag next to a wooden box about the size of a two-slice toaster. "Looks like you enjoyed Perkins," she says flatly, flipping the lid of the box open.

The comment catches Leanne off guard. She hadn't mentioned Perkins to Beth. The only way she would know is if she followed Leanne's Instagram. About twenty minutes ago, she'd posted a photo of Hank in the diner high chair. She'd tagged the location so that the caption about taking Hank "back to her roots" would make sense to her followers. Whenever she posted photos there, she had a general audience in mind, maybe a few specific people, but Beth had never been one of them. A few of her latest posts run through her mind, and she thinks of Beth on the receiving end. Beth seeing Leanne's homemade pizzas in her light-filled sunny kitchen; Beth seeing the images of her book—first the advance reader copies and then the real thing; the bottle of those placenta pills she'd taken postpartum; that image of the Republican senator Leanne hates next to a cartoon turtle accompanied by Leanne's political rant; the video of Hank sucking on James's knee as if it were a nipple; the latest poem that "broke her heart wide open." For a solid second, Leanne can see her life as presented online through Beth's eyes and she hates it, hates the faux intimacy of it. Intimacy, she thinks, is this. It's scooping out your dead husband's ashes for your stepdaughter.

But aloud she says, "Yeah. It's"—she hesitates, looking for the right word—"it's interesting to be here with Hank." Hank is twisting in her arms now, becoming restless. She surveys the hardwood floor at her feet and doesn't want to put him down. The floors look grimy, not recently mopped. She steps further into the kitchen. In the corner of the room is the antique breakfast nook, a small dark wood table and banquette. Leanne sets Hank down on one of the benches, hoping he'll stay ensconced. She digs into her pocket, retrieves the car rental keys, and hands them to him. When she turns around, Beth has scooped the ashes into the bag and is sealing it closed. Then she steps around the island and toward her and Hank. She holds out the bag but doesn't look at Leanne. She's looking at Hank. She smiles, acknowledging his presence for the first time. Leanne takes the bag. She says thank you.

But Beth is still looking at Hank. "Your grandpa would've liked to meet you."

Hank shakes the keys in the air and squeals, and for a second, Leanne catches a glimpse of her, of the Beth that Brittany must see. The non-monster. Grandma.

"Do you know what you're going to do with them?" she says, nodding at the gray, sooty mixture.

Leanne looks down at the bag. "My first thought was the Pacific Ocean, but he never liked the beach, huh?"

Beth shakes her head. "No, he didn't."

"I guess I don't know. I'll have to think about it."

No one says anything for a long moment. Instead, they watch as Hank scoots himself off the bench.

"Well, I guess we'll probably go. He'll just get himself into trouble here."

Beth nods, watching Hank as he moves past them, walking back into the mudroom, as if leading the way.

"I really do appreciate this," Leanne says. The end is within sight, and she feels the impending relief of a duty fulfilled. "I know you and Brittany aren't fans of mine." She reaches for the doorknob.

Beth sighs. "You're at the phase in your life where everything is new, everything's beginning." Her voice has changed, and Leanne stiffens. "But just wait," she says.

Leanne looks at her. She can see the disdain behind her eyes. "I am carrying my dad's ashes."

"The world's not as pretty as you think it is."

Leanne feels like she's been tripped, like she's been pushed to the ground. "I don't think it's that pretty," she says, and then bends down to take Hank's hand. "C'mon, baby." She pulls open the door with the same hand that's got the bag of ashes and then tugs on Hank's arm to pull him out with her. Outside, she drinks in the fresh air. Her throat had already started to itch from the smoke. Hank toddles down the two steps.

Leanne won't look back. She scoops her baby up into her arms. She walks to the car thinking: *Dignity. Dignity.* She buckles him in as quickly as she can. In the driver's seat, she takes one last look at the house, at the peeling paint, at her old bedroom window, at the impossibility of that campaign sign's declaration, and she forgives herself for running as far away as possible—for going too far—and for never wanting to come back again.

75

In a moving box in the back of the office closet, Leanne finds her childhood copy of Roald Dahl's *The Twits*. She has just hung up with one of the moms who sends her daughter to that day care up the street. Leanne visited yesterday along with Hank.

She has an idea for a story to tell, but she's still in the research phase, the wondering phase, which has led her to *The Twits*. She wants to remember how it ends. She flips to the final pages. *Oh, right.* The monkeys that Mr. and Mrs. Twit were so cruel to take their revenge. The Twits end up with their heads glued to the floor. Unable to right themselves, they get a case of the "Dreaded Shrinks." They shrink entirely—until they become nothing at all.

With the book still in her hands, she hears the ping of her phone. She finds it in the other room. It's a text from Mona, who accepted Leanne's apology over the cat stunt with a wave of her hand. ("Elspeth's always had a stick up her ass.") She has sent the link to the *INEZ* profile. Leanne can see the title of the article along with a little thumbnail image of Regina looking deadpan at the camera while standing next to the giant birdcage in her living room. Leanne doesn't want to click on it, but then Mona sends a follow-up. It says: *Trust me. You're gonna want to read this.*

It's enough of a push. And so she does.

Under the Microscope with Regina Mark
Oct. 2, 2016

By Sarah Montgomery @sarahMTGMRY

When I'm assigned to profile Regina Mark, the Los Angeles–based designer and co-owner of the high-end homewares store R.M. Goods, it's not because of a poorly written blog post warning mothers about the dangers of vaccination. No. At our first meeting, on the patio of a West Hollywood restaurant, though the blog post already exists, I don't know about it.

I don't know about a lot of things yet—like the history of germ theory, which appeared after and eventually replaced something called filth theory. No. When I'm assigned to profile "L.A.'s tastemaker" as deemed by *C Magazine* in a piece titled "California Cool," the word *filth* is not supposed to come up at all.

And at first, it doesn't. At lunch, I take careful notes of what's in front of me: Mark's strong jaw, red lipstick, tanned skin, blue-gray eyes, and brown hair pulled into a voluminous topknot. Of her clothes, I write, "moneyed and man repeller." She wears a tailored but loose cherry-colored sleeveless button-down dress that evokes the ease of Eileen Fisher with the chilliness of Anna Wintour. But mostly, I observe my own enjoyment. "Funny and comfortable. Almost soothing?" are my exact notes. I chalk this up to the fact that Mark and I have a mutual acquaintance; we both have infant daughters; and we live in Los Angeles. It's not until we've eaten our lunch that I even ask her about her store, her products, and her point of view as a designer. "Simplicity and quality are the key things for me," she says. "I'm not trying to reinvent the wheel. I know that. My goal is always the same: timelessness. When I'm designing, I ask myself: Will I still like this in ten years? Would I have liked this ten years *ago*?"

After the server drops off the check, Mark pulls up Instagram on her phone and follows me. Then she asks if she can take a photo of me and post it—"just as a story," she says, referring to the portion of the app that is timely, that will be gone after twenty-four hours. Most writers when profiling someone else try not to be a part of the story themselves, but when I acquiesce, and then later, from the comfort of my idling parked car, see my own image reflected back at me within her account with 18K followers, I realize that it's too late. I already am.

The very next day, I receive a deluge of texts from Mark. The first, a serious-faced selfie as she nurses her thirteen-month-old, Ursa Major Mark. The second, her white-lacquered desk covered with stacks of neatly folded textiles, with the caption stating: "Meanwhile . . ." The next, an image of Ursa's nanny, Margarita, "the glue keeping it all together," who appears smilingly caught in the cross fire of her employer's camera phone.

In another message she invites me to a dinner party she is hosting that night. Her "dear friends," the pop-folk musician Howie Robbins and his documentarian filmmaker and anti-circumcision-advocate wife, Mari Lisbon, would be there. In another, she wants to know if I can meet for lunch at the Soho House; she can put me on her guest list, she says, followed by "No pressure. I'll be there working all morning anyway." But I can't make it to either of these. What about the following week? I text back. And so we make plans to meet Thursday afternoon at her house.

In the meantime, I do my research. I stop by the sprawling R.M. Goods. The store is immaculate. The walls and floors consist of the same knotty pale hardwood, like the interior of a large modern Swiss chalet. I briefly imagine living in the space and can almost feel my cortisol levels decrease. It somehow even smells like the Alps. (Later, one of the employees tells me they burn a kind of incense called Nordic Wood.) That night at home, I find myself on Redfin looking at teardowns I might be able to afford and then rebuild in the vein of a Scandinavian yoga retreat center.

But before I have too long to consider this alternative lifestyle, I find two Instagram messages waiting for me from Mark. The first one reads:

I know the profile is probably supposed to focus on me and my textiles, but I feel like people overlook the other important work I do: 👐 ✍️

This is followed by a link to her blog, *RMarksthespot.com*. When I click on it, I'm led to a post titled "We All Want Our Babies to Be Safe." I read it and realize with a steady and growing horror that Regina Mark is an outspoken vaccine resister.

I don't write Mark back via Instagram. Instead, I begin reading up on the claims she makes in the blog post. I armor myself so that by next Thursday, when I knock on the door of her West Holly-wood three-bedroom Craftsman with guesthouse, where she lives with her husband, daughter, three cats, and a bird, I am ready for the debate. But when Mark opens the door, she greets me without a hint of the controversy within her very factually evasive blog post. "Come in, come in," she says warmly, kindly, with the unhurried face of someone who has just woken up from a nap. It's a strange moment, and I wonder if she assumes that I haven't vaccinated my daughter either.

"Let me show you around before Urse gets home and needs to nap." She motions me to follow her through the living room, but I cannot because I'm frozen to the spot staring at one of the largest, most modern-looking birdcages I've ever seen. It's white and angled into the shape of an A-frame house. When Mark sees what's distracted me, she backtracks. "This is Rosie." Rosie is a parakeet. She has a cornflower-blue chest, black-and-white wings, and is quite stunning.

"Say hello, Rosie," Mark says.

"Hello," Rosie crows, and I look to Mark with surprise.

"She's great," Mark says, already moving into the kitchen. It's just off the living room, so I can hear Rosie continuing to say hello as Mark pours me a glass of sparkling water. One of her three white-haired Persian cats sits on the countertop nearby. "This is Harry," she says. "You're not allergic, are you?"

I shake my head as she hands me the glass.

"Good."

Smoothly if not rotely, she walks me through her home, revealing the pristine rooms I've already seen via Instagram or previous magazine features. Everything is sun streamed, beautiful, and tightly curated, like Mark herself. And though the house was built in the 1920s, there's no sign of atrophy. Time has lent character and charm only. Not a thing is out of place until we reach the guesthouse, which since Ursa was born has become Mark's office and extra storage for her textiles. When she pushes open the door, her lips vanish into her face. "Oh," she says. "I told him to put these away." She's referring to a stack of white rectangular boxes, each one about the size of a thick hardcover book, piled up on the floor, just to the right of the small foyer. The letters *MRE* are printed boldly across them and then in smaller letters *Meal, Ready-to-Eat*.

I ask her about them and note her irritation as she explains: "They're basically army rations, like in case of an earthquake." She shakes her head and steps further into the space, motioning to a large framed corkboard filled with tacked-down pieces of fabric and magazine images. "This is my inspiration board," she says with an air of pride. I peer in. Many of the images are of animals: sheep in a green meadow, a lone polar bear walking across light-blue ice, a duck with multicolored plumage. There's a postcard of an Ellsworth Kelly painting and a Matisse-like drawing of a vase of flowers. Written across a magazine image of what looks like a version of the interior of her store—a kind of wood-walled and wood-floored chalet—are the words *Waldorf Pink*. I nod, tell her it's all lovely, as we slowly find our way back into the living room.

She's wearing a loose-fitting cream-colored jumpsuit, and as she sinks into the cream-colored sofa, tucking her bare feet under her, she almost disappears into the white abyss. I feel like I've waited long enough, but instead of asking her directly about the blog post, I ask her about this recent measles outbreak. "It's really sad," she says, her eyebrows pointing downward.

"And you're not worried about Ursa?"

She inhales. "This is going to be part of the piece?"

"That's what you wanted?" I say, and an odd moment follows. She looks a bit confused, as if she didn't remember the Instagram message at all. [Editor's note: Mark has since denied sending that direct message; however, the editors of this magazine confirmed that the message does exist within the author's account.]

"Look," she eventually continues, "as a parent, I think you have to choose your battles." A cat approaches her slowly, coolly. She pets it gently. "The number of shots babies get right now and in such a short amount of time—it's unprecedented. And kids are having serious reactions to them."

Vaccine injury. This is the main focus of the blog post. For the layperson, a vaccine injury might conjure an image of a swollen arm or redness at the spot of the injection, but when I Google it, I find that the term casts a very wide net. Things like autism—a developmental disorder that has been continuously and repeatedly shown to have no causal relationship to vaccination—come up. Likewise, the idea that any kind of untreatable severe reaction to vaccines exists, according to the World Health Organization, is simply a "common misconception about immunization."

Mark shakes her head. "I think that in a decade or two, we'll all be surprised by what's actually happening. And in the meantime, I prefer to listen to my fellow mothers and my own intuition."

"And just roll the die with infectious diseases?"

"If you want to put it that way, sure. My dad actually had measles when he was a kid, and now he's a seventy-two-year-old triathlete who still works sixty hours a week." She laughs.

This general lack of fear of (mostly) bygone illnesses is something that seems common in the anti-vaccine and/or vaccine-hesitant community, and in some respects it's understandable. Most Americans under the age of fifty have never witnessed the ravages of measles or tetanus or heard of a baby dying from rotavirus. And in the United States, deaths from these afflictions *are* rare. That's because vaccination rates nationwide are still very high, and American children for the most part aren't malnourished and/or exposed to other diseases like tuberculosis or HIV. But in developing countries, the mortality rate from measles—for example—is closer to 10 percent.

"All of this is actually part of the reason I started making baby blankets," Mark says now. "I don't know if you know this, but so many of the blankets you're sent home with from the hospital are made with synthetic fabrics, like polyester, which can take up to two hundred years to biodegrade." As she speaks, another one of her cats jumps up onto the couch as well and is received by the other, the one Mark is petting, with a sound that I can only describe as a bellowing E.T. It's a horrific, alien sound, which must also set Rosie off, because she starts squawking and flapping her wings. "Okay!" Mark says. "It's fine. She can be up here too." And then she shouts toward Rosie, "Rosie, please!"

It makes me listen more closely. Rosie is saying something. And then I hear it. "I'm trapped!" Rosie is cawing, and I look to Mark with confusion.

"My husband taught her that." She shakes her head and rolls her eyes. "He thinks it's funny."

Now seems as good a time as any to mention that in my research for this piece, I hit upon an internet conspiracy theory that Mark kills her pets. The origin seems to lie with the disappearance of her dog Bunny from her social media accounts, and also first-hand accounts of cats coming into and disappearing from Mark's life without rhyme or reason. Later, when I ask about Bunny, she frowns. "She had severe, really destructive anxiety. Giving her up was so hard." She has also left some comments, unhinged at best, on a Los Angeles animal rescue's Instagram account. (A Reddit account has kept track of these.) (Mark denies making them.)

But in the present moment, once the animals quiet, I ask about the relationship between making baby blankets and opting out of vaccinating.

She becomes animated. "You have a kid, so you know that overwhelming feeling, when the baby comes out, it's just . . ." She pauses, looking up at the ceiling. "I want to say it was a holy experience even though I'm not religious. And I think I realized instantly all the things we *do* to children—and how, at the end of the day, what I want for her is to be *free*. So, yeah, at first that manifested itself in this idea that I wanted her to be wrapped in organic fabric, but the idea has continued to influence my work. One of the colors in my current collection is Waldorf pink, which is a color used on the walls of Waldorf schools—a kind of school I'm really inspired by. And this pink they use is such a lovely, calming shade, and it's typically painted with a watercolor effect, so that the children can get a sense of the world beyond the walls. Like the walls aren't *really* a boundary."

I mention an article in the *New York Times* about parents of babies too young to get vaccinated whose doctors encourage them to stay inside during measles outbreaks, the implication being that the walls of their houses or apartments probably *do* feel like a boundary after a week or two.

To this, Mark smiles. "But you know what I mean. Children are their own beings. Instead of . . . this thing we must 'immunize'"—she uses air quotes here—"the minute they come out of the mother. You know that the current standard vaccine schedule includes one coming within hours of being born?"

I do know this. It's the hepatitis B vaccine, of which Dr. Bob Sears, author of *The Vaccine Book*, a popular book among parents who don't vaccinate or who choose to delay vaccination, writes:

"This is an important vaccine from a public health standpoint, but it's not as critical from an individual point of view." What he's saying *without* saying it is that hepatitis B, which is mainly contracted via sexual intercourse, is only a risk for a certain kind of baby, that is, a baby whose mother has an STD. (It feels important to note here that people can be infected with hepatitis B without knowing it and can therefore blindly pass it on to their partners and/or their babies—no matter their standing in society.) And, when the hepatitis vaccine became routine for all babies, sometime in the eighties, it saved thousands from eventually dying of cirrhosis or hepatocellular carcinoma.

But Mark has already moved on. "That's another interesting thing," she says, "even the terminology we use for vaccines: 'shots' here in the US and 'jab' in England, they're violent words! It's like, these babies just got here. I mean, can't we just leave them alone for two seconds?"

"But in protecting your daughter from this kind of violence—as you say—you are exposing her and potentially others to another kind."

She pauses before responding. "I mean, I understand that's what many people think. But still I'd rather take my chances with nature, with the natural world."

When she says this, I can't help but think of the cache of MREs sitting in her guesthouse—a kind of immunization against nature, no? And if we're talking terminology, let's talk about the word *cache* itself. It's from the French *cacher*, which means "to hide." Indeed, Mark had clearly intended for the MREs to be hidden. It makes me wonder what else one might intentionally conceal.

When I'm first assigned to write this profile, I don't know that measles is caused by a virus and hence is a "viral illness." Nor did I know how vaccines work. Now I know enough to get by at a dinner party; I can talk about "surface proteins" within vaccines that evoke an "immune response." Even still, I feared measles and trusted vaccines to protect me. That hepatitis B vaccine that is standard procedure for newborns? My daughter got one, and yes, mere hours after she came out of me. I remember hesitating for a second when the needle revealed itself, but then I decided that the doctors knew best. To be clear, I don't regret this decision. I simply realize my ignorance going into motherhood.

Germs are hidden from the naked eye. But filth is not. It makes sense then that filth theory—the nineteenth-century notion that unsanitary conditions, open sewage and the like, caused and spread disease—would come before germ theory, the now widely accepted and proven idea that germs, aka microorganisms, are what cause disease.

When I was first assigned to write this profile, I had already heard of Regina Mark and R.M. Goods. But still, I Googled her. I clicked on her website. I remember thinking that the textiles seemed plain, pedestrian. But then I read the recent feature about her anniversary party in *À la Table*. I scrolled through her Instagram. I saw that she had many followers, that she and/or her products had been in *Architectural Digest*, *Martha Stewart Living*, and *Sunset*. As markers of her success stood in front of me, I reconsidered my own assessment. Maybe the products aren't plain? Maybe I'm plain.

But with all this talk of epidemiology, I now want to take a closer (microscopic?) look. I think about my Saturday visit to R.M. Goods with nary another customer in sight. I go again to the website. This time, I notice its homespun nature and the way many of the items are "out of stock." I click on the stockists—the stores that carry her pieces: there are three locations in California, including her own store, and one in New York City. The lone store in New York is Up + Down, which is run by Linus Lincoln, the brother of Agnes Fass, Mark's close friend. The store in San Francisco that carries her items is owned by Cecily Mark, her aunt. The other one is a store on the east side of Los Angeles, owned by a woman with whom Mark recently traveled to Mexico City.

I reread some of the previously published magazine stories on Mark. Within the *À la Table* one that covers her fourth anniversary party, I recognize Thea McManus as one of the party's invitees. McManus is an acclaimed interior designer as well as the sister of the editor in chief of *À la Table*. I flip through *Architectural Digest*, and among the names on the masthead, I spy someone with the last name Pincher. (Mark's husband and the co-owner of the store is Val Pincher.) I research and find that the *Architectural Digest* staff member in question is Mark's brother-in-law. The story titled "California Cool" for *C Magazine* is written by an Elspeth Gluck, a high school classmate of Mark's.

I become curious as to why *this* magazine wanted to profile Mark. She's not launching a specific new product or store or even throwing a half birthday. I ask my boss, and she says that Mark's publicist pitched her. She forwards me the email from a "Pegasus Publicity" at gmail.com. I Google Pegasus Publicity and find no online presence whatsoever.

Hidden in the timelessness of these quilts and blankets, is there also a *design-lessness*? A *less-ness*?

An ex-employee of R.M. Goods, who speaks to me anonymously, tells me that instead of putting anything on sale, "Val [Pincher] would sweep the unsold product into a giant garbage bag and take it away." To where? This employee didn't know. She tells me that the bulk of the sales were the furniture and baskets—both of which R.M. Goods sells on consignment from other makers. And also that Mark's mother, Mimi, would come in often, sometimes spending hours or more rearranging the displays. She says Mark's mother talked wistfully about a store she had in the late seventies. I find a record of this store within a 1981 article about shopping in Beverly Hills in the *Los Angeles Times*: "Across the street, M.M. Goods has high-priced

American-designed millinery. A black, lavishly feathered fedora costs $1,400."

But over the phone, Mimi Mark dismisses the endeavor. "Oh, but it was nothing like what Reggie has created. I was so naive. I didn't know anything about branding or publicity. And then I had my kids and the real work began."

Back in Mark's West Hollywood living room, our conversation is interrupted by Margarita pushing the front door open with baby Ursa just behind her in the stroller. Mark jumps up to greet them, cooing at her daughter as she unbuckles her from the restraints. Margarita appears to have a story to tell Mark and launches in. As they talk, the door opens again. This time, it's Val. It wouldn't be an understatement to say that he barges into the room with the energy of the Kool-Aid man. "Talk about sucking the day's dick!" he shouts.

"Oh, sorry," he says when he sees me. He's wearing spandex shorts and a t-shirt with ample sweat marks. "Just got my PB on the one-mile climb."

Mark looks at me and shakes her head. "He sets himself goals on the StairMaster at the gym." She returns to her spot on the couch, this time with Ursa in her arms.

Margarita and Val disperse. Regina breast-feeds her daughter, and the room falls quiet again. "You know," she says, looking up from her baby. "Sometimes I have so many balls up in the air, I feel a little crazy. But after I published that blog post, I heard from so many moms thanking me for writing it. There was really only one commenter who didn't get it. And that one person did get under my skin a bit. But then I texted my friend Mari who does activist work, and I said to her: 'Am I crazy?' And she just texted back: 'No! The world is what's crazy.' And I just think that's so true. I mean, look at this election. It's a shit show."

Ursa spits up on Mark and begins to cry. It feels like a natural—almost *pure*—end to the visit. "I would hug you, but—"

Mark shakes her head, looking down at the spit-up on her jump-suit. Margarita rushes in to retrieve Ursa and starts patting her gently on the back. "Let me know if you need anything more," Mark says as she opens the front door for me.

Maybe it's just the general commotion that has set her off again, but as the door swings shut, I distinctly hear Rosie calling, "I'm trapped! I'm trapped!"

76

Almost immediately, an Instagram account called RosieTheParakeet is born. Rosie posts about her caged life. She gets 2K followers in a day.

In Leanne's Twitter feed, writers she follows are debating the merits of the piece: Is it working to expose and take down a segment of anti-vaxxers, or is it simply giving them more publicity? Others are copying and pasting snippets along with the eyeroll emoji. One person writes, *I'd call on stores to stop carrying Regina Mark, but I don't want to get in the middle of a family issue.*

Regina herself stays quiet.

For about thirty-six hours. After that, she posts the header image used in the profile, the one of her standing unsmilingly next to the birdcage along with the following caption: "You have enemies? Good. That means you've stood up for something, sometime in your life."—Winston Churchill.

Leanne moves through the comments just long enough to learn that Winston Churchill didn't say that.

77

Hank has officially started at the day care up the street, so Leanne has the house to herself for three consecutive hours Monday through Friday. That first morning on her own, she writes down a to-do list.

1. DAD'S ASHES

2. How to Become Rich in Loss

She's going back and forth on what to do with number one. The second item is the title of something she thinks she wants to write.

But at first, she mostly spends those quiet hours without Hank reading. She finishes the book about vaccines. It's so good. She picks up *Howards End*—a book her dad had sent her years ago—and is surprised by how funny it is. She loves the Schlegels from the beginning.

Until one morning, she opens up her journal. She starts writing: *The Twits but they are mothers. Koala Life but she's a mother. Cher and Tai. Emma and Harriet. But . . . they are mothers!*

She imagines a scene she wants to write: a mother pushed to the edge, but instead of breaking down quietly and within the four walls of her house, she takes her meltdown public, to some kind of town-hall meeting of mothers.

Once she begins making decisions for her characters, she makes a couple for herself. She'll bury her dad's ashes in the backyard; she'll mark the spot with a giant rock.

She finds a rock quarry just outside Los Angeles where they can buy one. It may look a tad strange in their little backyard, but she's willing to risk it. She's always liked those dry California landscapes with the occasional boulder. She thinks that when they eventually move from this house, they could even take the rock with them.

On a Saturday, the three of them drive to the quarry. They pick out a beige trapezoid-shaped stone.

The next Saturday, she digs a small hole in the back corner of the yard. James and Hank watch as she pours the ashes in. They help her cover them with dirt. And then she and James maneuver the rock on top. It's not easy work. They start sweating in the dry October heat. Hank toddles away to another corner of the yard. She sees him pushing his plastic dump truck. When they have it just where they want it, they stand there in silence.

That was a lot of effort, she thinks.

It was, she hears someone say.

78

Months later, Leanne and James attend a friend's thirty-fifth birthday party at her house. It crosses Leanne's mind that this friend has stayed in touch with Regina and that she may be there as well. But this mutual friend isn't that fancy. Leanne doubts Regina will drive across town for it.

So when she's making her way through the small crowd with a fresh glass of wine and sees her ex–best friend for the first time in over half a year, it takes a moment for her brain to register it. *Oh, right. You.* It takes another second for Leanne to decide how to be, a decision that is influenced by the dual facts that she is a teeny bit drunk already *and* Regina has chosen to wear her blazer by allowing it to drape over her shoulders instead of putting her arms through the sleeves. Leanne smiles but with restraint. "Hey," she says, and then nods at Val, who is by Regina's side. It seems as though they've just arrived. Regina has a clutch in the crook of her arm, but neither is holding a glass of anything.

"Hey," Regina says back. She smiles with her arms crossed.

"What's going on? How are you guys?" Leanne offers.

"Good, good. Busy. The same." Val smiles, seeming to agree.

"That's good." Leanne says it with a note of surprise. "Because that piece in *INEZ* . . ." The words just come out of her. "That must've been a lot."

Regina rolls her eyes, though Leanne can see the tension in her jaw. "Yeah, I mean those profiles are . . ." She shakes her head and shrugs. "Well, you know. Like that review of your book in the *L.A. Times*," she says.

"Right." Leanne says it slowly. She takes a breath. She looks at her old friend dressed like an off-hours European prime minister. And then: "Although, *if* we're being honest." Was she really going to be honest, face-to-face, after all these years of smiling and acquiescing? Of having her lines memorized and playing her assigned role with deference and ease?

She would have to use this as a writing prompt for her students: Two characters are having a conversation. One begins their sentence with *Although, if we're being honest.*

A bad review is better than no review.

No. She can do better than that.

If you're going to take a shit, it may as well be featured in the Los Angeles Times. *You taught me that, Reej!*

No, no.

Although, if we're being honest—

I hate you.

Does she? She thinks of Regina's Instagram feed. Still so serious and with so many self-portraits. Sometimes, yes.

But *How dare Schlegels despise Wilcoxes, when it takes all sorts to make a world?* It's a sentence from *Howards End* that she'd copied into her journal.

Leanne didn't like to think that she had needed Regina. Or Beth. Or even to some extent her own mother.

She would have much preferred to believe that she would have arrived on the right side of things without these women. But really: it was because Regina had been stupid and ill informed that Leanne had attempted the opposite. *Because* Regina was unable to see wealth outside of affluence, because she'd been so sure of herself, Leanne became suspicious of both: money and certainty. Because Beth had been mean and because Winnie had been careless, Leanne was careful with Hank. And would be careful with herself. Starting *now*.

She looks at her friend again. She smiles and repeats herself. "*If* we're being honest, I gotta get out of this conversation."

Regina responds with her eyes first. She blinks them one too many times. "Of course," she says, calling to mind those moments when Leanne has asked something ridiculous of her phone's virtual assistant, but the phone doesn't miss a beat, responds right on script.

"Go, enjoy!" Regina adds after another moment, shooing Leanne off.

Leanne looks at her and stares for half a second. She nods and then gives a glance to Val before slipping back into the folds of the party. She spends the rest of the night mildly aware of her ex-friend's presence but one hundred percent free.

EPILOGUE

During her next teaching session, Leanne learns from a student that Earl's book, *Who Are You Calling Cuckoo?*, ended up selling for $550,000 at auction. Also, two *Finding Dory* producers have optioned the film rights. The release date is TBD.

ACKNOWLEDGMENTS

When I thought this book might not get published, *one* of the things that made me sad was not being able to publicly thank people, which leads me to:

Thank you, Megan Lynch. You understood this book right from the beginning, and for that, I'll be forever grateful. Likewise, I want to thank Sarah Bowlin for seeing what I was trying to do and for believing in the project when I couldn't on my own.

I want to thank my dear early readers: Alison Harney, Anne Zimmerman, and Kristen Iskandrian. As well as my dear later readers: Bill Morris, Edan Lepucki, and Melissa Seley.

I want to thank Mary Anne Madeira and Kara Norman for that deep female friendship I crave; Mark and Marsha Bookman for their consistent support and for always taking my calls; Ella Cojocaru and Donna Bloom for strength; the Polies for much-loved conversation; and all of the *Mom Rage* listeners and supporters. You know the behind-the-scenes details!

I want to thank the people whose work fueled me: Sheila Heti, Eula Biss, Clarissa Pinkola Estés, Miranda July, and Luca Guadagnino.

I want to thank my mom and Bruce.

I want to thank my kids, Teddy and Isaac. They inspired this book; they sabotaged this book. They made it so much better.

But most of all, I want to thank Matt Bookman. You've always tried to give me a room of my own—even during a global pandemic with a year's worth of first-grade Zoom school—and I am deeply, eternally grateful for you.

ABOUT THE AUTHOR

Amelia Morris is the author of the blog *Bon Appétempt* (named one of the twenty-five best blogs of the year by *Time* magazine) as well as a memoir by the same name. Her work has appeared in the *Los Angeles Times*, *McSweeney's*, *The Millions*, and *USA Today*. She is also the cocreator of the podcast *Mom Rage*. She lives in Los Angeles with her family.